DOG
BOY

Also by Eva Hornung
writing as Eva Sallis

FICTION

Hiam (1998)

The City of Sealions (2002)

Mahjar (2003)

Fire Fire (2004)

The Marsh Birds (2005)

NON-FICTION

Sheherazade through the Looking Glass: The Metamorphosis of the 1001 Nights (1999)

TRANSLATION

Yahia al-Samawy *Two Banks with No Bridge* (2005)

EVA
HORNUNG

VIKING

VIKING
Published by the Penguin Group
Penguin Group (USA) Inc., 375 Hudson Street,
New York, New York 10014, U.S.A.
Penguin Group (Canada), 90 Eglinton Avenue East, Suite 700,
Toronto, Ontario, Canada M4P 2Y3
(a division of Pearson Penguin Canada Inc.)
Penguin Books Ltd, 80 Strand, London WC2R 0RL, England
Penguin Ireland, 25 St. Stephen's Green, Dublin 2, Ireland
(a division of Penguin Books Ltd)
Penguin Books Australia Ltd, 250 Camberwell Road, Camberwell,
Victoria 3124, Australia
(a division of Pearson Australia Group Pty Ltd)
Penguin Books India Pvt Ltd, 11 Community Centre, Panchsheel Park,
New Delhi – 110 017, India
Penguin Group (NZ), 67 Apollo Drive, Rosedale, North Shore 0632,
New Zealand (a division of Pearson New Zealand Ltd)
Penguin Books (South Africa) (Pty) Ltd, 24 Sturdee Avenue,
Rosebank, Johannesburg 2196, South Africa

Penguin Books Ltd, Registered Offices:
80 Strand, London WC2R 0RL, England

First American edition
Published in 2010 by Viking Penguin,
a member of Penguin Group (USA) Inc.

1 3 5 7 9 10 8 6 4 2

Publisher's Note
This is a work of fiction. Names, characters, places, and incidents either are the product of the author's imagination or are used fictitiously, and any resemblance to actual persons, living or dead, business establishments, events, or locales is entirely coincidental.

Library of Congress Cataloging-in-Publication Data

Hornung, Eva.
Dog boy : a novel / Eva Hornung.
p. cm.
ISBN 978-0-670-02149-9
1. Abandoned children--Fiction. 2. Feral dogs--Fiction. 3. Human-animal relationships--Fiction. I. Title.
PR9619.3.S244D64 2010
823'.914--dc22
2009041481

Printed in the United States of America

For Philip Waldron

I

The first night was the worst.

Romochka sat on the bed as a chill crept into the apartment. All his attention was focused on the apartment door.

The building was buzzing, strange. It was filled with curses and screams, as if all the residents were awake, drunk and angry. People were dragging stuff along the corridors, down the stairs, until their voices faded and the bumps and squeaking wheels receded. He could tell people were leaving. Tromping back and forth to get their things, then gone. None of them sounded like Uncle. Every curse, every stumble and scrape, was followed by nothing. No scrabbling at the door, no turning of the key. No familiar hinges sighing. No stumbling entrance. No hairy-nose-breathing in the gloom—only his own frosty breath. He was the only one there, breathing the gloom in and out.

He had been angry with his uncle for weeks, but this anger vanished as the evening lengthened. His eyes slid to the door. He had not seen his mother for a long time, more than a week, and since then Uncle had taken their possessions away piece by piece. First their clock, then his mother's wooden shelf that had been her mother's. Then other important things—the square table they used at breakfast, the two chairs, the television that flickered. But Uncle was never late home except on pension day.

Darkness now filled every corner. Romochka climbed stiffly off the bed and yanked at the electrical cord. Nothing. He scuttled to the electric hotplate that sat on top of the shelf beside the coat rack. He knew it was forbidden but reached up nonetheless and turned both cracked knobs. His heart beat hard in his chest.

No click, no friendly orange eyes on the knobs. No ticking in the metal plates up out of his line of sight. Nothing.

He shuffled over to the heating pipes. A bottle clinked and rolled away from his feet. He stretched out his hand.

The pipes were cold. He snatched his hand back as if scalded.

In the bathroom there was no hot water. The phone was dead.

'Someone,' Romochka said crossly to himself, 'has been a selfish fucked-up bastard.' He climbed back into the bed and deep under the cooling quilts. He repeated it, as if grown-up speech could bring them back, but his voice faltered: his heart was beating too hard. He put his thumb in his mouth and tried to slip into that thumb trance that had once carried him, wide-eyed, through anything. But he hadn't sucked his thumb for a while and it had lost its perfect shape.

With the exception of the phone, none of this had happened before.

He warmed up under the quilts. His nose and forehead, poking out of the gap between quilt and pillow, were uncommonly cold. He stared at nothing. Rain fell without sound, making dim striations across the rectangle between the curtains. He fell asleep with the strange notion that the outside was coming inside, and that he had to defend what little warmth he had left. When he opened his eyes in the darkness, he was scared by the unfamiliar rush of cold air onto his eyeballs. The window was brighter than before: the first snow was falling. The swirl and eddy of tiny snowflakes made the stillness in the room awful. Layers of silence cocooned his body: nothing stirred in the bed, in the room, out in the hallway, or anywhere in the building. Silence changed everything. The cupboard loomed, enlarged. The padding on the door gleamed in the odd light cast by the window. His ears moved, tweaking his scalp as he strained to hear something, anything; but the building had died and shut out even noises from outside. He could hear only the gurgle and hum of his own body.

The next morning his uncle still had not returned. He got up, glowering fiercely at nothing and everything, and put on far more clothes than he would normally have needed. Feeling bold, he went to explore outside the apartment. There could be no doubt, were he caught: he was up to no good. He would be beaten and locked in the cupboard.

The air was cold and silent. He checked the communal kitchen and was astonished to find that the stove, the sink and all the fridges were gone, leaving a very dirty empty room. Even the inbuilt kitchen furniture was gone, and pipes stuck out here and there from the wall. Muck and dust hung over the old wallpaper that had been behind the benches and stove.

The toilet was still there, so he used it. It wouldn't flush. There was no toilet paper and nothing at all in the cupboard behind the toilet. The communal bathroom looked almost normal, except that it was dry and its usual humid air had gone stale, leaving only a smell of mould.

He was all alone.

He wandered back to the apartment. Its ordinariness was now scary. Only the cold air gave away the desolation of the rest of the building. His adventurous mood faded and he turned this way and that with rising terror. He raced suddenly to the cupboard, wriggled in and closed the doors, just as though he had been caught, roundly slapped and thrown in. He began to sob as he had many times before, and his ears really did burn with heat and pain. He sobbed harder, then, and rocked back and forth until he fell asleep.

Over the next two days Romochka ate everything he could find in the food cupboard and didn't bother to clean up. He ate the half packet of biscuits first. Then he crunched through a cabbage, raw potatoes, cereal, rice and macaroni. He got a stomach ache and lay down. When he felt better, he managed to open the two tins of mackerel and ate them. He ate a box of sugar cubes and even tried to chew through a raw onion. There were two jars he couldn't open, one of preserved plums, the other cucumbers. He thought of smashing them but was too cautious. His mother had told him: *You die if you eat food out of smashed glass.*

He raided every forbidden space. There was little of interest and nothing edible in any of them. He pulled clothes out of boxes and hauled everything out from under the bed. His mother's dresses were pretty but flimsy, and one tore as he tugged them from their hangers. He held her peacock dress to his face for a while, breathing in. Then he laid them all gently to one side and went on rummaging. His mother had a little brown coat with fur cuffs, waist and collar. *It is so warm*, she said often, *that you don't need anything on your legs.*

It was not to be found. He gave up. He put on so many of his own clothes that he found it hard when he had to wrestle them down to go to the toilet. He tugged the mattress off the bed and threw everything warm onto it, then spent most of his time in the pile he had made. He was in big trouble if Uncle came back. He wanted Uncle to come back just to show him what happens if you don't come home on time.

After three and a half cold days and three long, unlit, icy nights he decided he had to leave. There was no particular reason he could see for his uncle and the phone, electricity and heating to leave and not come back, except that his mother had suddenly not come back—and, more recently, the furniture had left and not come back. In his short life his uncle and the phone had in general been less reliable than his mother, the heating and the furniture.

His stomach churned with apprehension as he moved aimlessly around the apartment. Going out to the street alone was forbidden. *If you ever set foot outside, both Uncle and I will kill you, first me, then him.*

But there was no food.

He procrastinated. He explored the other floors. It no longer surprised him that the building was eerily still and dark. He climbed to level four and knocked half-heartedly at Mrs Schiller's, knowing that she wasn't there. The door was unlocked. He pulled it open and walked into her apartment. It was still a shock, even though he had guessed there would be changes. Her big two-room apartment was empty and strewn with rubbish. A harsh light spread over everything from the undressed windows. Outside, treetops with a few golden leaves tossed in silence in the wind. He stomped back to his place.

For a moment he hesitated as he stood in the doorway. The apartment had an insistent homeliness, a pull on him that made him walk in as if things were completely normal. He sat down on the ripped sofa bed and looked around for his mother, ignoring the gaps where the television, table and bookshelf were supposed to be. He walked out, turned, and walked in once more but the strange effect had died away.

His stomach rumbled. He grabbed his red bucket and put a black velvet ribbon that had belonged to his mother in it. He ran down the three flights of stairs, past the burnt apartment on level one and down the main stairs. The buzzer that released the lock didn't work, but there was a thin white line between the door and the jamb. He threw his full weight against the door and it swung outwards, letting in blinding light.

He dropped his hands to his sides. Hunger and cold had pushed and pulled him down the stairs, but, for the moment, they had all but disappeared. It was a nice late autumn day—a high white sky, dry but very cold. The fleeting snows of two nights before had melted straightaway, but it was cold enough to snow heavily now. His spirits lifted. It couldn't be all that hard to find food and warmth. Grown-ups managed all the time, with or without money.

From the outside, the building looked unnaturally still. It was an old building, with many broken or ice-cracked panes in its outer windows. None had curtains and there was no movement in the darkened rooms beyond. There was no sign of anybody, except the signs that they had left quickly—trails of debris led from the door; drag marks and the imprint of handcart wheels through clumps of dust, dropped tissues and indeterminate things crushed to pieces under many feet.

Romochka stood in the doorway, watching people passing by on the pavement. They were almost all familiar but he didn't know any of their names. They belonged in the neighbour-hood. They came and left and came back. But no one who belonged to his building appeared. Maybe he should catch an eye, tell someone that he was all alone. They would take it seriously—you weren't supposed to be outside all alone at his age. He watched for someone familiar who didn't frighten him. Maybe the shaven-headed guitar man from the blue building three street doors from his. Maybe the fat lady from the corner tenement. She had three big nasty kids, but they weren't with her today. Maybe the old lady in the pretty cream lace scarf, carrying her two bulging avoski. He could see a loaf of bread sticking out the top of one, but it wasn't enough to make him talk to her. In the end he didn't try to catch any eyes. He was overcome with secretiveness and mistrust. His mother's voice rang in his ears: *Don't talk to strangers.*

He stood on the step curling and uncurling his cold toes inside his boots, not looking at anyone. He rocked back and forth a couple of times. His bucket knocked against his thighs. He put it down for a moment on the step and clapped his mittens together, stopping half way, palm to palm. In an adult the pose would have suggested prayer. In a four-year-old it suggested indecision so profound that his body had shut down in order to let him think.

The lane was almost deserted. Frozen puddles here and there gave a dull gleam, wrinkled like the eyes of dead fish. A car roared past, taking advantage of the sudden freedom of no traffic. It disappeared and for a moment nothing moved. It really was bitterly cold, and he knew he had better get moving soon. Still he waited. He was old enough to know that the street belonged to cars and the footpath to grown-ups and big kids. Little kids (and right now he felt particularly little) had no space in the world outside.

The next rush of cars cleared and a large yellow dog passed by on the other side, heading down the lane. Dogs, he said to himself, are warm. He had cuddled Mrs Schiller's hairy dog Heine many times, and he had a sudden vivid memory of Heine's warm belly skin and stinky breath. He picked the bucket up again and stepped out through a gap in the fence and onto the footpath. He clattered and rattled down the lane in the same direction as the dog. His mother had told him never to go out the door, never to wander off, never to go down the lane by himself even if Uncle sent him. She also told him: *Never go near street dogs. They have diseases that can kill you.*

There was no one there to chase him and tell him off, which gave his transgressions a certain hollowness. He was so cold and hungry. Had his uncle staggered around the corner and cuffed him a few times, then dragged him off to some new place to live, he would have sobbed and snivelled but he would have felt much better.

The lane cleared and he crossed in order to be on the same side as the dog. Now he shivered with excitement—he was definitely where he shouldn't be, where any little kid shouldn't be, doing what a little kid shouldn't do. She stopped just ahead, sniffing the corner of a building. He peered at the dog's belly where a double row of breasts swung as she walked. She turned and looked at him for a moment, then trotted on faster than before, moving in an easy confident way. Her pale yellow hair was thick around her neck. Everything else around him was grey and murky; so, he told himself, she was the only dish on the table. His mother had said that about their apartment, about Uncle, about the flickering television; and about him on those nights when she didn't work.

Romochka couldn't keep up. The pavement was slippery with black ice, his layers of clothes bulky and he had to walk flat-footed to stop himself from sliding. An alley led off to the left from the lane up ahead. The dog turned in and, when he reached the corner, she was gone. He sat down on the cold concrete, the bucket beside him. He couldn't feel his fingers inside his mittens. He curled up against a drainpipe that ran up the wall next to him. A faint warmth seeped through his clothes from the pavement: there were people up in this dark tenement somewhere.

His mother had said many times: *Don't go near people. Don't talk to strangers.*

He'd already done an awful lot of things his mother wouldn't like.

He didn't get up. The warmth from the heating pipes under the ground made him listless. He was around the corner from home but his legs were too heavy to do their job. Even his emptiness was too heavy, pressed into the ground by his sleepy bones. His head was too heavy.

A freezing drizzle fell. The black ice on the pavement

began to shine. The gutter filled with black sludge and the white lines on the asphalt disappeared in a reflective sheen. His blue mittens glittered with tiny droplets. He shut his eyes.

He heard a faint noise that was more than the whisper of rain, and much closer than the cars on the lane around the corner. He opened his eyes. Two dogs were taking up all the space in front of him, present just as suddenly as if he had been on one page of a picture book and had now turned to the next. They paced in front of him without taking their eyes off him, crossing each other's paths again and again. One was pale gold all over with a tail that curled back on itself, the other huge and black with cream paws and mask. Both were bigger and clearly nastier than the one he had followed.

They moved around, urgent with some purpose. They stared at him, eyes big and yellow. The rain spangled their fur. He liked dogs, but even he could tell these dogs wanted to hurt him. The dogs snarled at each other just as if he were a dish laid out in front of them and there wasn't enough for two. He wondered whether it was really possible for a dog to eat a boy. He frowned at them fiercely.

Struggling with his clothes, he used the drainpipe to pull himself up. The dogs jumped back. Then the dog he had followed appeared out of the shadows on the other side. She looked at him as if waiting: head high, tail low. He let the pipe go and crossed the alley towards her. She didn't move. The two dogs closed in behind with a rub of hair jostling for space and the snicker-snap of bickering. His dog had her ears up.

'Doggie,' he said, and she tipped her head very slightly to one side. One of the dogs behind him growled low. His dog lifted her lip over long teeth and growled back, a growl that travelled around him and was aimed at them. He felt the agitation behind him settle and, glancing back, saw that the gold dog was sitting now, watching. He reached his dog, put out his hands. She flinched, hesitated for a moment, then sniffed his face, his chest, his mittens. She was standing still.

Then she waved her tail from side to side, slightly, thoughtfully. The other dogs came up to her then, their heads weaving low, and they licked her face. She licked them each in turn, licked his face too, placing a sticky kiss on the corner of his mouth, then she turned and loped at an easy pace up another alley leading from the first, one he had never entered. People were filling the streets again, trudging, skittering and sliding along the pavements, but he paid them no attention. He focused on his dog and followed closely, the kiss freezing on his cheek. The other two dogs fell in behind neatly, without jostling.

He wondered what these dogs ate for dinner and his stomach sizzled painfully. He suddenly remembered his bucket, back by the drainpipe. *Leave something behind, and you can kiss it goodbye.* He faltered. Then he trotted on.

They had gone around a corner or two and were weaving in and out of parked cars when he realised he was nearly lost. He thought of stopping. He remembered that the apartment was cold and dark, empty even of his uncle's smell, and then, before he could think anymore, he *was* lost. He concentrated on what dogs ate for dinner. He pictured bowls of diced meat and cabbage, all in a row, with one extra for him. But perhaps dogs couldn't afford diced meat. Perhaps a soup, made with big bones, potatoes and onions. Or chicken soup with noodles. Maybe just potatoes. Hot and steamy. Mashed and buttery. Then he remembered: dogs don't have money! They steal

13

everything, or get given it! It could be anything. Cutlets! Kolbasa! Dumplings with meat! Chuk-chuk! Donuts! Saliva filled his mouth.

They passed throngs of people who were making their way home or to shops after work but no one stopped the boy or asked his name. He was a boy; his companions dogs. There was nothing to show that he was following, not leading. They looked like three obedient dogs, and he like a boy master— neglected, young to be out alone, but everyone knows without thinking that a person with dogs is not lost.

Three dogs and a boy passed through the populated thoroughfares of the precinct to more deserted lanes. Gates and mesh fences sagged, street walls crumbled. In the distance, apartment blocks were stacked like dishes in a rack, their windows glittering. Close up, weeds filled all gaps. They passed by low buildings with no balconies: offices and warehouses and factory sheds. They passed rows of identical five-storey tenements with cracked tiled façades and a few unkempt birches in the raked yards. They breathed in the smell of cooking onions and cabbage. Inside, people were preparing their evening meals, sitting or moving around in warm rooms, arguing, tired, sipping hot tea or soup.

They slowed only to cross roads or skirt cars or people, then picked up pace again.

A lane opened to a vista with no more streets. Ahead was a meadow filled with oddments of rubbish, ringed with buildings, all unlit: factories or warehouses without people. Then the three dogs did stop and eddy, sniffing in the corner of the street wall and the field fenceposts, moving around the boy,

14

ignoring him. The three dogs peed quickly, here and there. Then they trotted on as purposefully as before. He followed, staggering now. They slipped one after another through a hole in a fence and crossed the meadow through blackened weeds. They made a ragged trail through the icy grass, one track wide and one dainty. At the far side of the field, he stumbled and stopped, swaying on his feet. The lead dog dropped back and waited, looking at him, so he nodded, turned and trudged on.

They squeezed through a gap between a brick wall and a fence post, and then they were among abandoned construction sites. A car passed up the potholed lane and a few scruffy people walked by. A man was lying in a heap against the street wall, asleep. He had been rained on and smelled of wet wool and old urine. The dogs stepped wide around him but otherwise paid no attention.

The boy's strength was almost gone when the mother dog disappeared through a broken gate. They all in turn slipped through into an ancient courtyard. Here there was a tangled mess of dried grass and a dead orchard of five apple trees, their trunks bearded with lichen. Above, a brick façade ended in a broken cupola silhouetted against the sky. It was a church, a blackened and roofless ruin.

The dogs' lair was in the basement. They entered through a hole in the floor and clambered down a pile of rubble along a narrow, much-used path. Inside was dark. Somewhere puppies yelped and yabbered.

And so it was, trotting with three dogs through ordinary lanes, past ordinary tenements, past ordinary lives, a lone boy crossed a border that is, usually, impassable—not even imaginable.

At first he didn't notice.

Romochka could see nothing at all. He was assailed by a stench, pungent even in his cold nostrils. Then he made out a wide cellar with holes here and there in the roof. The two younger dogs had flopped down on the floor to one side and were scratching and licking themselves. They didn't seem to have any food. He could see some distance now. His dog had trotted to a far corner and was being greeted with delight by four small puppies. He crept close and squatted on his haunches as she was licked and squealed at. He watched as she lay down and the puppies tumbled over themselves to suckle. He could just make out her dark, shining eyes watching him as the puppies pushed and grizzled. He noted her thick hair, her tidy feet, with pale tufts sticking out between her shadowy toes. She was motherly to the puppies: firm and distant and bossy. He wondered what dog milk tasted like, and edged closer. His stomach gurgled. She watched him steadily. The warmth of the nest, warmth of the squirming bodies, rose to heat his face. He dropped to his hands and knees, to his belly and wriggled towards her. She growled, steady and low, and he stopped. Then he inched closer, again, eyes averted. She was growling softly when he reached her flank and the full heat of the puppies. He curled himself slowly into that warm bed and pulled off his freezing mittens.

He could smell the puppies now, warm and spicy-milky, sucking, sucking. He could smell her too, stinky and comforting. He didn't move except for an involuntary shivering. She growled on but didn't move either. This growl was for him. But it was a mind your manners growl, not a get out of my sight growl and he waited, minding his manners. Then she stopped and began licking her puppies. She reached over and cleaned

16

his face too. Her tongue was warm and wet, sweet and sour. He licked his lips and tasted her spit and the faint taste of milk. He wormed his cold hand towards her belly and grabbed a puppy. It writhed, grunting in displeasure as he pulled. It took two hands, but in the end he managed to yank it off the teat. The puppy squealed and snuggled, nudged deep and found another. Romochka wriggled himself close, buried his cold nose in the mother dog's hair and sticky skin, and then the hot milk was his. It slid, rich and delicious, down his throat and into his aching belly.

His anxiety floated away and wellbeing seeped through him. After a while his hands warmed up and he reached for her damp belly and stroked her with his fingers as he drank, feeling out her scabs and scars and playing his fingers along her smooth ribs. She sighed and laid down her head.

Romochka woke up in the solid darkness of the night. He had never experienced true darkness. No streetlight filtered in through blinds; no orange clouds glowed through gauze. He held his hand in front of his face and could see no dim fingers. He filled his invisible body and although nothing about him had changed, in this darkness he felt enlarged. Warm bodies clambered over him, burrowed around him. He grabbed hold of one and tucked it to his chest. The puppy whined and wriggled, but he held on harder and it stopped struggling. Its rapid heartbeat settled and he smelled its milk-and-leather breath.

He smiled in the darkness. If his mother walked in now, she'd find him well-dressed, warm, full. He hoped she would, just to see that he could manage without her, without Uncle. The mother dog's mouth loomed near his face. Her whiskers

17

tickled his lips and he breathed in the heated stink of her mouth. She licked him and he smelled her saliva as it dried and stiffened on his face. The other two adult dogs settled their heavier bodies inside the nest against his back. He drifted away.

The cold woke him. Light filtered into the cellar through the broken floor above, enough to see that the big dogs were gone and the puppies had deserted him to roam. They moved clumsily near the nest, tails up as they tracked scents. They pounced on each other, play-fighting, tumbling and snarling. He sat up and tucked his knees to his chest as best he could in his bulky clothes. He was cold, hungry and grumpy. There were no blankets. The bed was made up of some damp solidified rags, a lot of hair, gritty stuff and old feathers. He couldn't find his mittens. He looked balefully around and didn't bother to get up. The cellar showed no sign of provisions.

The puppies, seeing him sitting up, scampered closer in, bumping against him and tugging at his sleeves and leggings. He grabbed one as he had in the night, wrestled it into his coat top and held it in. When the puppy stopped complaining, he opened the top and looked down at it. The puppy's eye gleamed in that dark hollow. It reached up and began licking his face with exaggerated movements, licks that were almost nips. He stroked its white head. Then he noticed that the other three puppies had stopped playing and were sitting on the nest, pressed against his sides. They were watching the entrance to the cellar, tails wagging expectantly.

The mother dog entered and the puppies went wild, wriggling, whimpering, leaping on the spot. Then they raced around her, springing to lick her mouth as she stalked to the nest. The white one inside his coat struggled so violently that he couldn't hold it.

Even Romochka knew that breakfast had arrived and he reached out his hands in delight to his Mamochka.

On that first morning Romochka gave the puppies names. He surveyed them proudly. Brown, black, white, grey. All his! Then another day he gave them other names. Then he forgot their names and forgot that he had ever looked at them as a boy looks at puppies. Their breath filled the air around him, their bodies warmed him, and they fought with him for their place at the milk. Their weight pressed against him and their tongues left a milky trail on his skin. His hands reached for warm mouths and bellies, scruffs—throwing, wrestling, tongues meeting.

There were just the three adult dogs in the family. Their heavy bonier forms dominated the lair when they entered. His Mamochka, milky, clean-mouthed, strong, was the leader. The other two were her grown children. He could sense it in their familiarity and subtle deference.

The two big dogs were heavy enough to shove him, and were not tender with him. He learned quickly that their tolerance was enough for his siblings, and it was also enough for him.

His suckle siblings were all milk-spiced, but the three older dogs had strong saliva and rank muzzles, each different, unequal in experience. They carried their own body odour on their tongues, their own signature in faint urine, paw, skin and anus—and their authority in their teeth, clean and sharp. They carried their health and their abilities in their kiss. He tumbled over the puppies too, kissing each dog on their return to the lair, then smelling their necks and shoulders to see what they might have done, might have found today. He, like the puppies, found the smell on their mouths and bodies tantalising; but he couldn't read the stories.

Mamochka knew more than the other two. Her teeth ruled the lair. Mamochka raised her head and shoulders from her puppies and that was enough to end fights or quell food rows. She silenced bickering between Black Dog and Golden Bitch by looking their way.

Mamochka knew how to choose between risk and danger, and her wisdom and experience were evident in the crisp stories of her muzzle and shoulders. She didn't try every fascination for possibilities, follow every cold trail just to see what had happened for someone else. She didn't roll in everything wonderful that she found, but wore just one strange stink as a cloak or a disguise. Mamochka went where she thought she would get food and felt fairly confident that she wouldn't risk too much getting it. Mamochka also knew humans and bore the scars left by both affection and brutality.

The two younger dogs were all health and foolishness, all action. They were at the mercy of scent and whim. They were exciting to smell over, exciting to be with. The puppies would savour their adventures until the older dogs threw them off. Golden Bitch had signs of Mamochka's courage and cunning. She was a darker grey-yellow than her mother, with a cream face mask fringed gold and grey. Black Dog, her brother, was the biggest. He had a broad, heavy-muscled body, thick haired like his mother. He was visible in the gloom of the lair as a floating face mask over a chest triangle and light belly and legs. Black Dog vacillated between courage and cowardice, foolhardy until fear overwhelmed him. Then he became vicious or timorous, or an odd mixture of both.

For a little while Romochka was much like a fifth puppy, a dependant to be fed and guarded. He was shoved, tumbled, bitten and licked. He was told off and shamed. For his part, he tried hard to please and became downcast when he was snarled into submission. For a while he emulated the puppies in everything. They grew rapidly and soon outclassed him in every way he could see. He practised their agile moves. He tried to listen to what they heard and to smell Mamochka before she appeared, the way they did.

Yet he could do many things they couldn't: for one thing he stroked Mamochka while he drank.

Ж

For weeks, Romochka was contented. He lived as in a dream. The good beasts rubbed against him in the dark until he became beast too. Day and night flickered in the background of a more urgent cycle: cold and warmth, hunger and a full belly. The old world above disappeared from his mind, except that it took the warm dogs from him when they left to forage and sent them back with cold, wet fur or manes of ice and snow. That old world was reduced to smells on dogs, and the many different foods they brought back with them. Rats, mice, ducks or moles, even once a roasted chicken. Once they all came in with loaves of bread, another time with cold cooked potatoes in their mouths. Romochka adapted quickly to eating anything he was given and to sucking and chewing at small bones and knuckles for hours. Mamochka treated him with disarming solicitude. She made sure he got his pieces, along with the four puppies. She licked him clean, pinning him down with a paw. He let her do anything—even though he had the size and perhaps the strength to stop her—so delighted was he to be included. When Mamochka was gone, he slept in a pile of warm bodies or played with the puppies, imitating their growls and yips.

Golden Bitch and Black Dog accepted without demur that they too had to care for Romochka. He could remember when their faces were the faces of strangers and their scent unremarked: he could remember their eyes when they had wanted to eat him. He savoured the change. He measured himself in their eyes. Mostly they treated him as another puppy. A cursory greeting when they entered, then to be shrugged off; snapped at for overdoing play, snarled at for nearing them when they were eating. But Romochka had what no puppy could aspire to. He could stand up and lift his eyes and face high above them. In their own way they loved him and provided for him just as they would for any puppy. Yet, subtly present, was an altogether alien pleasure they too discovered in pleasing him. Golden Bitch began to stand apart from him, watching and listening. Black Dog smelled him over not just to greet him, but with a recurrent air of curiosity.

The puppies gave warmth and simple physical pleasures. They were also fun, a gang of four playfellows. He didn't think of them at first as different from each other, but because he could see the white one most clearly in the gloom, he grabbed her and dragged her to him more often than the others—his

22

closeness to White Sister had its beginnings before he even really knew her. Pressed into his body, night after night, White Sister moulded herself to fit Romochka, to fit not just his body but his moods and thoughts.

The temperature dropped steadily and the days became shorter. For a while Romochka wore only a few of his clothes inside the den, so charged and heated were the bodies of the puppies, but piece by piece he put them all on again. The puppies played night and day and slept deeply only after feeding. Slowly his own sleeping patterns changed.

While the grown-ups were out hunting he explored, following the puppies as they trailed smells from one end of the cellar to the other. He ran back to the nest with them when they startled rats or heard scary street noises. The cellar was divided by wooden pillars that held the frame for the floor above. The far corners were filled with junk—mouldy clothes, piles of wood, empty bottles. A statue lay on its back at one end, face serene above its pointed stone beard, chipped fingers peeping out from under wide stone cuffs. It was too heavy to move and Romochka soon lost interest in it. There was enough rubble and wood to build pens, then interlocking corrals with secret escape routes that the puppies had to hunt for and squeeze through. Romochka built mazes. Once the puppies understood the game, they played with increasing skill and enthusiasm. He led them through jumps and tunnels, turning on them savagely if they made a mistake. The puppies learned quickly to watch him and follow him closely, to do what he did, to delight in doing what he suggested. Then they would all lie down together, biting, wrestling, pouncing. Then they would lick each other. Then they would sleep. The older dogs would return every time to a fully rearranged lair, something that startled them at first.

In daylight, he became the leader of the puppies. Before long, under his shrieking and pushy direction, he and his litter siblings were team-hunting the rats, unsuccessfully but with increasingly elaborate plans. But he was crippled at night, and the days were getting shorter.

He remembered the chilled apartment and the smell of his uncle as if they were a bad but tantalising dream. He remembered his mother, too: dreamily, but without pain or discomfort. Her phrases, her perfume-and-sweat smell, were fixed memories rarely touched, as distant as the stars. He had dreamed that faintly coloured, faintly odorous world—then woken up to live here in the rich smelly darkness and in the rub of hair, claws and teeth.

Ж

Romochka was trying to make the puppies listen to a story. He had become bored with puppy play, with the repetition of stalk, chase, wrestle, growl, maul and sleep. He rolled onto the nest, opening up his belly, and they all piled on. Then he found he didn't want to do anything more. He grabbed White Sister and forced her to sit still. She stayed where he put her, waiting bright-eyed for his idea to take shape, yipping at him in encouragement. Then he grabbed Black Sister and tried to force her, growling and squirming, to do the same. She pulled back her

24

tiny top lip from her teeth and did her best to look really mean. He held her down. Then, when he got the chance, he wedged as much of Grey Brother as he could between his knees and grabbed Brown Brother by the scruff. Black Sister was nipping him in earnest now, and he had to let her go. She snarled and snapped at his hand, then sat down anyway, curious. He grabbed a rag and tried to tuck them in but only White Sister would let him. He held onto a corner of the rag as Black Sister grabbed the other corner and began tugging. Grey Brother wriggled out from between his knees and grabbed another part of it.

Romochka squealed suddenly at them all. He let go of Brown Brother, slapped Black Sister and Grey Brother. Grey Brother yelped, Black Sister snarled. They both gave him a look, then grabbed the blanket again. Romochka was so annoyed he began to cry. He turned his back on them and tapped his lap for White Sister. She wriggled in and looked up at him. He keened on for a while, then gathered himself. It wasn't going as he had planned, but White Sister was doing her best to pay attention.

'Once upon a time,' he said. He felt the other puppies behind stop at the sound of words. He cheered up. 'Once upon a time there were some dogs. Very good dogs who always brushed their teeth.' He giggled. He couldn't think for a moment what to say next.

'One was the best, one was the worst, one was the bravest and one was the scaredest.' He was very pleased with the words falling into that dark space, pleased with how much words were changing everything. But just then the puppies behind lost interest. White Sister tried to pay attention, but Grey Brother trotted off and found something alive under a beam.

Brown Brother was pulling at Romochka's clothes, and Black Sister, head held high, was making off with the blanket. White Sister held still for a moment longer, then leapt off his lap and scampered away.

'Stupid dogs!' he shouted, but words had lost their spell.

Snow fell more frequently and stayed on the ground above rather than melting on contact. Romochka had not thought to leave the lair in the weeks he had been there, even to see the day. But he didn't like peeing inside, although the puppies did all the time. Even he could tell that his pee was smellier than theirs. One night he scrambled up to the icy upper floor and peed in the corner furthest from the lair entrance. Golden Bitch watched him in consternation from her sentry point, but didn't move to stop him. Mamochka and Black Dog followed and stood beside him. It was freezing cold up in the ruin; dark, but not pleasantly so. The touch of icy wind was unfamiliar and he was rattled by the darkness over the uninhabited waste lands and the lights of the city. He scuttled back to the hole with the dogs following. This became his ritual. Mamochka often smelled his pee spot thoughtfully and then guided him, with nips, back to the lair. He could tell that his pee worried them. Poo Mamochka ate. At first he thought this was funny, but she ate his poo and the puppies' poo, and soon he didn't notice.

He knew when the dogs were pleased. He could feel it and see it in the way they used their bodies. Their joyous wriggle and the smile of a sweeping tail were an immediately comprehensible body of happiness. Mamochka's contented sighs in their bed filled him, too, with bliss. He knew when someone was annoyed, because they bit him. He learned teeth: the friendliness of a gesture that held teeth low and unthreatening, and slowly all the gradations from bared-teeth threat, lip-veiled threat, and teeth set aside or used for play. He found himself quickly fitting in with teeth serious and teeth playful, reading easily the bodies around him with eyes, fingers, nose and tongue.

Everything was ritual. He began to emulate the greeting, in which every absence was healed. He made his body joyous too, his head low, mouth small; he yelped in delight and licked the mouth corners of the elder dogs as they entered. The greeting was also the moment of all confessions. Body joyous or body contrite, pure of spirit, or guilt-ridden, waiting for punishment. The dogs all confessed truthfully to each other at first meeting, crawling low, with face averted, then rolling over to take whatever punishment was theirs. Usually their abasement was enough. If the puppies had exceeded their boundaries, or eaten Golden Bitch's bones, or ripped up the bed and spread it around, they told on themselves as soon as an adult entered.

Romochka could not bring himself to do the same. He lied, body joyous, and both Black Dog and Golden Bitch were bewildered and disturbed. They bit him less and less. Mamochka still punished him, making him roll over onto his back when she discovered his smell outside the lair or in the destroyed nest.

One evening it snowed on and on into the night and then, when the late day came, everything was changed, muted. The light inside the lair had dimmed: the parts of the floor above that were exposed to the sky were covered.

Romochka felt one of the big dogs very near. It was Black Dog, eyes shining, tail waving. Romochka understood, yipped and followed. Black Dog led him outside and Romochka blinked in that forgotten light. He had not been outside in daylight now for more than a month. The sun glimmered, a white plate in the flat grey sky. The earth was pillowed in white. Black Dog shone black against the snow. The cream eyebrows and mask gleamed uncommonly. His long winter coat made a thick scarf over his neck and shoulders. He turned bright eyes to Romochka; he was excited too. He licked Romochka's face and capered to the church door. Romochka skidded after him in socks, squeaking through the powder snow. Black Dog peed on the broken door, then led Romochka out of the building. The apple trees were white figures, each twig highlighted. Every stick, bent grass and broken beam in the courtyard had a mantle of snow. Black Dog led Romochka to the gate, and, for the first time, outside.

Everything had changed. The trees were a lacework of white above billows of white and shadow. Romochka looked back towards the city. The ranks of apartment blocks too were changed, their façades ornamented with the geometric pattern made by snow on a thousand balustrades and window sills. He couldn't remember ever having seen that snow was beautiful.

Black Dog yipped and Romochka turned to watch him pee on the gatepost, then out on the lane on the far corner of the street wall, on the near corner, and then on the next building, which was a three-storey concrete construction so unfinished that every floor had filled with drifting snow. Romochka then carefully did the same markers as Black Dog, holding in

28

enough pee to last. Black Dog checked their trail and was happy. He trotted back inside, turning at the lair entrance to look back for Romochka, tail waving. No nipping, now, just friendly telling. How polite! Romochka was delighted. He sought out Black Dog in the bed when they all settled, and, hesitant, offered to curl up with him. Black Dog stretched out in invitation, and, as Romochka twined his arms around that thick neck and buried his face into that heady male coat, Black Dog sighed and licked the boy's face for the first time with true tenderness.

After that, Romochka peed carefully on the markers; and all the dogs, he knew, would smell it and know that he was doing his job.

Winter deepened. Romochka went up to the frozen gloom outside only to pee. The long darkness upset him. The light in the lair was an almost interminable, blank nothingness. He would wake up refreshed and ready to play, only to find his eyes opening on darkness upon darkness with no relief. Daylight when it came made only a feeble glow near the entrance hole. At first he stayed on the nest, miserable and shivering, waiting with increasing annoyance for the shy day.

In the darkness of that first midwinter he would find White Sister at his hand the moment he thought he wanted her, and before he reached for her. She came to him now and then simply to keep him company and he found that his fingertips knew her better than the others.

He listened to the other puppies play all around the lair without him. He waited for light to filter in, or for the grown dogs to come home, or for the puppies to tire and come and play a little or sleep with him. But the puppies soon discovered that he couldn't see them and they started new games. He found himself pounced on from nowhere and mauled; leapt upon, wrestled, kissed, slurped and savaged. He stopped sulking and started listening. He could hear where they were in that large expanse. He could hear the giveaway sounds of them sneaking up on him. He couldn't tell at first which one was which until they were on top of him. He knew when it was Grey Brother who landed on him, because he darted in and away with agility. Black Sister bit hardest. Brown Brother was clumsy and indecisive about which bit of him to grab and snuffled a lot while he thought about it; and White Sister was a different build and the lightest.

Then he found that he knew much more, things he had known before without noticing. They each tasted and smelled different. The boys had a rank musk. White Sister and Black Sister smelled pungent, in his mind girlish—they shared something with Mamochka and Golden Bitch. They all pounced and scampered in different ways. Brown Brother would slide across the floor as he changed direction in a chase, scrambling and scrabbling, panting hoarsely in his excitement. Romochka found that he could tell whether Brown Brother was being chased or doing the chasing. He caught fear or the absence of fear in their excited breathing. White Sister he knew as soon as he had his hands on her, or her paws on him. He knew her out there in the darkness too: she could hold herself utterly still in a hunt, and he found he could guess when she was near him, stalking him, by sensing a solid patch of stillness among all the currents and crosscurrents in the darkness ahead of him.

He warmed up and his spirits lifted. He sat up in the nest, craning his neck this way and that to pick up sounds, trying to time his defence from their attacks. He giggled sometimes in an excess of anticipation; and then had to try to control his breathing so that he would hear everything. Then it was on: the rolling fighting tumble as one puppy after another piled on top of him, he laughing and gasping and trying to throw one off, bite another, pin down another and clamp his knees over a fourth. He soon learned not to expose his belly or neck. He poked holes in his woollen hat for his earholes and then pulled it down over his face and neck for some protection. But he was always sore, and Mamochka would lick his wounds every time she settled down to take care of them all.

He found that he felt larger, more agile, in the dark. A blow from his paw seemed to have the strength of four dogs. In the darkness his sense of himself became fluid. His teeth lengthened and his bite was deadly. All weakness dropped away.

After a while, he began to leave the nest, feeling out the floor and walls. He found the old rubbish and bones and the rough wooden beams across his path where they had been before shape and warmth drained out of everything. Things were more or less where he had left them, but in the darkness it was all changed and new, icy to touch. He no longer rearranged anything. He became absorbed in memorising every element of the lair. He ran cautiously in the dark, skin prickling for the consequences of misjudgement, running with hands outstretched until the beams rasped against his fingers, then running in the direction of the wall where the path should be clear. Soon he was able to run and jump obstacles in the darkness. He could run around the outer wall with his fingers to the frosted bricks, chasing and being chased. The puppies fell in with the new games, tracking each other and him.

When they were all tired, they fell in a heap on the nest and slow-licked each other to sleep. He took off his hat and let tongues envelop him. All five of them licked each other's faces at the same time. Then, when Black Dog came home, he took Romochka, never the other puppies, out across the courtyard to the unlit street. After the silence in the snow-bound lair, this half-forgotten world jarred. The cold bit into his face and hands and made him fumble and hurry. He found his eyes so raw and fresh that the fires burning in the distance flared. The pinpricks of the city burned. Snow lay like a deep orange cloud; the cloud above spread like a deeper orange snowfield. He would go back inside with dancing lights leaping just behind his eyes, on and on.

He rediscovered Black Dog each time as someone seen: someone with eyes glittering and wet and kind. Black Dog was the only dog he really saw all winter. He stood beside Black Dog as a boy stands to a dog, and he stroked Black Dog, even in the darkness, with his hands not his tongue.

Every waking session was wildly exciting. Every return of the grown-ups was a delight—in them and in the plenty they brought with them. Every mealtime was a loving struggle for more until his belly was round and full. Every sleep time was a deep peace. He was obedient and cheerful in doing everything the grown-ups asked of him. He was enchanted by their affection and by their lavish attention to his wee and poo and his personal cleanliness. He was careful to show good manners over bones and food, if also showing self-respect in guarding his own fiercely. To his brothers and sisters he was imperious, inventive, playful, but also solicitous. He could spend long happy hours stroking and licking their relaxed and bliss-filled bodies. They passed him chance kisses and sniffed inquiries as to his wellbeing. They ran to him if something scared them; then, strengthened by him, they bristled and snarled.

If there had been hot beef soup, everything would have been perfect.

Romochka was startled when he saw a large pale patch moving in the darkness by the grey entrance hole, and realised that White Sister had become a young dog.

Midwinter was over and the days filtered in, weakly at first, then longer and stronger. In the returning daylight their new faces and forms became familiar again, and he noticed for the first time that Golden Bitch touched him less than the others, and that he knew her least from the long winter rub.

Golden Bitch treated him with the distance and tolerance accorded all puppies, but where the puppies also got her disdain, Romochka got her attention. She didn't do anything with him. She sat on her haunches, neat and collected, breathing in the smells at the entrance hole, watching him. There was nothing hostile in her regard but nothing else overt either. Over time this glance became less introspective and keener. She pricked her ears at the sounds he uttered and the games he played with the puppies, but didn't move from her post. He bumped into her only if the puppies rolled that way, yet she never did anything to punish him. He became used to feeling her regard turned his way and seeing her eyes bright in the thin gloom of daylight. This gaze was his main contact with her. She was often the last to lie down on the nest, and so was at the outer fringe when he was at the centre, curled half asleep with the four young dogs and Mamochka.

Romochka enjoyed Golden Bitch watching him. He knew that she liked him. He didn't guess her bewilderment, so he aimed to get what the growing puppies now occasionally got—an affectionate licking. Not a cleaning such as Mamochka would give, but a definite, approving kiss, and an occasional invitation to learn something when she brought a live rat or mole into the lair. He imagined a day when her satisfaction at his learning enveloped him too. But whenever he leapt in to show his skill, she would sit back on her haunches and watch him: interested, but without participation or encouragement, just as she watched from the entrance hole.

In late winter, with the young dogs' larger bodies hemming Romochka in, testing his strength now with their vigorous play, a discord crept in among the five siblings. One week Romochka felt them all as equally playful, if different from each other. The next week one of them was no longer playing. Black Sister slipped from being funny as the snappiest, sharpest-toothed and sharpest-witted to being savage and genuinely angry. She ruined the fun they had been having and Romochka was annoyed. As the balmier air seeped in through the snow, the lair became a place of unexpected explosions, incomprehensible fights.

When the big dogs were away, there was no one there to check their fighting or bring peace. They ganged up on Black Sister playfully but she bit Romochka hard and often and reduced White Sister to submission, snarling and snapping until she had the lighter dog on the ground baring throat and belly. She ignored or rebuked her brothers and spent time alone on the nest. At the same time Grey Brother provoked the anger of the adults more and more. He tried repeatedly to sneak outside after them or to slip away unnoticed while the others were playing. If Romochka set up a maze for him, he deliberately wrecked it, or climbed over. Sometimes he climbed the statue, and barked, inviting Romochka and the others to catch him, and then refused to do anything except be prey. Romochka started games with Grey Brother only for them to fall apart as Grey Brother decided to look at him as the hunter and to tease just out of reach. Romochka couldn't catch him and was too annoyed to team-hunt him.

They were denbound. The air was deliciously warmer every day but the atmosphere became close and wet. Everything was damp. Romochka's clothes chafed horribly on his skin but cooled to freezing if he took them off. Sores on his ribs and thighs got bigger and more painful every day. Puddles formed on the cellar floor and soon the nest was the only part of the lair that was not covered in slabs of ice and sodden snow. At night all Romochka could hear was the split splat of drips and the sliding splosh of falling chunks. Then, one day, spring sunlight broke in and sucked everyone outside.

Romochka crawled through the hole, wriggling towards the sun. He looked up and saw blue. A car slid past in the slushy lane, engine whining loudly, and his ears prickled at the raw sound. The sky was a patchwork of rain clouds. The puppies followed him out into the ruin. They were such big lanky dogs! The five of them raced through the snowdrifts, all tensions forgotten. Outside the grey snow still covered everything, but it had slumped, sapped from underneath.

Then it rained, making a white curtain in the sunshine.

35

Romochka stood up on his hind legs and danced, his mouth open. This whispering water, falling on the snow, seemed to him something he remembered from dreams.

Over the next month the mountainous snow crumbled, shrank and vanished, leaving the black ice-sludge and mud of spring-time. The heavy grey and deep smoke blue of winter were gone. The earth was black and grizzled with dead weeds. The snow-burnt grass was lifeless, but, above it, the tree branches were dusted to their tips with a haze of green. Even the trees in the courtyard had sticky reddish buds on a few branches. Broad puddles reflected the green, bringing it to ground early. The view up the street towards the allotment was a swathe of these green and blue winking eyes in the cracked asphalt. Romochka stood in the empty lane in front of their lair and held his hands up to the white spring sky, pointing his fingers the way first leaves sprout from the buds. Just as he had danced in the rain on the grey snow, he danced now in the mud. The four young dogs made wide muddy tracks sprinting around him, tongues out, heads up, ears back. Then a car came sliding up the lane, wheels spinning in the mud, and they all dashed for the ruin, playing fear.

Ж

The young dogs had a lot to learn, and Romochka with them. They were allowed to play in the upper floor of their ruined church, and then, little by little, in the grass under the orchard trees. To go outside the courtyard to the allotment up the street they had to have adults with them. They went every day and sometimes at night, avoiding morning and evening when people and cars filled the lane. They learned quickly to track each other back and forth across the wide muddy space of the allotment. But there was no following Mamochka, Black Dog or Golden Bitch past the empty field or down the trail over the waste lands and long grass. If Romochka tried, they growled. If he tried again, they warned him, and if he persisted, Mamochka nipped him so harshly that he yelped. She was now the only one who reprimanded him with teeth.

Black Dog marked out about half the allotment as a territory for them to play in. Every wake-up, the four tumbled out of the building, pretended to test the air the way the grown-ups did, then tracked their elders out to the allotment. They would trot around Black Dog's markers, considering them thoughtfully, then abandon themselves to play within the boundary of that invisible fence. Romochka trotted around with them but could not smell what they could. He had to watch their reactions to messages and read the news from this. He found he knew immediately if they were smelling a stranger's or one from their own family.

Golden Bitch or Mamochka would be lying down somewhere in the rubbish around them. Romochka would only see them raise themselves up and walk towards the puppies if he or one of the others stepped outside the boundary, or if a strange dog approached the allotment. When Black Dog minded them he played too, more often than not. He taught them all to hunt insects, something he hadn't grown out of: the happy victory of downing a grasshopper and the respect to be shown to bees.

They played in daylight, twilight, moonlight, starlight, cloudlight. Rain and mist. Light time and dark time and the time of shadows when dogs looked larger and stronger, and their eyes shone in silhouetted faces.

Romochka's raw skin got infected and he had to take all the tormenting clothes off for Mamochka to lick away the pus and scabs near his armpits and on his inner thighs. In time his body grew accustomed to being damp. His chafed patches thickened and he slept near-naked with the dogs to dry himself and to get new sores licked. He began to separate his many garments and hang them up on lengths of wood the way his long-ago mother had hung damp clothes on heating pipes. Then he started dressing White Sister and Grey Brother in his clothes for sleeps, giggling at them and how much like him they looked. His thinner clothes dried out nicely on big warm dogs. Soon he was dressing all his siblings every night. He began to wear as little as possible.

His new daytime world above the lair was not the one he had left behind in the autumn. He noted, first with surprise, that cars, houses, shops, people and cooked food, even when these were seen, smelled, dodged, evaded, were now somehow fixed in place, even unimportant. They were ignored as eyes, ears and noses sought movement; real, interesting little shifts in the grass or waste lands that meant danger or food. There was so much in the new world to be learned that he quickly forgot anything that didn't touch him. This new world had immutable laws. It was divided into realms of danger and safety; it had clear enemies and its own demons.

He learned to notice dogs above all and learned that strange dogs were bad, without exception. They were to be treated with care and hostility. Any breach of territory was deliberate and unfriendly, to be met with controlled aggression or retreat. He learned that the most dangerous were lone dogs who had no clan. Onetime people's dogs, as Mamochka had once been, but these now lawless and unpredictable. He learned that the allotment was his family's and its pathways were closed to strangers, but beyond it there were the comings and goings of many other clans—open trails. He learned that the lair was secret, and that there was a prescribed pattern on entering and leaving. He learned about the hunt. He noticed that anything a young dog caught was his or her own, but anything a grown dog caught was everyone's.

If it hadn't been for Golden Bitch, Romochka would have felt an easy confidence about his growing knowledge. He wanted, above all, Golden Bitch's acceptance. He wanted her to stop watching him so eagerly. He waited for her to boss him and teach him to hunt mice. But he never got a puppy's easy, loving licking from Golden Bitch, or a young dog's lesson. There was an awful day in midspring when he was so happy that he scampered up to her, leapt and threw his arms about her muscular body as she guarded the territory in which they were playing. He felt her stiffen, then quietly sink into a controlled body of deference. Her ears were back and her eyes soft, and she licked her own nose again and again. Then she dropped very slowly and deliberately out of his arms and onto the ground. She rolled and presented her throat.

Romochka was horrified and bitterly hurt. She had said something that could not be unsaid and that threw everything awry.

Golden Bitch soon came to weave with pleasure at the sight of him, and to lick his hands and mouth in greeting. She always watched him with that same yearning interest. Romochka in turn could never forget that he was not a dog to her. He was also not a dog to Black Dog, but everything between Black Dog and him seemed accepted, easy. He was conscious that Golden Bitch was waiting for something from him that he didn't comprehend.

One day Mamochka, Black Dog, and Golden Bitch led them all together outside the playpen and to the other side of the vacant lot. Sunlight filled the world, and the allotment glittered with yellow dandelions. The young dogs were quivering with excitement. At the far end, they all squeezed through the fence and then clustered to one side. There they stopped, sniffing everything. Romochka could remember this place, but it seemed utterly changed. He savoured the memory, curious. He had been a boy then, with a missing mother and uncle, following a strange dog. He remembered how cold and hungry he was. How unknown the trail ahead. Now the allotment was the threshold of home, redolent with familiar smells, a place of impending safety, even boredom. He was a dog now. His mother was a dog. His brothers and sisters were dogs. He watched keenly as the young dogs smelled everything in long deep breaths, tails stiff and thoughtful. What could they smell? He tried, but it just smelled like pee.

This was the first meeting place. Only later did he realise that here they could know when and where everyone had headed out hunting, who had returned and what, if anything, they had caught. Here they could smell whether the approach to the lair was safe, and here also strangers left messages, a little way off if they were neutral; in the meeting place itself if aggressive.

Ж

The rubbish mountain rose dark and squat above a forest of birch, larch, spruce, pine oak and alder that stretched from the far side of the mountain to the horizon. The old cemetery hugged the base of the mountain at one side, almost invisible under its tree cover. The concrete block wall that stood between the cemetery and the invasive slide from the mountain could just be seen as a thin white line from the construction sites. Beyond the cemetery was a highway, flanked on the far side by more distant apartment blocks. The cemetery came within a hundred metres of the dogs' ruined church. All between was long grasses and marsh.

At the edge of the mountain, the waste land ended in a bank overlooking a shallow basin of rubbish. Whether water actually flowed out and away to some cleaner watercourse was unclear. It was a natural declivity that wound its way along one side of the ancient yet ever-growing mountain. In spring it was a sodden, treacherous pool, hard to cross and quite deep in places. In summer, the river of rubbish seemed to move in this bed in an imperceptible slide. A bucket seen from the eastern slopes of the mountain might two weeks later be seen in the centre of the southern curve. There was no clear trail across this shifting bed of debris.

In spring, summer and autumn a heady invisible stream, a potent current of chemical rot, flowed from the mountain into every crevice before it dissipated in the air around the apartment blocks, leaving a faint, almost sweet ester that persisted even underground in the metro station beyond. The forest produced its masses of flowers, its nestlings, its fruits, nuts, berries and mushrooms; the land went from muddy, to green, to richly grassed, to gold, filled with hares, moles and innumerable creatures, all as if the mountain had no effect. Dogs and people who lived here, if anything, welcomed the beacon of the mountain. It was their permanent compass.

The next time the dogs headed out, they went straight to the meeting place and then further. Mamochka took Romochka and, to his chagrin, Brown Brother, who was the clumsiest. Black Dog took White Sister, Golden Bitch took Grey Brother and Black Sister, and they all split up to hunt in the wide world. Mamochka, Romochka and Brown Brother filed across the waste lands, then picked their way as best they could across the rubbish river into the heady atmosphere of the mountain, with its grind and rumble of machinery and its stench. Once they crossed to the mountain itself, they had to watch for dogs and people, and perform the open paths rituals for each dog they met.

For the first time in months, Romochka came close to people. Men and women scoured the mountain, heads down, moving rubbish around with sticks and handmade hoes. Small children searched too, or rode on the backs of their parents. They paid him no attention. Mamochka led him and Brown Brother in wide circles to avoid them and he guessed that around people there were closed paths too. He could tell that Mamochka thought they were dangerous, and he remembered that they were strangers and that he should never talk to them. Both his mothers now had told him the same thing.

Mamochka skirted the mountain and headed for the birch forest and the shanty village on the far slope. Romochka's step danced with the excitement of it all. Brown Brother's tail was up and plumy in the breeze, and every now and then he barked just for the sake of it. Mamochka was purposeful and silent, and they followed, scampering and play fighting now and then.

Up ahead four ragged men were yelling, while beating something at their feet with their hoes and sticks. It roared and gasped, heaved and flailed. Romochka thought it must be some large beast they were going to eat, or that had perhaps attacked them. But then they all suddenly turned and walked away and he saw that it was another just like them lying groaning in the rubbish. As he passed by he could smell something that reminded him of Uncle. His step quickened. Mamochka ignored them.

A lot of dogs lurked around the shanty village. Some were tied with rope, to stay and guard the shack of their owner. Others were friendly with people but not pets exactly: stray dogs who had discovered the kind-hearted, dogs who hungered for reciprocal warmth and affection. These dogs kept their freedom. The people they loved were generous to them, flattered by the dog's affections, but neither owned the other. Their paths could diverge as inexplicably as they had joined. The dogs skulking at the fringes were scared strays, sick dogs, crippled dogs, hovering in close for any chance of scraps. Others were like Mamochka and Brown Brother: feral clan dogs.

These all knew each other and knew who was from a strong or a weak clan, and whether they should stand with deference or ritual aggression. The pet dogs and the clan dogs were the only semi-permanent residents. The others came and went.

The village and the forest immediately behind it was all open trails. No clan could close it: it was too desirable as a food source and too unsafe. Uniformed men charged in now and then, demolished everything, arrested or robbed the people and killed the dogs; then, in a day or two, the village would be rebuilt.

That first time, Mamochka didn't let them stay long. They circled the village and saw many dogs and people. Romochka saw a blind dog, a three-legged dog, four or five miserable dogs tied up with rope. Mamochka made it clear that some dogs they met were to be feared and some were not but he didn't yet know why and neither did Brown Brother.

No dogs were friends. All people were dangerous.

The foray gave Romochka a lot to think about. He lay in the lair with the others and saw the unfriendliness of outside dogs over and over again. He saw the four men beating the other man. He heard again the screams and fragments of other lives that came from the huts.

'Alyosha! Get me the meat grinder from Kyril's!' 'Oujas, Valodya! Go wash in the pond!' 'I'll skin you alive, I will.' *'Bla-ack Raa-ven, La la laa li la...you tell my...la la li laa...'*

His mind ran through all the images of mothers and small children going about their business, so profoundly separated from him. There were no older children in the village.

Mamochka took all the young dogs in turn to the village to learn about dogs and men. Because Romochka had to go with Mamochka, he went every time. It was a good place to find rats, although once they had one they would have to fight for it. With her help they usually kept their rat, but they had to learn when to defer. Romochka was shocked the first time he saw Mamochka, confronted by a big black dog, drop the rat and veer away stiffly with her hackles raised. After that he learned how to recognise the individual members of the forest clan. They were a much larger established clan with a lair some-where in the forest. Mamochka never crossed their closed paths. Her hackles rose whenever she saw or smelled one and he learned slowly to recognise this and to step carefully himself. In time the hairs at the back of his own neck rose with hers and he developed an awareness of territory that was almost unconscious.

By the end of the first week of forays Romochka was dis-mayed at what a poor dog he made. He was completely dependent on the four siblings, again, to know right from wrong, and Mamochka didn't let him hunt with anyone except herself, so little did she trust him to take care of himself. If he chafed at the rules and got silly or playful, or tried to tempt the others into a game, she bit him.

Worst of all, he was next to useless. His heart burned as he lay awake in the den thinking about it. He could see in his mind's eye the four, noses to the ground, knowing things he couldn't see or smell. He saw them curious, delighted, intrigued, doubtful, frightened, worried, elated; saw them slow down, deviate, turn back or speed up, stop and listen in reaction to what their nose could pick up. He saw them hunt, tracking something until they flushed it out, and he could see on their bodies the moment they crossed a boundary into closed paths to do it. He could recognise the apprehension of a hunt in

45

someone else's territory. Yet he could smell nothing. He had tried by himself to trail Brown Brother across the allotment. He thought he had it. He turned round to see Brown Brother proficiently trailing him.

How would he ever hunt properly without a nose? He felt his nose and his small teeth in deep dissatisfaction. He rubbed his palms over his hairless arms and felt his callused hands and long broken fingernails.

From the first meeting place there were trails through the waste lands and marshes to the mountain, the cemetery, the forest and the city, open trails that were the same every time, that skirted other clans' closed paths. On the mountain, at the edge of the cemetery, and in the forest there were other meeting places. The trail home or outwards always took these in and everyone (except Romochka) could read whether the region had been safe and fruitful.

He learned mountain, cemetery's edge and forest but not the city. He didn't even know that a trail led there, back to where he had come from so long ago. He learned to skirt the apartment blocks and the abandoned construction sites and warehouses that lay between them and the city, abutting the highway at the far side of the cemetery. The blue-tiled apartment blocks, with their vast fields, playgrounds, and gangs, were open paths to all dogs. No clans lived there, although many pet dogs did. But he learned over time that the mysterious closed paths around people were unpredictable, and that the gangs were one of the greatest foes.

He learned that the warehouses nearest the allotment and the heated tunnels that passed under them were inhabited by older children, and he learned to stay out of their way. They were loving to dogs but brutal to children and adults outside their own clan. Their haunts and meeting points were scattered with the plastic bags they held on their noses. When he first began to notice the warehouse gang, Romochka picked up a plastic bag. It had a clot of grey in the bottom and a faint, oddly pleasant chemical smell. For a while he picked up these discarded bags, held them to his face the way he had seen and sniffed for the unique smell of these big children, but he stopped when he found his nose was useless for a while each time he did it.

The small clan in the abandoned church held a territory precariously. Humans were no threat. The church was too broken and cold to give shelter to the homeless and had long ago been replaced by a new church on firmer ground, the dome and spire of which gleamed above the treetops some distance from the side of the mountain. But they weren't safe from other dogs. They were weaker and fewer than some of the other clans, and were also at times attacked by clanless dogs, especially when foraging alone. Clan dogs circled each other, displayed their teeth but rarely fought. No dog could afford to be injured in a fight, and no small clan could afford to lose a dog.

They were extremely cautious, and the trail leaving the church was indirect. Romochka learned to leave the lair through the allotment. From immediately outside the ruin, he could see down the lane and all between them and the mountain, but he learned to turn, cross the allotment first, close the path afresh at the last meeting post, then head for the mountain from between the construction sites. The trail to the mountain was a clearly marked single track through the weeds at the edge of the cemetery. He learned to trot along this path in single file, watching for everything that moved or made a sound. He knew from watching his family that they smelled and listened for opportunity and for danger, and he tried with his eyes and ears to do the same. He ran slightly hunched, swinging his head from this side to that.

All people were dangerous, without exception. They were like demons at the fringe of everything important in his world, but they were also familiar. Out on the mountain or among the birches, a stranger stood out as much to him as to anyone else. He got to know regular visitors by sight: the truck drivers who wound their way up the mountain to dump refuse; and the two backhoe drivers who both smoked the same brand of cigarette.

The people of the mountain and village were his too, in a way. The one-legged man who clinked and slopped as he hobbled; the old woman who shouted *Ivan! Iva-aan!* Sights, sounds and smells. The smell of flowers that hung about the skinny woman with the broken mouth, and around her long-haired daughter. Romochka knew them all without even looking. The loners and the parents, the lovers and the children. He skirted them and forgot them.

Ж

The troubles of late winter were long gone, but a subtle tension still entered the lair with Black Sister and lifted as she left. The tumult her anger had brought into the lair settled, but no one forgot it. With Romochka present, she was almost never playful. They all learned to temper their play, and their affection towards Romochka, when she was with them, especially in the lair.

Romochka might enter the lair with Grey Brother to find White Sister, Brown Brother and Black Sister playing without reserve, the air thick with the smell of simple happiness. At the sight and smell of him Black Sister would drop away and go to lie alone on the bed, leaving Romochka to take her place in the game. Later she would savage him for an imagined incursion into her sleeping space. Increasingly Black Sister's personal space even when she slept on the nest was hummed out, mapped for any who rubbed against her.

But Romochka found that if he shared a bone with Black Sister and growled at all others, then his difficult sister was transformed. Where there had been snarls and painful savaging in the dark, there were licks. She made room for him next to her with elaborate gestures, then fought off all others, half playfully but at least half in earnest. As summer approached and Romochka went out of his way to give her the exclusive moments she craved, Black Sister's jealousy abated.

Black Sister's feelings were constant or predictable; Romochka was changeable. Sometimes he pushed one of the other dogs into the invisible electric zone that surrounded her. He could start savage fights, especially between her and White Sister. They faced off at each other fiercely, as Romochka stirred up trouble between them.

One day Romochka and Black Sister routed a rat in the late spring flowers in the courtyard. It shot into the ruin, across the floor and then through a gap and into the lair below. Black Sister sprinted for the entrance and scrambled down into the empty lair with Romochka following, yelling in excitement. Black Sister sniffed out the trail, but it was clear that the rat had gone to cover under a pile of crates, slats and other timbers that were too heavy for Romochka to move. Black Sister crouched down, tail wagging, eyes shining in the gloom, snuffing away at the gap under the wood pile. She turned to him with a look of such hope and expectation that he was stirred. She trusted him to help her get that rat, she really did! An urgent pride flooded him. He would, no matter what.

She watched with keen interest, yapping at him now and then as he rummaged for something that might do. He picked up a long birch branch and went up to the gap. Black Sister stayed crouched low but wriggled to the side to make room. Her body quivered as she laid her chin flat to the ground to see what would happen. He shoved the branch under and began jabbing wildly here and there. Black Sister jumped over, her head jerking this way and that, and he knew the rat was on the move. Black Sister stopped stone still, and Romochka gave one last jab.

The rat shot out of the pile, Black Sister ducked and snapped. She had it. Romochka crowed and jumped on her, rolling about on the floor. She shook the rat hard and then scampered as fast as she could around him with the rat in her mouth, pretending he was after her. Then they both threw it and caught it, and threw it, pretending it was still alive and had to be got again and again.

The rat was well shaken and bedraggled. He opened its mouth and peered at its long yellow teeth, so unlike a dog's. How strange to have teeth rising, not descending! He pushed his finger into its cooling mouth to feel how sharp they were, how they gnawed and nibbled. Yes, that explained rats. He would keep these teeth, a memento, and use them for any ratlike needs he might have. Any small grinding of pretty things, anything special.

Black Sister was watching him. She reached a polite paw towards the rat, looking bright eyed at him. He handed it over and she pulled the rat open with great delicacy, then inclined to him. He was delighted. They lay down on their bellies and spread it out. This was, he decided, his favourite food. He chewed through the slippery ribcage to its soft centre, keeping the head in his fist to make sure Black Sister didn't crunch through it and eat his treasure.

Romochka lay on his back with his head on Black Sister's flank. He sucked the stripped skull clean; she fumbled with the tail between her creamy paws and mouth. Every time she dropped it, he reached over and handed it back to her to prevent her from moving. He tied the skull into his hair and picked up the smooth birch branch. He rolled it around, feeling each end. One end was slightly narrower than the other. He held the narrower end and swung it lightly in the air above him.

He remembered long afterwards that the day he decided to make himself a club and a treasure collection was also the day he and his difficult sister were happiest.

Ж

Mamochka avoided the city. The hunting grounds of shanty village and forest were safer, and even there Romochka could feel her steering him away from throngs of people. They were

51

an urban dog pack surrounded by a great city, yet through spring they lived a life of field, mountain and forest. The days heated up, green seed heads formed and ripened where there had been flowers, and spring slid into summertime. The forest was filled with plenty: inexperienced young birds, late nests, baby hares and the leftovers from picnickers.

All in one week Romochka's clothes fell apart. They had already become tight and strained but then the old padded coat, discarded in the heat, was ripped up by someone and scattered throughout the ruin. His jumper tore as he pulled it over his head. He split his trousers, and then ripped a whole leg off on some rusty wire on the mountain. He had a close look at everything else. His undergarments were full of holes, frayed and almost translucent in spots. His hats had vanished. His toes poked out of his gaping boots. He frowned at his bare arms. If only the hair would grow.

The next day out on the mountain, he looked for clothes, not food. It was clothes season. By the end of the day he had a pile of remarkably clean and sturdy things. Three boots, each big enough to go on either foot; enough socks for hands and feet; three pairs of trousers, one even a child's size; a pair of shiny blue tights; some long sleeved garments and, best of all, a thick military coat. He even had some string to tie loose things tight around his skinny waist.

He got changed and tried his new appearance out on the dogs as they entered the lair. They growled, hackled and barked at his strange shape and smell and he was hugely gratified. Then he basked in their avid attention to every detail of his dress.

Through the early summer they drank from puddles and

pools where they found them. Sometimes they lay in the lair, panting and thirsty through the long day, waiting for evening so they could head out. Then Romochka found an old red bucket out on the rubbish riverbed. He filled it with fresh water from the tap on the outside church wall and wrestled it down the rubble pile and into the lair. From then on they had fresh water and he was inordinately proud whenever he saw them drink. He changed the water when it began to taste funny, found a new bucket when the old one cracked, and kicked it over and glared at them all when he was annoyed with them.

Late summer was hot and easy: plentiful for all the clans and lone strays around the mountain. Romochka got used to being dry again. His sores healed, faded and were forgotten. He forgot too his dependence on his ears in the darkness and was accustomed now to using his eyes in the long daylight. He felt the strong bodies of his brothers and sisters begin to fill out and become adult. He himself had become hard and wiry and very fast. But he was far from being as effective as the dogs.

More than anything, Romochka wanted to succeed in a hunt and bring home a real feed that he caught himself. White Sister had brought home a ham she'd managed to steal from somewhere. Black Sister, sharpest and fastest, had caught and killed a heron. She'd been hunting with Golden Bitch around the ponds in the depths of the forest, but it was Black Sister who carried the bird in proudly. Grey Brother got some kittens, also with Golden Bitch helping. Brown Brother, so big and clumsy, had even managed: he had brought home a french loaf. He got wedged in the entrance of the lair trying to bring it in, and Romochka, giggling, had to show him how to turn his head sideways and enter loaf-first. When Brown Brother laid down the loaf they all hung back, waiting for him to decide that it was for all. All of them except Romochka had made the shift to proficient hunting and were honoured for it.

Nonetheless, Romochka was aware that he was useful. The household refuse end of the mountain was easy to get at but soon picked over. He had a sack, several buckets and plastic bags, and he would hover around the back of the rubbish trucks, darting in for anything edible. This was a hunt that took three—one to sniff for him, one to snarl at people and dogs who were there for the same reason, and he with his hands to find, grab and hold on. But it was dirty hunting, and nothing about it made him feel that he too had grown up with the others.

To raid the cemetery, moving from grave to grave to pick up the small offering of sweets and cookies that were left there, was more difficult. Just after dark the cemetery was overrun with dogs and people all doing the same. Romochka dreamed of leaping up to snap a graceful neck and bringing home something fresh all by himself.

Conscious of Golden Bitch's occasional glance, Romochka thought he knew what she saw. His brothers and sisters hunted now for all. He alone still needed help. As summer advanced, however, his ability to gather things began to fill him with quiet pride. His hands could do what their paws and teeth could not. His haul these days from the fresh dumps was plenty indeed, and, with his brothers and sisters guarding him, he could ensure that he kept what he found.

With so many of them hunting and with Romochka's rubbish and sweets collections, they were a good-looking clan, if grease-discoloured. Romochka's ribs disappeared under a layer of muscle.

Some nights they went up to the ruin or the allotment to sing. They sang to all the clans of the mountain that their summer was joyous, filled with plenty, their bodies strong and sleek and their hopes high. They sang their own strength to the overarching sky and the spangled city. The other clans sang in the distance too. But when Romochka threw back his huge head and joined his shining voice to his family's chorus, the clans of the forest and mountain fell silent.

Something was happening with Mamochka that Romochka couldn't smell, but everyone else could. They all lingered over her and followed her around the lair, savouring it. Everyone seemed happy and excited. Mamochka enjoyed their attention—up to a point: she drove them off if they got too engrossed in what they could smell on her. Then there came a time when they seemed to smell her as a ritual dance, but there were no snarls or reprimands. Each in turn circled her then left her before she got angry. All except Black Dog would dance for this moment around Mamochka at every meeting, each with the same deference, then fall back and watch as Mamochka and Black Dog played and fought and played again. Then for two days Mamochka and Black Dog mated and did nothing else: joining, locking, panting, parting. They stayed stuck together for long stretches, exhausted, focused only on each other, with day passing into dusk. Even Romochka could smell them now and he tingled with a heady excitement. He felt the pressure of an obscure happiness. He watched in tune with the other dogs, who were lying with him around the edges of the dance. There was no envy. A serious satisfaction hung in the air, and in this he half guessed that they all, himself included, had worked and hunted, for this; and that with Mamochka and Black Dog's dance their summer was fulfilled.

Ж

A silence filled the cooling air. The birds were still and the strange, gold light of autumn slowly took hold across the forests and through the trees of the parks and highrise yards.

Then the golden autumn was over early and suddenly. Three deep frosts burned everything that was delicate, blackening some leaves, freeze-drying others and tinting all with brown. For two days the waste lands smelled of haymaking, or tea: grass and leaves dried by ice, not sun. Aspen leaves had fluttered like flocks of golden birds in tight formation. Now the trees were half bare, raggedly festooned. Romochka, the dogs, the grey crows and smaller birds guzzled the bright rowan berries that had been inedible before the frosts.

The cold came in from the north as never before. The rainless days were cruelly cold. The sky stilled to a solid disc and Romochka felt the air leaving his body and freezing. The city seemed to be stiffening in the too-early winter chill. The birch leaves tinkled faintly as they fell.

Then the snow began early and didn't stop. Every living thing was caught too soon. Still-green leaves in the undergrowth were coated in white. Snow fell from overweighted branches, and yellow leaves followed to make a discoloured carpet on the white beneath. The waning daylight on the mountain saw people and dogs eddying, noses and eyes turned upwards, northwards. The bulldozers and trucks that puttered ceaselessly through summer on the southern slopes of the mountain disappeared to wherever it was they hibernated. The cigarette smell of the backhoe drivers was a memory.

Romochka's family paced the lair, uneasy, and yet more the chill deepened. Snow would normally have made the lair cosier as it was sealed in, but this time they could only tell it was warmer inside when they emerged to a world colder each day than the night before. Romochka could barely struggle through the deep snowfall. Nothing was right.

In the gloom of the lair Mamochka stood over her three newborn pups, ignoring their mewling, listening. Romochka could tell she was worried and that she knew something that he did not. Then she blinked slowly, bent her head to the puppies and killed them. One by one, biting once through each of their soft heads. Then she lay down and, one by one, ate them. Bellies first, grinding through tiny cartilaginous bones until there was nothing left, growling even at Romochka if he made a move towards her. Then she slept a long while. Through the night he heard her slow-licking herself. She ignored him and didn't move to hunt. He slept fitfully, shivering cold even with the four cuddling him, even with all his clothes on.

With the weak dawn, which they heard and smelled rather than saw, Romochka found that they were completely snowed in. He crept to Mamochka's side, scared. She licked his face, then pinned his big head down with her paw and cleaned his ears. He let her. She growled when he moved towards her dugs, but he waited and begged until she gave in.

Black Dog and Golden Bitch burrowed in from the outside. They had been out all night and found nothing. They greeted everyone, carrying the cold in with them on their shaggy shoulders. They smelled the empty nest in deep snuffs. Then they waited with the younger dogs for twilight. Everyone would have to hunt.

Even in winter the mountain gave off enough heat to melt the heavy snowfall; and, with its cold heat, to send a steady beacon of faint chemical disturbance into the frozen forest and out to the tenements and apartment blocks. In its updraught, ragged birds—seagulls and grey ravens—wheeled and cried, looking like bits of windblown rubbish themselves. Snowstorms held everyone pinned in their holes or huts. In between storms, the earth was fluffy and evanescent; the sky solid as metal. Everyone hunted in the lulls. The hunting was variable for the dogs but hard for people. At winter's twilight, stooped figures trailed up and down the mountain or along the river, poking for scrap metal or wood, or digging for food. The mountain was ringed day and night with fires.

Close-up, everything around the mountain was movement. Snowflakes danced and drifted in the smoke that rose from the fires. People stamped and jiggled in their bulky clothing; dogs trotted continuously. The birds swooped and beat the falling snow in troubled eddies with their wings.

Romochka knew little of this. Denbound by the cold, he depended on the food the others brought in and the milk he drank. He waited for the first plunge in temperature to end and the snow to shell. That first fortnight of storms took its toll on everyone and when it lifted, Romochka couldn't stay inside. He put on all his clothes, grabbed his sack and headed for the mountain with White Sister and Grey Brother. It was a mild clear evening and the trail to the mountain was marked in the snow—man and animal had already been this way.

He was past the abandoned construction sites when he heard a faint music. He stopped. Singing, human singing, out by the mountain. The harmonies, with their dying fall, seemed to come down from the sky like snow or rain. They filled the air around him with something as faint and as lovely as the smell of spring flowers.

He would hunt later. White Sister and Grey Brother followed him unquestioning, trotting towards the forest and the fires. He liked the fires but had never been able to get near them. People here knew he was not one of them, and he guessed that he broke their rules, crossed their invisible closed paths and offended their order. Romochka was faster and more silent, and he had the dogs: he wasn't in any real danger from anyone. But he couldn't creep in and be friendly around a fire without being chased in earnest.

The music swelled and reeled him in. The men were lit up in orange light, roasting the hindquarters of a slaughtered dog. Its pelt and head lay on the stained snow. It wasn't a dog he recognised, and he thought from the smell that it was probably one of theirs, not a clan dog. Someone would be wearing that golden pelt in a few days. The smell of cooking meat was very good. White Sister and Grey Brother melted into the forest, and he slipped silently to the birch trees at the edge of the circle. The fire was so warm he could feel a little of its heat seeping into him, even from so far away. Men and women stood around it, holding out their hands to the warmth, all singing. The song was sad and beautiful, and although Romochka knew all these people by sight, sound and smell, they seemed now strange, transformed and mysterious. His chest burned with a feeling like hunger but closer to his throat. He wished he had something to gnaw on.

The women's voices rose and knotted the wild air, filling the nothingness above him with pain and longing. The men's voices, it seemed to Romochka, tried to scramble up into the sky from the earth and fell back, weeping for their failure. The women's voices fluttered, by choice, down the ladder set by their shifting notes and then stepped down to rest with the men in long chords, joined.

He felt he might burst with the need to scream, howl or run. But he stayed still, blended in the shadows to the trunk of the birch tree. The voices rose again in the same wild refrain and a hopeful croak or moan slipped from his own throat. A woman holding a large sleeping girl child stopped singing, turned and peered hard into the darkness. The singing continued around the fire, but he could hear from a sudden absence in the music that it must have been her voice that soared above the others. She was staring straight at him but couldn't see him. He held himself hunting-still. Her arms clutched the heavily bundled child and he made out the torn fringe of her coat silhouetted by the fire. Her mouth sounded wide, as though smiling into the darkness. He was suddenly very afraid of her.

She took a step towards him, and he saw her face clearly. He knew her, but had never looked closely at her. She was young and beautiful and had a huge scar that split her face down the middle from forehead to chin, breaking even her nose and lips. She only seemed to be smiling—her mouth fell around the scar that way. He knew which hut she lived in and knew the sound of her screams. He knew her thin daughter too. *'Irena! Irena! Don't go far!'* The same voice.

He was no longer afraid. His ears still rang with the high glory of her singing. On impulse, he stepped suddenly out of the shadows and stood, legs apart, arms at his sides. He heard an intake of breath. She knew him too. Everyone here knew he was not one of them, that he was wild and had dogs. She didn't move but looked fearfully into the forest behind him. His heart was shaking him, he knew he should run but still he made no move.

She tilted her head; he saw the fire illuminate full half of her lovely face. She was looking right at him now, into his eyes, and her face glowed in the flickering, sound-filled orange light. Then she opened her wide, broken mouth and was singing again, her back to the other singers, her eyes on him, her arms clutching her sleeping child tightly. He stood like a deer frozen in a beam of light, part of him rising into the black sky with her voice, swelling until he, Romochka, filled all the vast hoop of the night sky above the fire, the mountain and the forest.

She suddenly nodded to him, her mouth arcing around the black hole out of which her shining voice flooded, and he came back to himself. Eyes still fixed on his, she ducked her head then, in what he imagined was an acknowledgment, even a trusting farewell, and turned, still singing, back to the fire and the other people. He was so happy he couldn't bear it. He ran soundlessly, sensing Grey Brother and then White Sister swing from different parts of the forest into the trail behind him.

He went often to listen to the singing after that but it was only after many visits that he saw his singer again. She was alone and ill; her voice had lost the quality that had transfixed him. It fluttered like a sick bird that could not fly, and he was disappointed and annoyed.

He waited until she was trudging back to her hut and then slipped out of the woods into the light of her flame, just to see what she would do. She shrieked and clutched at her chest, gasping her fear. He was at first pleased, then suddenly very upset with her. She pulled herself together, and they stood facing each other in the deep snow. Her torch crackled between them, its light flickering on the pale forms of the birch trees. The sizzling rubber bound to her stick seemed to him very loud, and he dropped his eyes, embarrassed. Then she sucked saliva back from her open mouth and he looked up. She nodded again at him, but without the language of farewell in it, and, clutching the torch with one hand, she leaned slowly forward and reached out her bandaged hand. She brushed his cheek with the backs of her bare fingertips, her eyes smiling. He spun and bounded off into the snowdrifts of the forest, feeling as though, after all, she had sung as before.

The cold deepened. The dogs were restless, day and night. Hunting wasn't too hard at first: everything was struggling on the mountain, animal and human. The dead were quickly buried in snow, but they could make several trips out to any fresh carcass before they lost it.

Romochka's cosy life as a puppy the previous winter was like a dream. He had to stay put in the den, drinking from Mamochka whenever she appeared and eating what the dogs brought in for him. With all the dogs out hunting, and no puppies, the den was bitterly cold. Mamochka didn't have enough milk to fill him and barely enough to warm him up. He put on the tights, the three pairs of trousers, all the long-sleeved garments, pulled socks onto his hands, feet and head, and huddled in the greatcoat, shivering. He shook out a hair-encrusted blanket from the bed and wrapped it around himself. He tried to cajole a dog into staying with him, something only White Sister really understood. He would wait, shivering, cuddling her close until the others returned.

He slept fitfully and dreamed of the singer, her voice wringing the air with the power of a snowstorm, yet so sunny, so starlit, so strong a howl for a moon! Sometimes he felt tied and helpless within its knots and coils; other times he had wings and he saw himself and her as shining birds. Sometimes he dreamed she was his first mother and it was his name she was singing. He named her one evening, rummaging through his mind for the human word, gnawing away until he found the marrow he knew was there. Pievitza. The Singer.

He got used to the dogs pacing hackled and edgy in the den. They were not pacing merely to keep warm, as he was. He shared their apprehension but did not know what, other than the dark and cold, they were worrying about. None of them really knew except Mamochka. She knew what the cold might bring out of the northern forests, and she waited, pacing, infecting everyone with her unease.

One milder night Romochka escaped the den and headed off towards the mountain. The new snow had finally packed down enough to be easy to walk on, and this cheered him up considerably. He left the blanket behind and walked as briskly as his clothes would let him, swinging his club. He knew that Black Sister, Mamochka and Brown Brother were out too, somewhere nearby. Everyone else was in the lair.

It was dark, but he could see quite well. These days he could always see quite well in the outside dark. He headed along the trail to the mountain. He wasn't hunting; he needed the whole clan now to do that. Winter had made the mountain very hard. Even if he found anything, someone, human or animal, would get it off him. Tonight he wanted to listen to the singing; and he wanted to find some tool to shave down the handle of his new club. It was too fat for his hand, and the mountain had everything hidden away somewhere.

He rounded the corner into the open paths that crossed the waste land snowfield to the mountain but could hear no singing. He knew the fires were blazing—he could see a glow in the sky. Why were they silent tonight?

He sensed it: something was coming. Something bad and fast, and spreading out to the sides in front of him. His scalp and neck hairs rose. He suddenly felt how little he could see, not how much. He could smell nothing. His nose was wrapped up, but in any case the cold had dulled his sense of smell. He stopped just in time to see the thing form two eyes on a black fluid point straight ahead of him, break away from the wide shadow and become a huge animal rushing, rushing, rushing up and leaping in utter silence to fill his vision. He was on his back, winded, smothered, his face pressed into coarse hot fur, an alien stench, the sound of teeth.

Then everything was fearsome noise as he felt Mamochka leap from behind his head and land on its back, bringing it sliding and suddenly terribly loud onto the snow.

He rolled and wriggled away, struggling with his layers of clothing. He turned around in time to see the darkness behind him also become points that turned into leaping animals, and then Mamochka was writhing and yelping underneath them. White Sister, Black Sister, Brown Brother, Grey Brother and Golden Bitch and Black Dog were all on top of them, snapping and snarling. The snow squeaked as they struggled; the dogs snarled and yodelled, their homely voices mixing with the deep frightening clamour of the Strangers. Romochka wanted to run but stood where he was, swinging his club ahead of him blindly and shrieking through fear-clenched teeth.

The three huge creatures suddenly separated themselves from the seven dogs, then seemed to melt into the far shadow; but Romochka could feel them turn...and watch...and wait. The dogs knew. They didn't stop to check him or each other. They backed; the shadows followed. They turned and walked slowly until they were near the gate and the path to the den hole, then Romochka felt them all decide that he should *go! Go!* GO! and he sprinted for that cracked door, running and stumbling with them all hedging around him. He wriggled through as Mamochka and Golden Bitch turned and faced outwards, ears flat back and teeth bared, snarling and slavering into the darkness. Everyone else tumbled in after him. The shadows, he knew without looking, had become living animals again and were sprinting too.

After the scramble, panting and scratching to get into the lair, the dogs swallowed their terror and turned in the darkness to fight at the tiny entrance hole. The Strangers' smell was on them, around them, in their fur, in the air.

Nothing happened. They stood, hackles raised until the

smell faded from the air and they could lick its residue off each other and clean their gashes. They tested the outside air and emerged cautiously. The trails, theirs and the Strangers', were clear. The Strangers had faltered and then veered away at Romochka's first pee corner. Mamochka sniffed out their certainty, then their doubt and their fear in long breaths.

They were back the next night, the same three. Then, a few days later, five; then more. The days shortened. The cold clamped huge jaws on the city. The seven dogs slept in a jumbled pile on Mamochka's nest, with Romochka in the middle. The Strangers hunted him in his dreams.

Romochka would feel Mamochka lift her head. He could picture her in the darkness, ears pricked. She would murmur low and the dogs would rise from their uneasy twitching to mutter and pace. They were all together now. There was no lone hunting and the lair hummed like a summer beehive with their many voices.

Once the Strangers were close enough, circling the walls of their sanctuary, even he thought he could smell them, and he stared into the darkness, terrified, longing for Mamochka to stop growling and give the all-clear, to lick him and cuddle him.

When eventually she settled, and the feeling of relief permeated the dark space, they would leave warily and surround Romochka as he peed, refreshing the human markers that kept the foreigners at bay. Then at the dim daybreak they would go together towards the mountain, hunting.

They seemed safe enough in their lair, even though the starving Strangers knew exactly where they were. They travelled to the mountain only in daylight, and increasingly rarely. The other dogs of the mountain and forest had all but disappeared. Perhaps they moved into the city and were shot; perhaps they were eaten by the Strangers. Romochka saw a few he recognised as young dogs from former clans: they had crept in near to the fires and people around the mountain. Romochka's family had to learn to hunt near the fires too, moving as a pack through the vacant snowfield to the village, then dispersing in the shadows around the huts, to meet again before attempting to cross back to their den. If they could breathe the Strangers in the wind, they hung back in the village, waiting. They started to use daylight for the return. This left them just a few short hours in which to find all they needed. Returning the long way, weaving through the unheated and now untenanted warehouses and then the allotment.

It was midwinter. Night had altogether lost its summer depth and was an expanse of dirty orange above and below. Day was a brief visitation of many greys. Romochka could see the dogs' eyes and shapes in the gloom inside the lair only at midday. Otherwise he could see nothing, but could hear them and feel where each of them was. The Strangers were in the empty construction sites all the time. When they were able to get to the mountain Romochka hovered near the trucks, darting in at each fresh tip. He would try to gather enough food for the week in a small sack, but it took the whole family to guard him from other dogs and people once he had some. Then the race home under threat of attack from the Strangers. Grey Brother was the strongest, so Romochka slung the sack over his shoulders and ran next to him, steadying it, slapping and abusing the big dog into submission. He trusted the scouts, Mamochka and Golden Bitch, to warn of approaching Strangers. He concentrated on the sack and on Grey Brother. The rest hung close as his guard. After they had wrestled food home this way twice, Grey Brother understood and they became faster.

Romochka noticed in the twilight of the days that everyone in his family was smaller than before. Narrower. Ribby, with big heads, especially Mamochka. Their fat had dwindled so slowly he hadn't noticed. He felt his own chest. He too was a grid of bones under his hairless skin. They had an occasional fresh feed from a kill, and they had the fruit of their hurried scavenging around the mountain, but it was no longer enough.

Romochka still had his mother's milk. From then on, until Mamochka's milk dried up, Romochka would suck a mouthful from Mamochka and kiss it into a sibling's lapping mouth. They wove around, expectant, when he was drinking. His fingers got used to their knobbly frames and he didn't always share. Sometimes he was too hungry and bad tempered himself. Sometimes he would withhold it out of spite.

The Strangers called out to each other across the ruined church, still outside the charmed circle. They were starving too.

Romochka started making weapons. He sorted his collection of nails and spikes and found a length of metal pipe he could use to bash them through flat pieces of wood. When his hands froze onto the metal he had to pee on them to unstick them. His fingers ached terribly so he wrapped the metal in old cloth and put several socks over his hands. Mamochka licked his hands carefully in between his bursts of hammering, and he warmed them by burying them against her belly or between her thighs. He couldn't do anything without a dog handy to warm him up again. He asked Grey Brother, who was the hairiest and had the strongest teeth, to chew down the handles of things, slapping him off when he thought enough had been crunched off. He made a small stockpile of various kinds of club and nailboard against the far wall of the lair. In the darkness he tested each for swing. He was pleased with his own strength and his new array of teeth. He would smack those Strangers hard if they ever came near him again.

Ж

Romochka awoke from a fitful sleep and stiffened, eyes closed. Everyone else was awake. Despite their stillness, consternation was building in the lair. He didn't know. But they knew; and the Strangers knew. The wind had changed.

No smell came from the north, yet everyone prickled. As he scrambled to the far wall by his pile of weapons, he could feel them all in their positions: Black Dog and Grey Brother, the two strongest, near the entrance. Pacing back and across behind them: Golden Bitch, Mamochka, Black Sister, Brown Brother. He fingered the floor for the board filled with nails. In front of him, flat to the floor, he knew White Sister was crouched, ears flattened and teeth bared. He could hear her rattling snarl-breath and feel her fear. All of them knew too where he was and knew by now that he would be swinging his slabs of wood in the darkness. They stayed out of reach as they guarded him.

There was no smell. The snarl suddenly swelled among

them and he could feel them tense. There was still no smell. He closed his eyes to stop blind-staring the freezing darkness, gritted his teeth on a scream and swung harder. Each breath threatened to turn into a shriek of fear as it left him. He swung harder again, fighting the empty air.

Then the Strangers' smell was there among them, and the snarls of the family erupted in the chamber. Ahead there was a huge tumult, a crashing, compound tumbling, snarling, snick-snack, scrabble, huff, and then bubbling swells of fury. He heard Grey Brother yelp in pain as the fight rolled with crashing and scraping over towards the nest and back. White Sister in front of him shot forward, and then there were two fights up ahead towards the entrance. The deep unfamiliar snarls and gasps moved between one and the other. Strange yelling. Scrabbling at the dark entrance; fierce, strange screams again, and more scraping. He could hear Mamochka snarling through jaws clamped tight, tugging, and with each tug, a Stranger's deep yelps halfway up the tunnel. He heard them all latch on, pull, and then the hoarse breathing, a scuffle of frantic adjustments by the silent, concentrated family; more hoarse breathing, a dimmer struggle. Then quiet.

Everyone relaxed and he lowered his nailboard, shaking all over. He could smell blood. Mamochka and Golden Bitch dragged the dead animal to one side and everyone trotted around sniffing the story, trailing the one who had escaped up to the entrance. No one made a move to go outside. Grey Brother made an odd sound as he passed back and forth—he was using only three legs.

Outside the Strangers howled and everyone hummed and prickled. This time he felt them move with Mamochka to bunch just behind the entrance. White Sister was still flat in front of him and he sensed that there was no one except her between him and the entrance. He was panting, holding his board out in front of him.

We are the only dish on the table, now. Suddenly he saw his first mother's face, her wry expression and wide, sidelong smile as she said that. He hadn't tried to picture her for a very long time now and couldn't normally drag her face into memory. It was such a pretty face! Hairless though, and with very short teeth. He held onto the image. She had managed somehow to get past the Strangers, to come checking up on him, making sure he wasn't sucking snot or holding onto his penis. She wouldn't approve of either the dogs or the Strangers. She'd tell them all off, and then she'd smack him one, too. They'd all slink away with their tails between their legs and their bellies, eyes and teeth low to the ground and he'd slip into his warm bed in a warm, lit-up room, and he'd hold onto his pisya and snivel until she came in, all dressed in her red glitter dress, and she would tuck him in with a biscuit and hot milk before she went out hunting. How wonderful. How delicious! All this would vanish.

This time he felt the Stranger come slowly through the icy hole, wait, and then drop into the lair. It stopped. The dogs were silent, held by Mamochka. He felt the new presence thickening the air, blocking the flow from the ice hole to him, and then he thought he felt it stiffen at the sight of him and White Sister, who had started growling, high and mean. Then he heard the faint pressure scrape of powerful hind legs. Everything slowed down. The Stranger had leapt and was silent, airborne. Would land once only: yes, there! Thud-scrape.

Airborne again, huge, filling the darkness, flying over White Sister's swelling snarl towards him. Now!

Romochka swung as hard as he could. He fell back against the wall as his nailboard stuck fast into something and was ripped out of his hands. White Sister's high snarl was in the same moment muffled, buried deep in flesh, and then he smelled the tearing of hot guts. White Sister and the Stranger crashed together to the floor in front of him and the far end of the lair exploded in snarls and yells, yelps, scuffles. He heard Mamochka's snarking snarl, and the swallowing increments of her fierce grip.

He heard slithering down the ice hole and another explosion of snarling and scuffling. Two fights split, roiling in the darkness to far sides of the den, and he faced the icy hole unguarded. He thought he felt another Stranger, and another, and another, all leaping at him just as the first had done, but... no, they were phantoms. He was yabbering now, patting frantically to his left for another weapon. He calmed down a little as his fingers found his club, and then he realised White Sister was still right near him, busy. Tensing, then regripping. The subtle, unmistakeable noises of throttling against the feeble scraping of the disembowelled animal.

The lair stilled to other rattles, scrabbles, crunching guttural growls. He could smell blood everywhere, and death. He schooled his ears to seek their voices, since all his sense of them had gone haywire. He could hear Golden Bitch, Mamochka, with kill grips. Black Dog roaming free, growling in the airflow from the ice hole. White Sister, breathing easy now but still gripping, just beside him. Then a scuffle and Black Sister too, with perhaps a hamstring grip. Then, in the nest, Grey

72

Brother panting in pain, low to the ground. Brown Brother…
he reached out into the darkness and his ears crawled with
foreboding. Nothing.

Nothing, and again nothing.

Slowly the tension in the lair eased. He could hear normal
breathing and movement, but the pressure in his chest began to
build. He stumbled forward, reaching blind and disoriented
into the wrecked space. White Sister came to his side and,
holding her, sobbing now, he inched forward towards where
the others had clustered and stiffened.

The dogs sniffed long and hard, and then, with the last
warmth of Brown Brother in their nostrils, turned away,
ignoring that bloodied mass as if it too were a Stranger.

Romochka couldn't let it alone. His fingers fluttered over
his brother's body, wriggling into every wound, poking and
prodding. He licked the bloodied face, whimpered. Whined as
a dog then swore and cajoled. He curled up with Brown
Brother as he had many times. Not even White Sister came to
him as he sobbed, gasping, trying to ease the emptiness the
dark and the Strangers had opened up inside him.

The huge body cooled. Romochka was driven shivering to
the nest and the warmth of the others.

All of them were injured, except Romochka. Grey Brother
was hurt worst of all. His foreleg hung limp, a mess of crushed
and clotted flesh above the joint. White Sister had a flank gash
from the attack of the first Stranger. Mamochka's beautiful soft
ear was ripped. Black Sister had a tear down her face that
would later give her an even more dangerous appearance. The
others had neck and shoulder bites.

They lay together, licking each other, concentrating on each wound. By the time they had finished, the corpses were crisp with icicles and as solid as rocks.

The dead saved them. They had enough frozen meat to last them until the smell of spring seeped up through the snow, daylight strengthened and people drove the Strangers from the waste lands, forest and mountain. They stayed put in the lair, cleaning out their wounds with unhurried licking sessions, conserving their strength. Grey Brother recovered slowly. Romochka fed him chewed-up pieces and lay with his arms around him to sleep. For a time, he beat the others off if they approached Brown Brother's corpse. Then he forgot, and that heap became a Stranger to him too.

No Strangers tried, after that, to enter the dogs' den. And the dog extermination operation that cleared the city of nearly all starving homeless dogs missed them altogether.

Ж

The daylight and the warmth in the air pulled them from the lair. Romochka stood in the lane in front of the construction sites, breathing deeply. The snow still lay in thick drifts, covering everything, but the trees stood bare and free. Something about the black lace of the trees against the sky spoke of freshness, even though not a single green bud was to be seen. The snow banked against the trunks, splashed now with weak sunlight, had a defeated look. It was losing its hold, sucked away into the melt underneath. He could smell it, dank with rotted autumn leaves and the promise of mushrooms. He could hear it gurgling quietly away to itself, waiting to rush out and make everything horribly muddy. The flock of clouds in the blue above had gentle pale grey centres. Clouds that would never snow, he thought, his heart leaping. These spring rain clouds made him so happy! He cut a tight circle with a quick-step scamper. Soon they would all be in the forest playing, in the grass, in the green green grass! Everything sick and dying would have vanished with the winter, the fat would fill them, smooth out their boniness and make them all bigger; the world would be new again.

That night Romochka insisted they go out for dinner and get something fresh, warm and bloody. He was utterly sick of the frozen carcasses, utterly sick of the smell of them, utterly sick of the hard work to chew frozen meat off the bone, utterly sick of peeing on his own food to soften it up.

II

A small boy about six years old is walking just inside the forest, weaving through alder, linden, oak and birch. It is a picturesque season: creamy sunlight slides over mottled trunks; fine white branches and pendent leaves wave in the breeze. The air is filled with birdsong and pollen. White blossom hangs in clumps on the rowan trees at the edge of the forest and cemetery. Yellow archangel flowers, lily of the valley and wood sorrel speckle the glades. The sweet scent of linden flowers thickens the air and, up close to any linden tree, the song of honeybees adds to the subtle din of birdsong, electric-cable buzz and distant highway.

This place is one of those odd pockets of Moscow where forest takes over and city fades to sound only. It is a tiny frontier—part of a tattered wilderness interspersed with city, more city, then fields, dachas, villages—the beginning, in dribs and drabs, of the unending wilds that stretch northwards into myth.

On the brink of the vacant lands the buildings are a strange mixture of the older highrise apartment blocks with blue-tiled façades and new projects—excursions reclaiming the grass and swamp, begun in high enthusiasm during perestroika and then abandoned through ever-lengthening temporary delays. The spikes of rusting construction girders and concrete façades stand at the edge of the untended fields, marshes and copses of birch forest. Electricity pylons carry low-slung lines over the fields and into the forest. A few green and brown dachas huddle together in a copse under one of the nearer pylons, looking like a marooned fragment of a village, which is what they are.

He scuffs his feet along, kicking anything solid ahead of him.

The residents of the rubbish mountain and the forest know him and leave him well alone, even go to great lengths to avoid him. What stands out at first sight is his mane of matted black hair. It sweeps back from his brow in a tangled ropey mass that reaches the middle of his back. He is, like everyone here, filthy and dressed in several layers of motley clothes and rags. He is uncommonly healthy for a child of this place, his body straight and wiry. His physique is harder and more agile than that of any normal child. He is more dexterous and twists through his spine more quickly than humans ever do. He swings the rough club in his right hand with easy proficiency. He is almost silent, except for the snarls that can rattle through his nose and teeth.

You cannot guess his parentage exactly, except that he is dark-eyed and faintly Tartar, pale-skinned under the encrusted filth. He has good features: broad cheek bones above a wide mouth and excellent teeth, but it is hard to tell whether he could look pleasing. His black, slightly Asiatic eyes would meet yours, if you came upon him by accident, with a kind of naïve hostility and mercenary appraisal: disconcerting in a six-year-old. He also smells worse than any bomzh. But this isn't why people avoid him. There are many odd people on the mountain, and as a child he would normally be easy pickings for predators.

People avoid him because he is never alone.

It is whispered that his dogs can appear from nowhere and there are more than twenty of them. They are bigger and stronger than normal dogs. His own long, sharpened fingernails have the strength of wolves' claws. He is a demon, some say, who eats the flesh of humans and wanders alone in the form of a child to tempt people near. Others say he is a genetic mutant escaped from top-secret laboratories. Even the sceptics are, nonetheless, aware that he is dangerous. A ripple spreads across the mountain and forest at the sight of him. People wedge their shanty doors shut and watch him through cracks.

Their own dogs bristle and growl uneasily, snuffing the air as he passes. That dogs fear him adds immeasurably to his reputation.

Through the gentler seasons, the dogs and the people who live in the ramshackle huts on the forest edge of the rubbish mountain leave each other alone. They share a territory and share its hardships and provisions. They share its dangers.

Militzia, charged with fighting the twin threats of disease and crime, and trying at the same time to supplement their own meagre pay-packets, patrol the mountain and the rim of the forest. They destroy the shanty huts and round up people, shooting pet dogs in front of their owners. Last autumn the clean-up was in earnest: an unprecedented attempt to remove homeless people from the city centre and get rid of the increasing number of stray and feral dogs. Moscow was to be a showpiece, the government TV stations proclaimed. The streets were swept, the canals cleaned by wide armed barges; dog registration was half-heartedly imposed, a census taken, residency permits audited. Stray dogs and people were hounded and bullied to the outskirts and beyond.

In winter things are different. The militzia season is more or less over, at least out in the open by forest and mountain. The bomzhi survive by working or begging in the city, there to be preyed upon by the militzia waiting outside factories on payday; or supplementing their income through beggar protection rackets. The enmity between feral dogs and bomzhi is seasonal, and winter is its peak. Clan dogs break into any hut that seems unusually cold and fight other packs off the fresh meat they know they will find. If humans notice, they might beat the dogs off with flames and shouting and sticks, but still at times neighbours find a chewed-over frozen corpse when the dawn-dusk seeps like milk into the sky.

Out here, in this land of the dead and the discarded, the bodies exposed when the snow melts in spring are unremarkable. People of the city call them snowdrops. The municipal authorities and the militzia collected more than three hundred this thaw.

In spring, life returns to a precarious normality. For now, men and dogs get along in mutual wariness and muted hostility. The weather is mild; pickings in city and forest are good. And they have a shared enemy.

Ж

82

Romochka kicked through the leaves and junk. White Sister, Grey Brother and Black Dog were with him. He could see Black Dog scavenging by the river up ahead, looking like any dog out there by himself, minding his business. Grey Brother and White Sister were in the forest to his right, out of sight but watching over him. They were waiting for him to go deep into the forest for the hunt. He could feel their separate, reassuring presences, their patience.

He was hovering at the rim of the forest for no good reason, something that had lately become a habit. At first he had enjoyed the stir he caused trailing through with his siblings at his heels. But these days he meandered apparently alone, apparently aimlessly. He listened to fragments of human speech, repeated them in his head in wonder and misery. *'Yeah, I can get you a teev. Won't be fuckin easy but I can get you a teev.'...'I'll feed you to the dogs if you don't stop whining'...'You want wheels? ASK THE ROOF FOR WHEELS!'* If he saw people, particularly if he saw children, he would find a nice birch tree and whack it savagely with his club until its bark was pulped. Then he would saunter off again. He had begun to come close to the huts and the outskirts of the shanty village. Quite a few birch trees had his marks on them.

Today he saw nobody. The muster was over. These days, two men with guns came every morning to the village. They dressed in ordinary, if clean, clothes but their haircuts made them look like militzia. They smelled faintly of houses: cooked oil, sweat and soap. They lined up the men, women and children. Then they chose men with sores, missing limbs or scars. They took the babies off their mothers and gave them to other women. Young children too were swapped around, and then everyone was yelled at, loaded into a minivan and driven to the city. They'd return late tonight, and exhausted mothers would retrieve and feed their starving children.

He smashed some bottles with his club behind a shack but no one came out, even though he could tell there were children hiding inside, hiding first from the muster, and now from him. He knew they were watching him. He howled, eyeing the pretty lace at the window. White Sister and Grey Brother appeared and sat beside him, as he stared at the back door, but nothing happened. He thought of pulling away some of the polythene nailed all over the shack and crushing it into little pieces to provoke them, but changed his mind. The shack itself seemed special to him—it would be wrong for him to touch it. He headed off into the forest feeling restless, even disconsolate. He really wished he had some lace in his collection of special things, or better still, a big piece to hang on the front of his bower.

The singer, his singer, was gone these many months. Her hut too was gone, obliterated as if it had never been. He wished she would turn up again. If he ever saw her again, or her skinny daughter, this time, he told himself, he would talk to them. 'Hi,' he said conversationally to a slender tree. His voice was odd and croaky. He tried, louder, 'How are you?' Black Dog trotted up, startled, and licked his face, then fell in behind him with White Sister and Grey Brother. They set off at a trot into the forest.

When he was with the dogs he had no reason to fear bomzhi but they worried him, unsettled him. He thought about them a lot, mulling over what he saw them do. Territory and paths clearly mattered to them, but other than obvious zones around fires and houses, he couldn't see the boundaries, and this made him fear them a little. Sometimes they seemed to him just like sick dogs or lone strays. You couldn't predict when they would be dangerous. Some of them didn't know how to behave, either with him or with each other. They fought and yowled, ripped and tore each other over food and scraps of metal. They stole from each other, beat each other senseless, even killed. They mated even when one of them didn't want to. At other times they touched each other with a tenderness that filled him with confusion and longing.

At first sight and first smell, Romochka knew that to strangers, to house people, he himself was one of the bomzhi, the horde of the homeless, undifferentiated to the city people and the militzia. For a long while he had been charmed that he could pass as a bomzh but these days it troubled him. Today, like many days before, he escaped his vague unhappiness by returning to his usual activities: hunting, or home to the lair.

The forest was best of all in springtime. The dogs scented for him, and he climbed like a young bear to raid nests of eggs and fledglings. Black Dog always dug crazily for moles, although he rarely got one. They chased spotted deer fauns on sight but avoided young elk: they had fierce and powerful mothers. Around the spring-fed ponds the young ducks and other water-fowl were plentiful, if rather smart.

Romochka couldn't swim and didn't like getting wet, but all of them tried hard to fish, so enticing was that glitter in the fast running stream that ran from the prudi through the forest and into the city. Black Sister, always the fastest, was the only one to have had any success. She had stood up to her shoulders in the stream, staring intently into the water, again and again plunging her great head under. The one time she came up with that splattering wriggling meal of silver made them all redouble their efforts.

Today, however, Romochka was bad tempered and half-hearted, and they got nothing.

Ж

Grey Brother bounded along, joyous, and with the unmistakeable air of transgression. He led Romochka across the allotment with a spring in his step, his limp barely perceptible. Romochka thought Grey Brother was excited that it was, for the first time, just the two of them. He scampered too as he wondered what possibilities a hunt with his surviving brother would bring. Grey Brother was strong and a good hunter, although not as fast as he had been, and Grey Brother still enjoyed the forbidden more than the sanctioned. He liked to start fights with other clan dogs by flouting their boundaries, and he liked to sneak off by himself. He had been known to go out hunting with Black Sister, only for the two to return singly from different parts of the territory. Once he disappeared for more than a day and came home with nothing, the smells of strange dogs all about him.

Grey Brother marked the last meeting post and stood, quivering. He looked towards the mountain and hesitated. Romochka was about to lead off, but Grey Brother suddenly made up his mind and sprang off in the other direction. Romochka ran after him, yipping in delight. He had never gone this way.

Grey Brother was redolent with the smell of mischief and had a lot to show him. They roamed through the grassy verges by the highrises, along roadsides dodging traffic and joggers, past shops and kiosks. Romochka's spirits soared with the adventure of it. Then they came to the metro entrance. Around the squat glass building with its ever-swinging doors, Romochka saw faces he knew, people sleeping on small squares of lawn with their dogs or begging at the metro doors. He noticed that they recognised him too. And Grey Brother.

His high spirits slowly subsided. Grey Brother knew this place too well. He moved in a practised way from meeting point to meeting point. This was where the paper bags of half-eaten pirozhki came from. This was where they found whole loaves of bread. Cake.

His brows drew together. They had all duped him. They had all hunted in the city. All except Romochka.

Grey Brother noticed Romachka's changed mood and struggled to find something naughty enough to cheer him up. He tried scaring an old man but Romochka only slouched after him, deep in thought. They chased a cat half-heartedly, but soon gave up and trailed back to the allotment. Romochka didn't mark the post. He felt the treachery of his family keenly. He couldn't smell the city on them, and so they had hidden it from him. The dogs, who never lied to each other, had lied to him, all of them. Everyone, even the people of the mountain, went there day in, day out.

Grey Brother licked his hand with uncommon tenderness as they walked slowly back across the allotment. He didn't dart off to do something of his own, and Romochka was touched. Grey Brother didn't usually hang around being kind hearted.

Back in the lair he sat down away from the others and scowled at them. Mamochka didn't trust him and didn't expect him to hunt properly. From this day on, he told himself, I will be hunting in the city. He glowered at them—Mamochka lying on the nest oblivious to his resolve; Golden Bitch staring at him with furrowed brow from the sentry point. You can't stop me, he thought to himself. I'll show you all.

Ж

Romochka, White Sister and Grey Brother headed home with a jaunty air. He carried their catch in a large doubled plastic bag slung over his shoulder. Now and then they had to stop while he flopped it onto the ground to have a rest. He sighed with exaggerated contentment and pride as White Sister and Grey Brother sniffed it passionately, wagging their tails. They reached the last meeting place by the fence and he swung the bag around in a flourish to leave a message for the others. He peed on the last post, too, for the first time since Grey Brother had taken him to the city. He, Romochka, had brought something home, and it was extra special! He let Grey Brother lick his fingers as they made their way across the meadow grass of the allotment.

Everyone would know that he hunted, and hunted well. Every stranger visiting their meeting place would know that *he* was part of the family. Each breath filled him with a sweet happiness the closer he got to home and the further he got from the city and people. He began to smile delightedly to himself. It had been chancy, but in the end so skilful. He was bursting with it now, if underneath still a little shocked at what he had done. His ear still burned.

Romochka, White Sister and Grey Brother had sniffed trails in the maze of lanes around the shops, apartment blocks and metro station for a couple of hours, finding nothing much. They missed the one cat they chased; it ran at Romochka to escape, and he misjudged his dive.

He could tell from the way White Sister and Grey Brother lifted their noses that the woman lumbering up the footpath towards them was carrying something good. He felt dizzy for a second with the strength of his inspiration. He didn't think. He gripped his club, stepped out in front of her and swung it hard at her knees. The dogs held to the shadows, disoriented, not understanding his intention.

He missed. The woman stepped back, dropped her bags and cuffed him across the side of the head, sending him sprawling.

'Filth! Bomzh! Animal!' she shrieked, stepping up to kick him, but she got no further. The two dogs were on her. White Sister stood over Romochka, black eyes blazing, snarling and leaping to snap at the woman's face. Grey Brother circled her and began darting in and out from behind for nips. She swung, yelling in pain, to face him. Romochka grabbed the two shopping bags and ran, wrestling them along the road, around the corner and into an empty cardboard box next to a dumpster in the alley. He shut the box and sat crouched inside, listening. He was shaking all over. The woman screamed and screamed, but he could tell that White Sister and Grey Brother were no longer with her: the screams were very regular. His heart stopped pounding, although his head still throbbed.

He felt and sniffed through the bags. Chickens! Two! No feathers. Cheese! A big half round. Sausages! Celery, carrots, onions. Cucumbers. A liver! What was this big thing? He sniffed it, his nose still stupefied from the liver. A cabbage! There was a commotion of people now around the corner, and he could hear the woman still yelling and screaming. He waited, his hands feeling over the food until there was calm. White Sister and Grey Brother wouldn't be far. He knew they would find him. He would need them, to stop some big kid or dog thieving his haul.

Then he started to feel bad. It crept up on him. He saw himself again and again swinging his club at the woman. *Filth! Bomzh! Animal!* His first mother would have been angry.

'Filth. Bomzh. Animal.' He said the words over and over to himself, his own rusty little-kid voice scaring him in the darkness of the box. Something dissolved suddenly, some huge barrier between him and people. They had been in the untouchable fringe of his world; dangerous, like dogs with frothy mouths, yet irrelevant like those sick dogs, too. He started to cry softly to himself.

He heard the dogs outside tracking him, then Grey Brother's nose pushed through the flaps of the box. Romochka giggled in relief and madly licked that big head. He wiped his face and nose on furry shoulders. He backed out and pulled the bags out after him. He let them sniff the liver on his fingers and the chickens in the bag. They bounded around in delight and triumph, which cheered him up immensely. He loaded everything into one bag, put it inside the other, and off they set.

After that, Romochka and the three young dogs preyed on people. They kept as far from their own part of the city as they felt they could safely go, and with this their open path territory expanded considerably. They got a system going and Romochka no longer had to front up first. It was heart-racingly exciting. He would pick a likely victim, someone with shopping bags in a deserted alley, and saunter past them, or behind them, gleeful that there was no way they could recognise that he was a hunting dog. Then, when he judged the moment, he yipped. White Sister, Grey Brother and Black Sister would appear silently out of the darkness and hold the person at bay. Romochka would run hunched into the melée, take the bags and leave the three to keep the furious and frightened victim against the wall until he was safely away. Then the dogs would melt into the darkness again.

Romochka didn't let them do it too often and never in the same place twice. People would not put up with that, he told himself, if it happened too often. But it was his pride and joy. It was his special hunt with the three. He began to watch people the way he would watch birds to see where their nests were.

He became aware that the dogs each had a different view of people. Grey Brother would beg now and then, from a safe distance. Golden Bitch and Black Dog at times chased kids for the fun of it, and Romochka and the three joined in. When they were all together they could scare even adults, especially the diseased or drunken ones. These reminded Romochka faintly of his uncle, and he whooped as he saw them run from the hunting pack.

Mamochka avoided humans and had trained Romochka and the three to fear them. Yet, in time, he noticed that for all

91

her wariness Mamochka was also the most attached to humans. Unlike the others, she knew the human word 'dog'. He realised he had never seen her deliberately frighten people, and she would only snarl at them to defend him, Romochka, or (he guessed) one of her puppies. He saw that she had a basic respect and affection that extended to all humans they met, and he was chastened.

Perhaps there were other ways to get food from humans.

People were relatively kindly towards dogs, he discovered. He made White Sister and Grey Brother sit beside him on the street and hummed meanly at them if they snarled or growled, or even lifted a lip at anyone. They both sat, looking crestfallen—ears down, eyes sliding this way and that in discomfort, but quiet enough. He stood outside the Teramok cabin by the metro station with a plastic bag and accosted everyone who entered. He tried his croaky little voice on the long-rehearsed phrase: 'Please, give. Beautiful dogs, hungry.'

People looked at him and the dogs and laughed. They *were* beautiful dogs: one white; one gold and grey.

'What do you want from me, kid?'

'Food, please, for the starving dogs. When you finish.'

Many did come out and drop their leftovers into his bag. Even the Teramok workers did on occasion. He was all the more successful because he shook his head when they offered him money. Some people gave him coins anyway, and he accumulated a small cache among his treasures in the corner of the lair.

Things only got out of control if anyone tried to pat the dogs. White Sister and Grey Brother immediately lost their grip on the parts they were playing and snapped furiously, then tried to run away. He took to standing well in front of them, so

92

that he could intercept such hands himself, and say, nodding seriously: 'They are hungry. They bite. Hard.'

When he called the collection to a close, the three of them would scamper off, he with a spring in his step, they with tails waving gaily. Out of sight they would all check the catch, and he would kiss and make a big fuss of the brave dogs.

This kind of hunting was less fun but he felt good about it. He would come home with a heavy bag and everyone would eat well. He was sure Mamochka would approve. He watched other beggars and rehearsed their phrases. *For the love of Christ, give!* Professional beggars didn't mind him. Some even nodded to him as he passed by. Word soon spread in their city-wide network that the crazy dogboy was harmless and never took money, and so the beggarmasters left him alone.

As Romochka's confidence in his urban hunting grew, so did his ability in live hunts. He worked better with his siblings, and they learned quickly to cover his weaknesses and trust his strengths. He was a finer strategist than any of them, and they brought home good food regularly under his guidance. They began to look to him for direction, and to pay attention to his plans.

Ж

It was a daytime hunt in the city. Romochka and Grey Brother trapped the large ginger tom in a cul-de-sac, Romochka's heart hammering with excitement. He crouched, club extended. Grey Brother crouched too, ready to leap up or flatten his body, depending on what the cat chose to do. The dogs and Romochka generally chased cats on sight—exhilarated by the furry burst of speed as they fled, their fury and violence when cornered—but without real hope of catching one.

The cat stood still, back arched, tail bristling as thick as Romochka's arm. It bared its puny teeth and spat twice. Romochka giggled and yipped. Yes, that's what he'd do too, spit and think, spit and think. Grey Brother quivered at each sound it made but held back with uncharacteristic humility, letting Romochka lead. Romochka threw pebbles at the cat to make it choose, but it moved only slightly and kept focus. His heart leapt in delight, his belly jumping. They had a cat cornered, and what a cat!

Then the cat bolted, choosing to go for Romochka, as they always did. He was ready, and, as luck would have it, he felt his club connect. The cat roiled back across the open space before the wall and whipped itself upright in the far corner. There it waited, hooped and spiky, tempting them, daring them to close in so as to shorten their reaction time when it made a run for it. Romochka could see it all, and he held Grey Brother back, making the cat choose again.

It chose Grey Brother. It dashed under him, seemingly straight into his great, downward swinging jaws and descending trap of a body. Then, at the last second, it twisted upwards and wrapped itself, snarling, claws outspread, over Grey Brother's face.

Grey Brother yelped and staggered up, shaking his head from side to side, blind-staring into ginger belly fur while the cat sank its teeth into his brow. Romochka dropped his club and raced up. He grabbed the cat with both hands and wrenched as hard as he could, pulling five parts of Grey Brother's face up with the cat.

The cat let go just as suddenly as it had attached itself, twisted, and swiped Romochka across the face. He dropped it and kicked viciously, his rage bubbling up with the blood from the stinging gashes. Grey Brother had lost all reason now and was scrabbling for the cat in the corner. Then he had it in his paws, trying to bring his jaws through its flailing weapons as it yowled, raked him and wriggled free. But it was still trapped and by now Romochka was ready. He kept Grey Brother in check with fierce growls. The cat was his.

It fought with such feistiness, even when exhausted, that Romochka wished it hadn't died. He would have liked to carry it alive back to the lair, but in the end he killed it almost by accident with a blow to the skull. He was still very proud of himself to be bringing home cat for dinner. It was a brave cat, and good to chew. He decided he liked eating brave and beautiful things best. He kept its ginger tail in his collection of rat skulls, feathers, beaks, claws, iron nails, metal spikes and coins.

Romochka and Grey Brother had brought home the first healthy cat the pack had ever caught, and with that kill Romochka's place as hunter was finally established.

Ж

At the back of the Roma Restaurant, Romochka made friends with the cook. Mamochka apparently knew her. Romochka, watching from the shadows, could see his mother's fear and pleasure. His heart melted as the wary Mamochka bolted a plate of spaghetti and meatballs. The cook, big arms crossed over big breasts, talked softly all the while, and Mamochka's ears stayed flattened and her eyes soft and even half trusting as she ate.

The next time they went together with Golden Bitch and Black Dog, who both hung back in the alley while Romochka waited with Mamochka in the pool of light at the Roma's back door. Mamochka gave one small bark and sat down, expectant, her tail waving. The cook came out and stopped short at the sight of Romochka.

'Good dog Little Mother bring me here.' Romochka said quickly. Mamochka looked up in surprise at the sound of his voice, then licked his hand and continued to wag her tail.

'I thought she was a stray,' the cook said, frowning.

'Yes,' said Romochka. 'Me too.' He held up four fingers. 'Four dogs.' He called Golden Bitch and Black Dog from the shadows. They stood well back, reluctant, unconvinced. He pointed to Mamochka, to Golden Bitch, to Black Dog, then to himself. 'Four dogs, please.'

The big cook laughed. She had a gurgly, juicy laugh. Black Dog and Golden Bitch would have fled, but he and Mamochka held them there with their assurance.

'OK—dinner for four, Laurentia's best,' the cook said, still laughing, and turned back inside. She came back out with four bowls of steaming ravioli. This, thought Romochka happily, is the dog's dinner. She handed him the bowls, and he carried them one by one to the three dogs, then took the last one for himself.

'Nice manners, young man. Want a fork?' she asked. He

96

shook his head, blushing with pleasure as he shovelled the wonderful hot food into his maw.

Romochka, Mamochka, Black Dog and Golden Bitch trotted the long and dangerous trail home at peace with the world, their bellies warm and full. They saw a cat hissing and spluttering in a narrow lane and didn't even chase it. They howled at a military siren. They chased each other around in the vacant lot before their lair.

The Roma was open late. It was a long trail through hostile territories, human and dog, to get there. Skirmishes as they traversed closed paths, judicious retreats, all-out routs, lurking, waiting and slinking through the cold alleys; these were normal. They could get there quickly if they were lucky, but it sometimes took them half the night. Laurentia fed them all the leftovers after midnight in eight bowls. They would get home again sometimes just before dawn, still full-bellied and ready to sleep.

She blinked hard when Romochka first arrived with everyone.

'How many in the family, young man?'

'That's it,' he said.

She would watch, humming and murmuring, as he handed out the plates to the shy dogs, and then praise his manners when he served himself last. He collected the bowls for her at the end and occasionally felt her warm hand touch his as he handed them back. It was a delicious jolt.

He adored Laurentia. In time he took it as his due that his bowl was special—hot and fresh, not scraps.

'Where you living, then, wildchild?' Laurentia asked, pausing in the middle of a song in a strange language. Romochka looked up. He almost answered, then stopped, worried. Mamochka, could she speak, would never tell anybody. Not even the slightly foolish Black Dog would tell. A mental picture flashed of how assiduously Black Dog posted warnings. He wanted to tell Laurentia everything about himself. He stared at her, big-eyed.

'No place,' he said slowly.

'You warm enough in winter in No Place?'

'Yes, snug as a bug.' He put his head down, thinking furiously. He had tricked her with a lie. Would she be cross? He couldn't bear to look. Mamochka was whining softly now, worried. Time to get going. But he had to give Laurentia something special, just to say sorry. He looked up.

'My name is Romochka,' he said.

Laurentia beamed at him and held out her huge hand for his. 'Come!' she said.

Mamochka growled first, then all the others rumbled low, lifting their heads from their food and moving in as a pack.

'Shush shush,' Laurentia said, flapping her other hand at them. 'Good dogs—I'm not going to hurt your precious prince.' She kept her outstretched hand waggling in a demanding way at Romochka.

Romochka smiled his rare, sweet smile and put his hand in hers. She swallowed it in her huge palm, and he blushed deep red. She led him inside. They didn't go into the restaurant, which, from the smell, was down a long dark passage. He followed Laurentia as she ducked through a small padded door. She flicked a switch and a single globe lit up a narrow, jumbled room. On one side there was a low sagging bed that smelled strongly of Laurentia; a bench with an electric hotplate on one side and a three half-empty preserve jars on the other. A loaf of bread lay in the middle, one end sliced off, and a delicate dusting of crumbs spread over the bench. He could smell the dried end of the bread, and its soft freshness underneath. Everything was cosy and lovely. He couldn't believe Laurentia had invited him in. He guessed her quilt and bed were dry. Everything was so well set up, with little bits of food here and there, handy for any time you needed them.

He stared at a faded picture of a blue sky over a sunny city. Laurentia sighed and murmured, 'I'll go back as soon as I pay off those filthy scoundrels.'

She reached for a large jar of biscuits perched on a high crooked shelf, took out three and put them in his hand. Then she led him outside again.

'Scram, caro,' she said, 'before I get caught.'

Romochka drifted off in a haze of happiness. Mamochka sniffed him all over, concerned and impressed. He smelled his own hands. He could smell the sweet oil of the biscuits on one. On the other, he could smell Laurentia. Grease and cooked food, sweat and a woman smell, and, underneath that, a faint burnt smell, as if her old sweat had turned to ash.

Ж

Out of respect for Laurentia and Mamochka, Romochka all but gave up robbery with violence. Through the summer he did well with various forms of pilfering and begging, for which he used only White Sister and Grey Brother. He thought of Brown Brother occasionally: so slow to anger and happy to hang out with him for hours on end. Brown Brother would have been perfect. Grey Brother didn't mind begging from people but was fidgety and liable to vanish when Romochka wasn't looking. Black Sister was aggressive and bad for business. He could never get the snarl off her face.

Despite his extraordinary appearance and smell, the people of the city barely noticed Romochka. People moved with practised blindness through public spaces, silent and unsmiling, their eyes never seeming to focus, their thoughts turned inwards or dimmed. In the city, children who were pretty, clean and well dressed sometimes caught an eye or a smile, but unkempt children, or children who stank, were erased. There were too many, and the lost children of the city too overwhelming, for any one person to be able to cope with an awareness of them.

Some people did give food or money to children, but without conversation, fiercely incurious. It seemed they built this into their routine, just as they would going to the theatre. Romochka was drawn to the area around the metro entrance, placing himself to intercept these routines, seeking out his regulars with glances, reminding them that he was there. Even White Sister and Grey Brother knew some of their people. They waved their tails lightly when they scented the skinny lady who wore pretty clothes or the dvornik from the war museum who smelled of vodka and toffee. White Sister and Grey Brother were large dogs, similar in form with their twin curled tails and long legs. They both had large dark almond shaped eyes with black rims set wide on their handsome faces.

They had very red tongues and very white teeth and pointed, wolf-like ears. To be recognised and deferred to by these beautiful beasts charmed many people.

Romochka both encouraged and restrained the dogs: he didn't like them getting close to people, but their courtesy was a great asset in the hunt. His role was the boy-owner. He never dropped to all fours, or licked or sniffed the dogs. He didn't snarl unless he had to. He was known now as the boy asking for dog food, and some people from the apartment blocks sought him out to give him old cakes, bread, meat and bones. He collected so much good food that his family were shining and sleek—better looking than most strays or ferals. He didn't like seeing them eat rubbish off the mountain any more, and it was a long time now since he had hovered at the back of a garbage truck.

They were fairly safe around the metro. The uniformed men were nearly all crippled veterans with their caps in their outstretched hands. The skinhead gangs and the other street kids frequented slightly less populated places. When Romochka saw forest people in the city begging at the entrances to metro stations, or in the underpasses, in front of churches or hotels, he felt a pull. A feeling that they, alone among all others passing by, were of his kind. They knew him too. Recognition flickered between them, loaded with mistrust, unwilling; unable to flare up without incinerating the tenuous bond they both felt tying them to each other through their shared land. He treasured that thin glimmer. He actively sought mountain people for the sake of it. Yet only in the city was this thread palpable. On the mountain or in the forest he was, as always, their enemy.

The bomzhi watched this domesticated Romochka warily. Those who lived out at the mountain knew he was wild and that he had more dogs than just these two pretty performers.

Ж

Romochka had never seen anything like Mamochka and Golden Bitch's hunt. The dogs, he could tell, had also never smelled anything like it. It was a huge bird with glinting blue feathers, a long blue neck (broken and mauled), a white mask and a strange crown of blue-green. It was lying on its back with brown-feathered wings splayed. Its meaty breast rose high into the air, the very incarnation of plenty. The dogs put bellies to the ground and reached paws for a small claim, waiting for Mamochka and Golden Bitch to start. The two of them hovered proudly over the huge bird as everyone else smelled it over, snuffing deep into the feathers for the flesh beneath.

Romochka stuck his nose to it too, drawing in deep draughts of its feather musk and flesh. The death smell was new as new. It was still just warm. He stroked the fountain of feathers that formed its tail. They were as long as he was tall and thicker than a pile of clothes. He reached under Golden Bitch's growl, leaned over the bird and pulled at the wing to roll it over. It was so heavy! A real feed. How had they got it home unhindered? Then the tail rolled into view. It was covered in more-than-counting little pictures of eyes or water puddles, each the same as the last, glittering in the dim light. It was like the green eyes of springtime winking in the street. Romochka let out a small yelp of delight. He rolled the bird back and squatted down on that swathe of feathers. He was eager now to get on with eating. These feathers were his for after.

The dogs were wriggling, tails waving, ears up. Then Black Dog, Romochka, Golden Bitch and Mamochka began pulling the feathers off it in huge mouthfuls, clearing their choked mouths with tongue and paw, then pulling more. Romochka yanked handfuls out and threw them behind him. The others gripped and tugged at legs and wings on the periphery, and in no time they all pulled the bird apart. The wonderful rich smell of flesh and viscera rose in their faces. Everyone edged in, low to the ground, ears flattened, sneaking under and around the growls of Mamochka and Black Dog.

Romochka's hands slapped and wriggled around the grinding jaws, feeling for the bits he wanted. The bird was a male. He was a little disappointed but not surprised. Very colourful birds were usually male. He did love female birds: the flesh stocking of shell-less egg yolks arranged in a row from smallest to biggest was his favourite meal of all. He worked his hands deep into the cooling innards, feeling over and under the slippery sweetness for gizzard, heart and liver. His snarl swelled as he lunged slightly towards any whose muzzle came close to his hands. He felt the delicious taut globe of the heart and wrestled with the carcass to rip it out. It slipped through his urgent fingers three times, then the threads and sinews gave and it was his. He popped it into his mouth and couldn't quite shut his jaws around it. He struggled to bite, chew, growl and at the same time feel for the smooth flaps of the liver. White Sister was pulling the intestines away under him. He found the tight juicy ball of the gizzard and quickly tucked it under his clothes at his neck, feeling still for the liver before anyone else snaffled it. His elbows were out and he growled savagely, then he had the slippery liver in his fingers. Arms buried in the bird, he gently worked it loose with both hands. He didn't want it ruined with gall.

He sat back, happy. He felt the liver over until he found the gall bladder, bit it off gingerly and spat it to the floor. Then he stuffed the liver, too, down his neck against his chest, freeing his hands to help with the heart in his mouth. He pulled out the gizzard and chewed one side off, making an opening. He squeezed the grit and meal out onto the ground and settled down to chew through the rich flesh and its rubbery inner skin, spitting out small bits of grit and occasional feathers. He was humming now, rather than growling.

He watched the others as he ate. They were lying in the shape of a flower around the splayed carcass, all on their bellies with front paws claiming small parts for themselves. Now and then they inched in under the older dogs' snarls, reaching with deferent muzzles for more. Mamochka, beside him as always, snapped savagely at anyone who bickered or reached too quickly. Mamochka still watched Romochka's eating with a fierce dedication. Romochka's share was secure, stashed away under his clothes. Black Dog's too was unchallenged. No one would dare to squint at him and pin a piece of his with a hopeful, assertive paw.

Afterwards they each dragged small bits and pieces over to various corners to suck and chew and mull over. Romochka pulled the amazing tail feathers over to his play lair and began to arrange them here and there. Golden Bitch trotted over with the jewelled blue head in her mouth and settled with

Romochka to chew through the beak and small bones to the soft centre of the skull, but Romochka drove her out furiously when she bumbled through the arch he was building from the feathers. Then he raced after her, threw his arms around her neck and wriggled his fingers into her mouth as she growled. He wanted the crown. He snarled in her ear as she snapped at him, but in the end he was so persistent that she let him take it. He yanked the bedraggled crown fan from its topknot and handed the head back to Golden Bitch.

Back in his little lair, he felt it over with wondering fingers. Fine black stalks all gathered in the small nub of flesh at the base, each tipped with a tiny iridescent fan at the top. He hid the crown in his special hiding place among his miscellaneous beaks, claws, bottle caps and other treasures, all hidden even though he knew none of the dogs would be interested in them.

He sat on his pile of feathers and watched the dogs lying here and there around the feather-lined lair, each gnawing or crunching at a leg, wing, ribs, spine or neck held between their paws. He began building an elaborate rib cage out of old bones and feathers. He tried to get several of the tallest to stand upright by wedging their stems and then weaving the shorter ones here and there through the flowering ribs. He made the shorter ones all face their puddles inwards. They were the outside of the ribs looking in. He was the inside of the ribs looking out. He was very pleased for a while.

Then he collected as many small bones as he could find around and put them inside the bower, making limbs and a belly for the feather animal. He grabbed Brown Brother's skull and set it at the front. Then he took the crown from its secret spot and placed it in the belly too. He sat inside what he had made, with its full belly behind him, and the den in front. He was a giant animal, guarding.

He was diverted for days.

Ж

Summer passed into golden autumn. There were no puppies. Then, as the cold gripped the city, Romochka stayed active, hunting with the others whenever they were out. The long, denbound nights seemed a distant memory. Something was different this winter, utterly changed. He was colder sooner, struggling to warm up in the nest with the others, shivering as he trotted out to hunt. He desperately needed more clothes. He craved the occasional gifts of hot food. One night, sleeping fitfully in the nest, he reached for Mamochka and felt her smooth belly. He woke up.

It was going to be the first winter with no milk.

With the first big snowfall, the bomzhi by the metro disappeared. Romochka soon realised they and some of their dogs were inside the swinging doors, on the steps, or down in the underpass. He felt the hot exhalation each time the doors swung, and he longed to go down too into those warm tunnels and arcades.

He wasn't afraid of the metro itself. He had a vague memory of holding his mother's hand and boarding a loud train. But he was afraid of being cornered and caught by the militzia. So he hovered, feeling the warmth waft his way and vanish before it heated him at all, too wary to enter this other, closed trail of people.

Inside the warehouse fence, Romochka found two dead children with spraycans and glue but no food in their bags; and beside a dumpster, rolled in newspaper, he found a baby frozen solid. He didn't touch these. *Mamochka doesn't eat them, and neither do I,* he told himself. He wrapped the baby up again and left it for other dogs. The next day they all were buried under the snow.

The chill was so harsh that Romochka had to keep moving when he was outside. If he sat anywhere, Mamochka or the others chivvied and jollied him until he got up. They too knew that he had to keep moving. He wound a cloth about his face and wore two woollen hats, but still the cold bit into his nose and ears. He had quite a lot of clothes to put on, but he was only ever warm when he was asleep in the heated pile of dogs, and then only if he had a full belly. His bare hands ached and itched, and he tried to keep them inside his sleeves and in his armpits all the time. One day he was so cold that he thought he could not keep moving. White Sister and Grey Brother trotted, worried, at his stumbling heels. He headed for the metro and with his heart tumbling inside his chest, he pushed through the heavy doors, one after the other, to the warm interior.

He glared around, flanked by the two dogs, but no one paid him any attention. Bomzhi sat along one wall at the head of the stairs to the underpass, and he could see more begging or sleeping at the bottom of the stairs. House people entered and left, flowing up and down the stairs, parting to go round him. They wound their scarves up and put gloves on as they ascended, and unwound their scarves and took gloves off as they descended, but they all paid him no attention whatsoever. A uniformed official in a glass booth studiously avoided noticing him.

Romochka headed down the stairs into the warm dark belly of the underground. He unwound the cloth from his head and let the heat reach in to caress his frozen face. His scalp began to itch. He found a nice dark spot near bomzhi but not too close, and far enough from the glassed-in shops that lined one wall of the underpass.

He sat down with the two dogs, took his hats off, and then he just fell asleep, trusting the dogs to watch out for him. But White Sister and Grey Brother fell asleep too, trusting him to know what he was doing in this strange place and somehow trusting the miraculous warmth as if they were all little babies. The people flowed to and fro in front of them like an impersonal and congenial river. Then one young man stopped and took a picture of them with his mobile phone, and White Sister woke and jolted Romochka and Grey Brother with her growl. Romochka leapt up, looking about bewildered, while Grey Brother snarled and feinted a lunge at whatever it might be that had caught them unguarded. But the people just flowed by, and Romochka settled.

They were all blissfully warm, and all hungry. Romochka pulled out a grimy plastic bag to begin his begging for scraps. People weren't eating much here, but bit by bit they got something. Local people recognised the tableau—boy, dog, plastic bag—and didn't need him to say anything. Perhaps some were even comforted to see this familiar creature of their place. Since the scraps were for dogs, no one was shy about what they put in. Half-eaten stardogs, pirozhki, sloika. Shaurma or kartoshka skins. Anything they had been eating, and suddenly no longer wanted. It wasn't much, but they got some small bites for everyone at home.

Romochka began to get edgy and worried about the others, and about how cold he would become on the way home. He had no idea how long he had slept, and he had no idea what the weather was doing. He felt disconnected and disoriented. He tied up their takings and stowed them under his clothes to stop them from freezing on the way, and he put on all his toasty warm clothes. He shared a stardog with Grey Brother and White Sister to give them the strength for the long trek home.

Ж

Romochka hunted deep in the city, partly because he needed the metro station in order to thaw out on the way there and back. He headed for the train stations, the throngs of people, especially people eating, and he filled his bag with scraps, gifts of food, daring thefts. He usually took only White Sister because she was almost invisible in the snow. She stayed nervous and loyal at his side while they trotted swiftly through the streets, but he went inside buildings alone, meeting up with her again at their own peed-on meeting places. He learned the rhythm of people's stomachs, and hunted at the tail end of meal times. Often he ate all that he collected in the outward-bound metro stop to give himself strength for these hunts and then had to wait until people were feeding again. Once his bag was full, he headed home with enough miscellaneous foods to feed everyone.

And they had Laurentia.

But it was a long trail to any thronging of people with food on them and as fresh snow continued to fall, ranging widely became more and more difficult. The journey to the Roma and back took almost all night. It was a long hungry march in single file through territory after territory, human and dog, into the intensifying bewildering bustle, skirting the new army of snow workers and slow-moving vehicles as best they could; then a sleepy, almost dream-like trail home, with legs aching and the deadly cold encroaching. The snow was too deep and soft until they reached the scraped and salted streets, but these were very dangerous. They tried to keep to the less cared-for parts of the city: the alleys, building sites, railway lines. The snow banked high against the factory walls. On one occasion White Sister had to pull Romochka out of a snowdrift, tugging wildly at any bit of him she could get teeth into as he yelped and squealed.

Laurentia heaped presents on him. One week he staggered home with a stack of old blankets. She gave him a pair of some big kid's boots lined with sheepswool. He took these things with a serious-faced, awkward thanks. But the coat left him speechless. It was brand new, with tags hanging off the collar. It smelled of shops and Laurentia's touch, but no one else. He put it on, with Laurentia beaming at him. He wanted to get away. Her smile clung like cobwebs to his blushing face.

Once he was out of sight from the streetlamps of the Roma, and away from Laurentia's happiness, he wrapped the coat around himself in glee. It was lined with ticked fur that gave off an animal smell. It was thick and soft around his hands and face and neck. The coat itself was a pale colour, quilted, thick and warm. It had pockets. Mamochka, Golden Bitch, Black Dog and the three were itching to have a smell, he could tell, but he trotted on ahead, making them wait.

When they came to the first meeting point they all quickly checked the messages, made their marks and then gathered around Romochka to smell the coat. He squatted as all of them sniffed it over, as they buried their wet noses around his face and hands, breathing in that rabbit-skin smell. Black Dog lost all sense. His eyes rolled, he buried his nose deep into the fur next to Romochka's ear and began whimpering as he made chewing movements with his jaw. Romochka giggled and slapped him off, but Black Dog couldn't keep away. All the way home, the big dog had a crazed look in his eyes and found himself nibbling at Romochka's cuffs. He apologised every time Romochka whacked him but lost control of himself again immediately afterwards.

Whenever Romochka took the coat off, Black Dog's eyes followed it, and, to save trouble, Romochka hung it off a high rafter whenever he wasn't wearing it. For a while the coat changed the terrible winter for him and made everything easier. For a while it even made him more appealing to people when he went begging in the station; and it made them more appealing to him. Perfumes could not quite mask the skin and fur undertone on winter people: Romochka could smell sheep and fox and other unknown beasts. His coat made him feel a kinship with these fur-clad men and women. He was amazed, the first time he went into the bright lights, to see that the coat was sky blue.

The cold deepened. Even the blue coat could not keep Romochka warm. He risked hypothermia if he went very far at all. He got to the warmth of the metro some days, but no further, and he dreaded having to get home again afterwards.

He could not get enough food, and hunger made him raise supplicant eyes, not to the faces of passers-by, but to the food in their hands. Getting to the Roma had become impossible. He dressed in all Laurentia's gifts and wrapped a blanket over the top of everything.

Dressed like this, and with the dogs around him, he was more or less warm in the lair. Outside, his body was so hampered by his clothes and by holding the blanket in place that he was unable to do more than get to the metro. Then, by the time he got home to the lair, he was invariably freezing. He sought out the driest dog and cuddled close, shivering and shaking, while they gulped whatever food he had managed to bring home. He yipped urgently at them, hurrying them to come to bed. They all knew what to do now, and they flopped down around him, on him, with contented sighs as he patted them delightedly with his mittened hands.

Romochka stayed long hours in the metro, leaving only when he hoped the other dogs might have had time enough to get something or when his bag was full. Bit by bit his regulars re-established their routine. They carried their scraps from home and some helped in other ways too. The skinny lady gave him a stale cake and a pair of thick adult's mittens one day; on another the dvornik tossed a woollen hat with ear muffs onto the ground in front of him.

Then one day, as he stumbled out through the metro doors to the grey world above, a balmy air swept over his face and a new smell filled his nostrils. The thaw had begun.

Laurentia wept when she saw them and heaped Romoch-ka's bowl up again and again. She clicked her tongue at how thin he was. She laughed a lot and sang to them. She made an insect-squashing motion with one hand on the back of the other when he asked solicitously about the gangsters and militzia. 'One day the Roof will fall!' she said airily, and Romochka grinned too, although he had no idea what she meant. She even, to Romochka's shock and delight, held her breath, dived in and hugged him.

Ж

The city hunting territory was huge now. Its outer boundary towards the rising sun was a wide highway that roared day and night with heavy traffic, an afternoon and evening's trot there and back. Between the rising sun and the setting sun, the southern boundary was the wide brown river, so far away that they could only get there after thaw. It could take from sunset to sunrise to get there and back. Between the river and the sunrise was the Roma. To the north, towards the winter Strangers, the boundary was the edge of a wilder forest that Mamochka feared. It had elk tracks at the edge.

Within Romochka's hunting territory there were several metro stations and gradually he became familiar with them all. Spring and summer brought changes, however. Officials and militzia chased him if they saw him; a prohibition on dogs was sometimes enforced, and people veered sharply from him, clutching their noses, staring and frowning far more than they had in wintertime.

He no longer visited the stations only for warmth: he was people-watching. He knew there were trains far below. He could feel and smell them; vaguely, he could remember them. In his home metro he explored further, deeper. He headed past the shops near the entrance to the high atrium before the turnstiles and the abyss of the escalators. He watched people rise and descend; he watched them buy tickets, pass through the turnstiles and then disappear bit by bit: first their legs, then their middles, then their heads. On the other side of that arched maw blank-faced heads appeared, motionless shoulders, hands, legs. Then, when the feet appeared, the whole person suddenly moved and marched off.

He began to carry a few of his coins in his pockets and one day presented himself, frowning fiercely, at the cashier's high booth. He stood back so the cashier would see that he was there, then leaned in and reached up. To his dismay he couldn't quite reach the coin dish. He dropped his four coins on the bench near the little glass window. He had watched enough to know that more often than not these were wordless transactions, so he waited, heart pounding. It worked. The bored cashier barely glanced at him as he passed a ticket and two other coins back. He lost that first ticket on the way home.

He became practised very quickly. If the cashier waited, or looked annoyed and barked at him, he would put another coin down. Sometimes the cashier, as on that first occasion, gave him coins back with the ticket. It was mysterious and charming. It was something he couldn't begin to explain to the dogs.

After a while, adept at buying tickets, he began to think of using them to go through the turnstiles, just like everybody else. He watched closely. He would have to put his ticket in, *just so*; take the ticket from the machine, *so*; then march through. Without a ticket, the turnstile would suddenly burst into life and bash his legs and thighs with two metal arms. White Sister would have to go through low on her belly, below the range of the metal arms. He'd tell her. He saw teenagers jump over the arms and saw a dog go under, and he could see that the metal couldn't hit them.

He sat and watched for hours, daring himself to try it. He had imagined the sequence so many times that when he got up and walked forward it was as if in a dream.

The escalator seemed interminable. White Sister made herself small on the step below him and pressed her shuddering body hard to his knees. The snap of the turnstile arms above her head had scared her badly, and he could feel that the escalator was almost too much for her to bear. His legs too were shaking. He was both afraid and exhilarated, charged with the surge of power and weakness one feels when stepping over a boundary and into another's territory.

They got to the bottom, and his jaw fell open. He had never been inside something so lovely. It was a soaring vaulted space with great painted scenes in panels along the sides and on the ceiling. He stood, staring. Suddenly there was a shocking noise and disturbance in the air. He grabbed White Sister as she tried to bolt, growling in her ear, struggling to hold her there by will, for he could not hold her by strength alone. The noise rose to a shrieking, deafening metallic grinding, and a train settled stunningly at the platform. It quieted to a steady roar. Romochka and White Sister were blocking the end of the escalators with people flowing around them both in a mad hurry. Then he was growling in her ear

115

as the train's roar rose to a sudden scream again, until it lurched and shot like a forest snake into its dark hole at the other end of the station. He still had her, shaking hard against him, mainly because she could see no escape back up the dark escalator through the moving forest of legs.

He wrestled her off to the side and sat down with her between a rubbish bin and an ornate bench. The people on the bench stiffened, sniffed about, looked at him with tiny glances of angry comprehension and got up to move elsewhere. He murmured in White Sister's ear as another train screamed into the hall next to the opposite platform, stilled to a roar, emptied, filled, and screamed off, filling the whole huge space with deafening compound noise.

He kept at White Sister until her heartbeat settled. The monstrous trains came and went so often that she soon lost her flight reaction and settled into simple misery, clinging to him. Romochka smiled happily and began to look around at the fair, clean faces of the men and women, all depicted in rich colours, framed in carved stone. His heart burned at the sight of men and women hoisting a red tractor, men and women harvesting wheat, or building a brick factory in the sun. Men and women stern with resolve, pointing their guns at unseen intruders. Always sun-drenched, even though the real sky outside was the colour of river water.

He gaped, open mouthed and blank eyed. He ran his callused paws over the walls, staring up, not noticing or hearing the curses of the people who first tried to repel him with insults then scrambled to get away from him.

Crowds of people stood near the edge of the platform, each person almost touching the next, yet just distant enough to be alone. They were clearly not a pack. It was as if all these strangers had somehow agreed that their personal territory could be shrunk for the purpose of waiting for trains. People stared blankly up the tracks or straight ahead, none meeting another's eyes. Bomzhi, with slightly larger personal territories, waited for trains, lay along the walls or stood next to loaded, tarp covered trolleys. There were gang children and homeless children too. Some were weaving in and out among the people, asking quietly for coins.

Memories unfurled; his neck hairs stirred. He almost felt the ticket clutched in his hand, his other sweaty and warm in his mother's palm. Chatting, not noticing anybody. Not having to notice everything. He was suddenly filled with yearning for his lost smallness, for his mother's hand holding his. Then White Sister shifted against his foot and he realised his eyes were tired from watching the people flowing on and off the trains. The grand and beautiful pictures on the walls began to make his head ache and his empty belly grumbled. He felt increasingly as if danger were all around and he couldn't see or smell it. White Sister had been sleeping off her shaking terror on his feet, trusting his ease, but she woke up now at the smell of fear-sweat. He got up suddenly and they rode the awful escalator up to the daylight.

He had been home for half a day when he wanted to go back.

Ж

117

They all sat up, wakened suddenly from an afternoon snooze. Mamochka, Golden Bitch and Black Dog growled low, making a swelling, threatening chorus. Everyone's hackles rose and Romochka's neck and spine prickled. Someone was stumbling around in the ruin above them; rummaging, clumping, then dragging a beam from one end across the earth and weeds to another. They heard voices: there were two men in the ruin above.

Romochka scuttled to the wood pile and climbed up. The dogs paced, alert and scared. He could see legs wearing boots made of a yellow pelt of some kind. Romochka hummed a low, silencing warning, and the dogs dropped their voices and hovered in a group below him. They watched his face with such open trust that his chest swelled. He hummed his lowest, quietest note then stopped, listening. The second man's voice rang out over the other end of the cellar and Mamochka, staring at Romochka's rigid form, kept the others silent. The man in the fur boots grumbled just above them: 'It's a good place. What's that idiot on about?'

The other man murmured something indistinct.

'I don't fucking care—look around. We can build a house with all this stuff, and if everyone's scared of the place, all the better. Leave us alone, no problem.'

Romochka clambered down. The dogs paced miserably and Romochka listened with rising anger as the two men pulled things back and forth above them. The dogs looked at him, repeatedly, asking something of him. Mamochka licked him every time she passed, a deferential kiss that made him ache inside. Mamochka had never licked him like that; yet now, again and again, he felt her tongue on the corner of his mouth,

118

and he felt her waiting. *Waiting for him to tell them what to do.*

Evening fell, but it was not a comforting darkness. The men lit a crackling fire up above in the ruin, murmuring and exclaiming all the while about some beef they had obtained. The flickering light through the cracked floor made the den seem permeable, flimsy. The smell of cooking meat and onions filled their space.

Romochka climbed back up onto the wood pile and stared down at the family as they waited in a semicircle before him. They all knew now that the men were moving in, taking over their closed paths.

Mamochka gazed calmly up at him. Golden Bitch, sitting motionless at her post by the entrance suddenly got up and walked over to Mamochka. She raised her head and looked at him intently with ears pricked. There was nothing bewildered in her glance. She wagged her tail slightly. She looked like Black Dog—impulsive and eager. Ready.

He was dizzy with sudden resolve: he would drive the men out.

He leapt down, his body tingling. He hummed them all in close and bounded on all fours up the rubble pile and into the moonlight and firelight above. He felt their huge courage rise like a wind behind him. Golden Bitch was at one hand, White Sister at the other, and the rest following close. Romochka didn't stop to think. He bounded up the familiar blocks of stone and leapt to the nearest parapet. The dogs spread out in the shadows beneath him as he raised his shaggy head to the midsummer moon. He felt his fingers curl to the stones, and a howl bigger than his whole body welled and roared through his throat. The dogs howled in response below, hidden in the shadows. Then there was silence.

Both men leapt to their feet and turned away from the fire, peering this way and that.

'Alyosha, *what was that?*'

'Dogs? Calm down, Yuri—they won't come near the fire.'

Romochka stared down from his parapet. He felt, then, immensely powerful. He was not afraid of their fire! He cackled out loud and both men started. Mamochka was leading the dogs around the outside of the ruin and he waited, humming quietly, weaving them into a dance—a singing hum now, not a growl.

'Alyosha, *what is that?*' Yuri was pointing straight at Romochka.

Alyosha peered at the silhouetted form.

'A statue, a little lion?'

Yuri laughed nervously. 'It moved, I swear it did!'

'Hah! You're off your face, you moron. Stone don't move.'

Yuri shuddered.

Then Romochka stood up on the parapet, and both Alyosha and Yuri screamed. He howled again and all the dogs answered from around the outside of the ruin. He stood for a second, then leapt down, singing the dogs in closer. Alyosha and Yuri were both panting now. Wherever they looked they saw the glinting eyes of the six dogs. Romochka bounded on all fours just outside the clear light of the fire, then raised his voice, pulling the hum of the dogs with him into a crescendo. The two men screamed again and ran for the street door, the terrible slavering noise of the pack filling the air around them.

Romochka spent his first night as leader basking with the

pack by the embers of the fire and eating hot, half-cooked beef stew.

Ж

Each metro station had its own character. Romochka had roamed in a daze through gracious stone forests, palisades, mosaics, statue arcades and painted scenes, his mind strung taut with a strange, pleasurable pain. He had found children in the pictures, all pretty and fair-haired, pet dogs, and bigger creatures. He'd searched these crowds of many-coloured heroes, the crowds that never went home or hunted, and felt his heart pound in sickening delight. In these pictures, somewhere, he would find his singer, Pievitza—in all her sternness and glory, and she would be flat too, and identical every day, yet new; silent yet singing.

But today was different. He didn't gawp at the ceiling, or stare at his favourite painted panels. He walked down to near the end of the crowd and stood, sweating, at the edge of the platform, not looking at anybody, setting his face with the same studied and strategic indifference he had observed many times. This he understood well, and it pleased him. Mature dogs too, he told himself, would act as though the other were not there, not a threat, and so make themselves unthreatening too.

People looking round for the awful stench didn't have time to identify Romochka as the source. The train pulled in with a diminishing scream over the roar of its engine. The doors hissed open, and he was suddenly pressed from all sides by the crush of people pushing against each other at the edges to get

121

on and the flood of people pouring off. He found himself swept
onto the train, but once on he couldn't feel White Sister beside
him. People pressed against his body, and he started to panic.
He would have begun fighting to get away if the crush hadn't
suddenly separated again into discrete bodies, some seated,
some holding on above their heads, all avoiding each other's
faces or staring with unseeing expressions. The space around
him began to grow as people scented him and tried desperately
to get away.

In that widening space, Romochka dithered, craning his
head frantically. He lost his balance and fell flat as the train
lurched and took off, accelerating to its impossible speed, shuddering, clunking under him, grinding against the tracks. He
was on all fours, clinging to the bucking floor with open palms,
crying through clenched teeth. A wave of horror rolled over
him and then, through all that grinding, gnashing, screaming,
roaring, rattling and clanking, his ears twitched. He had picked
up a quiet, terrified whimper. Somewhere up the carriage
and down low. White Sister was flat to the floor up ahead
somewhere.

He began to wriggle forward on all fours through the legs
but then the train decelerated sharply and he had to stop
moving to keep his balance. People were shouting at him but as
a thicket of legs stampeded off the train and another forest
marched on, all the words were broken up and lost. White
Sister was still whimpering quietly somewhere ahead of him.
She hadn't moved. The train took off, the people began to part
around him, and he moved through that open space towards
her. Another stop, another exodus, and an even more crushing
surge onto the train. He was pressed against the legs of those

seated along the benches, people jiggling and bouncing in unison as the train bounded, swayed and rocked over bumps in the tracks.

The carriage was so full now that people couldn't get away from him. He wriggled doggedly between knees and was cursed and kicked, and then the train decelerated, stopped, and seemed to fill even more. He was crying with the effort, and thinking about starting to bite when he felt White Sister's tongue on his face. She was pressed tight under the seat behind the row of legs near his hands. He reached under to her happy face and cradled it. Someone high above him laughed kindly, and he felt a little better. He decided not to bite anyone.

He closed his eyes, squeezing the tears out, and rocked and swayed and bounced with White Sister until the people who smelled him began to desert that carriage and he could ease the dog out and cuddle her in his arms.

He wiped his nose and eyes on his sleeve and pulled himself together. He adjusted to the flying speed of the train and stood. He nearly fell again when the train suddenly decelerated and slid into the lights of yet another station, but he was too low and hemmed in to see more than a glimpse of the roof. He clung to a silver pole with one arm and to White Sister's body with the other, so that they would not be swept out of the door again with the sudden dissolving of people into that strange human river that had swept him on. People settled into their places, and then he clenched his teeth, eyes shut as the train launched into speed again.

When he opened his eyes, he saw immediately that the carriage was half-filled with kids, big and little. He could tell that these were not house kids. These were bomzh kids, street kids and gang kids, and he was suddenly very alert. He edged himself into the first free space that had a metal pole to hold onto, and he made quick hostile eye contact. The first kid to approach he snarled at savagely and made White Sister do the same. The kids laughed and talked about him, but they left him alone.

Then a terrible thought burst in on him. How many stops and starts? How many stations? He was probably further from home than he had ever been. This train had not really changed direction all that much apart from what felt like a long turn away from the sunrise. It was hard to know in the darkness.

He started to wonder whether it was really the same train that appeared in his metro station, or whether it was a completely different train each time. He tried to remember what had happened when he was a very little boy, and he vaguely recalled getting off trains. The phrase *catch the metro home*.

A horrible fear flooded his body then and he nearly blacked out. This train was carrying him further and further and he had better get off before it was so far that he would never find his way back. How far he must have travelled already! As the train pulled into the next station, he stood up and, with White Sister, stumbled out onto a strange platform.

This station was filled with trains and platforms and people flowing between them in steadily tramping hordes. His heart twisted in despair and he wished he could curl up somewhere and go to sleep. White Sister whined miserably at his side, her ears flat to her skull. He scrambled to the wall and then found an escalator.

Romochka and White Sister emerged into the daylight in

a completely unfamiliar part of the city. It was so different from his city that it might have been somewhere altogether unrelated. Unbroken buildings rose all around them, some exceedingly beautiful. The blue sky was filled at all edges of its vast basin with the intricate forms of grand and ordinary buildings, none of them concrete apartment blocks or factories. Grime-laden trees stood around here and there as ornaments, but there was nothing in sight that resembled a wild copse or a forest. There wasn't even any garbage.

Romochka was too devastated to hunt. He scrambled past people and cars and into a small park across from the metro station. After his shock he needed sleep more than anything. He found a broad, low bush and crept under its bower. Trams squealed and rollicked along their tracks around one side of the park, and a busy lane curved along the other. As he closed his eyes he could smell exhaust, car brakes, the kartoshka and pirozhki from the stalls and, closer, vodka. A lady sitting on a park bench nearby was sipping it, raising her whole handbag to her face for each gulp. The leaves had been raked out from under this bush, and the dusty bare earth filled his nostrils, smelling naked and wrong. He fell asleep, leaving it to White Sister to snarl at anyone who tried to push in.

It was evening, and he was cold. He cuddled White Sister close and stared out through the leaves at the weak glimmer of coloured lights.

They were lost. He couldn't think of any way to find out from people how to catch the metro home. What was the human word for his home? He couldn't think of one that anybody would know.

He trotted cautiously to the streetside with White Sister. Other than a cleanish drunk on the tramstop being shaken by two very bulky militzioner, and a street kid cleaning windscreens at the traffic lights, he could see no one homely. He could see no bomzhi and no dogs. It was terrible to be in a city with only one dog and to have no idea where the bomzhi would be. When he found them, he had a fair idea they would be strange bomzhi, not the mountain and forest clan. Bomzhi knew he was not one of them, as did street kids and skinhead gangs. Dogs knew he was not one of them as well, so here all he could hope to do would be to hover near bomzhi in the hope of becoming a little less visible, and more like a bomzh or a street kid to all the other clans: the militzia, the various clans of house boys, the beggarmasters and that indiscriminate mass of people, men and women and children, who lived in houses, carried zipped bags of various sizes and colours, and cleaned their clothes.

He would have given way again to despair, but White Sister's tail was up and plumy and her step jaunty. She looked at him repeatedly, waiting for him to lead the way, urging him to hunt. She was hungry. The burden of responsibility pushed him on. He crossed the road at the lights and, alert for any sign of militzia, began to look for a place where people gathered, eddied and ate. He needed a bag desperately if they were to beg for scraps, but this place was so poor in rubbish that he couldn't find one.

Finally he found a familiar blue dumpster in a lane. He climbed on top of it and managed to wrestle its heavy metal lid open. To his delight, it had plastic bags and mixed rubbish, including old bread, cabbage leaves and chicken bones. He threw as much out to White Sister as he could and stuffed two plastic bags into his pockets, along with the bread, some bones and cabbage leaves for himself. It was a while since he had had cabbage and he started to cheer up.

He nearly dropped the lid on himself when White Sister growled. He scrambled out, losing half a loaf of bread and pinning his hands between the lid and the rim. The two militzioner from the tramstop were at the head of the lane watching him. They were both equally heavy but one was shorter than the other. They were too substantial for him to consider running at them and dodging around or jumping. White Sister's teeth were bared, her hackles up, but her eyes were sliding to him. She was so far out of her paths that she didn't know what to do. For a second Romochka stared at the two men. They stood still too, but he sensed from their alert poses that when they moved it would be towards him, and for more than a casual hassle.

'Eh, you! Papers!'

Romochka didn't know the lane or where it led, but he turned and ran, his coat swinging. For some reason the militzioner shouted after him but didn't bother to give chase. He and White Sister pressed themselves into the evening shadows along the walls and made their way to the end of the lane, out into a maze of old shops and ornamented five-storey buildings.

They wandered on. His deepening impression of the city was its bareness; how hard life was going to be until they made it home. There was nothing to be found here. No rubbish gathered in these lanes, no piles of miscellaneous junk filled odd corners. There were no fields with old mattresses and other havens. The grass was all clipped short and no small creatures could find a space to live. Even the fringe of grass between pavements and buildings, that little mouse-run at the edge of everything, was not there. The ravens mewling and complaining in the parks looked well fed, but he couldn't work out how they got by—or how to catch them. It was a city of many different types of dumpsters but to his dismay most were locked. Here, too, it was as if bomzhi didn't exist and so far he had seen no single dog that wasn't clearly a pet.

The shadows darkened and the city's glimmer intensified to brilliant lights. Scared, fast-moving bomzhi began to appear here and there. Romochka saw a round hole open in the pavement, and a man in a properly filthy overcoat with bottles clinking in his pockets scrambled quickly and surreptitiously out. He swung his big head this way and that in the twilight, then pushed the metal lid to his hole back into place and walked quickly away. This frightened Romochka as much as it informed him. He didn't dare go down there; he might be trapped with them. He noted, too, the speed at which bomzhi moved on the street. They knew that they were not safe here.

It was a frighteningly barren and uncomfortable place. There was nowhere to stop and think. He was overwrought. He decided that he had to find a safe lair and worry about food and water tomorrow.

They broke into a fenced-off demolition site to get away from the unending tramp of feet and the proximity of fast-moving cars. The site was calm, the engines of the huge earthmovers silent for the night. They clambered over a pile of rubble nearly as high as a building. The summer air was heavy with dust and, as they settled against a lone corner wall in the rubble, Romochka realised how thirsty he was. White Sister panted.

The sounds and smells of the city were muted, but they slept only fitfully, waking at the early dawn. A clear sky arched above the city. It was going to be hot.

Romochka rubbed his gritty face and looked around. The site was piled high with a rubble of multicoloured bricks—some with pale blue paint and plaster on one side; some yellow; some wallpapered. The corner that had sheltered them rose like a broken tooth to one side, its chipped plaster shattered and torn at the top, but somehow both homely and strange up close.

The chains at the mesh gate clanked. Time to go. They climbed over the rubble to the far side, wriggled under the fence into an unfamiliar lane and away. They trotted aimlessly looking for anything that might feed them or give them water. They tried every dumpster and were chased away from the few that Romochka could open. It was a long time now since the cabbage, bread and chicken bones. White Sister's belly looked pinched high up against her spine. As they made their way down a small lane, following the smell of water, a faint music filled the air. Romochka was too thirsty and hungry, and too scared to think about music, but he did lift his head, jangled by the sweet sounds.

He stopped and reeled: he recognised these buildings: they were the flat cupolas and domes he had seen depicted on station walls, now made real and as round as peaches. Worst of all, in the middle distance, peeping through gaps between buildings, a vast brown water glittered in the afternoon sun. He began to pant, clutching dizzily onto White Sister. There could be no doubt. He shut his eyes to try to lessen the horror.

They were on the other side of the great river.

He could sense that they were a long way downriver from

home. They had turned the Roma way between the rising and setting sun but had gone much, much further than the Roma. They would somehow have to find a way across the river, then head upstream until he found the little bit of river he knew from the outer boundary of his city hunting territory, then head between the setting sun and the rising sun until he picked up the Roma trail, then home. And before that, they had to get food.

He sat down under a tree and rocked back and forth, whimpering. That escalator was so long, so deep underground! Could the train really have gone under the river? He'd never thought of the river as having a bottom. He tipped himself over at that and curled up tight around his empty stomach, but White Sister wouldn't let him be. She licked his face and hands, burrowed under him, nudging and cajoling. She stared at him intently, optimistically. He was the leader. She also knew they had to hunt and couldn't hunt separately in this place of unknown trails and boundaries.

By midmorning they found themselves above a wide, still canal that ran the same direction as the river. They dodged a sudden noisy horde on the footpath and stared down at the water. A steep paved escarpment dropped without a lip into the dark waters, and there was no way he could see to climb down and get a drink without falling in. White Sister whined as he hunted around for something to carry water in and something to lower it down, but this city, maddeningly filled now with the smell of water, hot bread, cooking meat and hot oil, was empty of anything one needed. They made their way along the promenade at the edge of the canal, looking through the wrought iron balustrade for any chance to get at the water. White Sister, ahead of him under the shadow of a high footbridge, suddenly ducked and scrambled. There was a shriek and a sharp crack: she had caught a water rat. Romochka's spirits lifted.

After the rat he felt a little better. He let White Sister lick the blood from his face and fingers while passers-by exclaimed and walked wide around him in flurry and disturbance. He ignored them. He was in no danger from these clip-clopping women and their pungent, soapy men. House people like this would hate to touch him, would never think to jump him, hold him down or beat him. He could see that this place was not a haunt for gangs, skinheads or bomzh children, so that left only militzia as the principal predator.

He was still terribly thirsty. White Sister panted and gulped, panted and gulped. The river was out of sight but very near, drawing this canal in. He could feel its presence like a huge animal hiding, ever moving. Its current wove sinuously through the air here and tugged at the sunrise end of the canal waters.

Sure enough, the canal opened up ahead, joining the great river. The balustrade ended suddenly, and here there were steps down to a wide concrete platform at the water's edge. He drank deep and splashed his face and arms in the water. The ripples settled and the dark water stilled. The reflected evening colours formed again into straight lines and the orange windows of the shaken buildings were almost perfectly aligned again.

More food, shelter, and a way across this river. He shook the water with his hands again, breaking the city into tiny scattered fragments of pink, orange, grey nothingness. He hated this city.

The river, at least, was smelly and reassuring.

It was evening again, and again he could smell food everywhere and hear music. The eyes of each passer-by gleamed momentarily on him, then studiously lifted, and he knew that in such a place there could be no invisibility. Sad music, men's and women's voices, floated from one building; another pumped a heartbeat and electric sizzle. He kept moving from street to street, White Sister trotting miserably at his heels. The city lights were every colour, and the high domes shone in the night sky, and everything was dreamily beautiful.

Romochka watched White Sister as they trotted. Her behaviour was bothering him. At first he couldn't work out who she was speaking to, who she was eyeing with that friendship glance and tail, that pleading, that little dip of her ears. Then he realised it was people. Any people. White Sister was so hungry now that she was begging, turning from him, breaking all the rules and behaving like a stray.

He was overcome with rage and disappointment. When she gazed at the next passer-by, inviting, he growled and kicked her savagely. She cringed, guilty, then slunk for a while at his heels, head and tail low, glancing at his knees now and then. But she couldn't help herself. She was starving and people had always been good to her.

The next time Romochka growled but did nothing. He felt very cool towards her; and wretched with an inner dismay. It was his job to find good hunting grounds and a safe lair and he couldn't do it.

Tears ran down his face. He had never felt more unhappy in his life. There was nothing to do but trot on. He dared not stop but had nowhere to go.

They were halfway across the bridge. The summer river moistened the air. He breathed deeply, and White Sister snuffed between the poles of the balustrade. The traffic roared too close, but still he felt better than he had since boarding the train. He stopped in the middle of the bridge and looked at the water far below where it swirled and settled. Could they trust this rich smell of water and putrefaction to pull them back in the direction of home? Then he noticed that White Sister was head up, snuffing another way, the way home, straight home. He felt suddenly peaceful. All would be well.

It all happened so fast that Romochka thought he must be in some terrible dream. They entered a courtyard that Romochka thought would be a shortcut, found no exit and, as they turned to leave, the world whirled into movement. The tramp and scuff of boots and yelling and shouting. It was so sudden and terrible that Romochka didn't know where to look. For a moment he stood, whipping his head back and forth, unable to comprehend that he was surrounded by a wall of uniformed muscle.

He made a dash for it, and the ground thumped him hard in the back of the head. He was brutally rolled over, his face pressed into the asphalt, his wrists wrenched and cuffed. Someone put a boot to his head while someone else tied his feet together. White Sister was snarling over the back of his head, and someone yelled, 'Shoot the dog!' as she was booted hard, and lifted off his body completely. He could see with one eye

133

half obscured by his hair as she regained her footing and turned to lunge, then someone very big stepped over him towards her, impossibly fast, and cracked her hard over the head with a truncheon. White Sister crumpled and Romochka screamed. She was moving feebly on the asphalt, struggling to raise her head, as he was lifted into the air. The men were shouting over him and he was thrown into the militzia van.

'Why didn't you shoot the dog? I ordered you to shoot the dog, Zolotukhin!'

The militzioner shrugged. 'I like dogs.'

A revitalised bustle and noise rose in the main station, and the door to the cells opened. Noise of moving bodies and excited voices swelled around a man who entered the cell corridor. The pack leader, Romochka guessed. His companions fawned: eager, informative. Romochka heard his own incredible hairiness, vicious nature, strange gait, amazing reflexes and stench—and their triumph in capturing him—all made into words and passed to the leader. He felt afraid. The leader came up to the bars and stared at him, unsmiling. Romochka stared back, equally formally, his spine stiff.

The leader turned and said in a cold, gravelly voice, 'What the hell do you think you are doing? It's just a kid. Get those cuffs and the gag off him.'

'It bites, Major Cherniak.'

'Get them off!'

The pack held back, and they all burst out laughing. The leader growled in exasperation. He unlocked the cell and marched up to Romochka, who crouched more tightly into his corner. The major leant down, holding his nose with one hand,

and untied the gag. Romochka waited a second, and then bit as hard as he could, holding and grinding his teeth into a soapy wrist. The leader straightened, yelling, shaking him by the hair and wrestling his hand free as Romochka tried to get more wrist in gobbling snaps.

'Give us a hand,' the major grunted, and the laughing men yanked Romochka's head back while Cherniak extracted himself. Romochka gave a choking growl.

'Just a kid, just a teeny kid,' one sang and pouted his lips.

The leader sighed, nursing his hand as they relocked the cell. 'That *is* just a kid, and a really little one too. What is the world coming to?'

The mean one snorted. 'Feral kids are worse than rabid dogs. Worse than adults too, and they reckon there's millions. Never solve anything unless we get rid of them. Put it down, I say.' He made a flicking hand gesture, pointing at Romochka's head. Romochka understood: he had seen guns. He snarled.

'God, Belov, you got kids. How can you say that?'

'That's no kid. That'll kill my kids given half a chance.'

The leader turned away and snapped at the others, 'Get him out of restraints by dinnertime. And don't cut his hair— you'll need it.' He stalked off.

As evening fell five militzi entered Romochka's cell. They took off the handcuffs and shackled his wrist to a ring in the wall. While two held him down by the hair, another untied his feet and ungagged him. He kept them at bay with his best perform-ance, but was bewildered when they put a huge bowl of hot soup and half a loaf of bread down on the floor beside him, and left.

135

Next morning he was held down and stripped. Then, as he yowled in pain and scrambled back and forth as far as his handcuff would let him, he was pressure hosed with cold water and left naked for a few hours until he and his cell were fairly dry. The station wasn't cold; he warmed up bit by bit and later they threw him a blanket.

Over the following days Belov's Dog became an attraction at the station. Officers from other precincts came, paid money and laughed loudly while Romochka was held down, pushed and goaded, poked and mimicked—his savage bite, raking claws and incredible speed shown off to a never-ending stream of amused militzi. They gathered to watch him eat, laughing, and they watched when he used the toilet, exclaiming over the fact that Belov had managed to train him. Belov said there was nothing like a high pressure water hose—it should be in the dog training manual.

Romochka kept within the boundaries of his dog self and never let on that he heard them. He was in disguise in the hope of some unknown future advantage it might give him. He lurked malevolently within himself, watching them, hating them and, bit by bit, despising them for what they didn't know. Days passed.

Hiding inside his dog self insulated him to a degree from his own thoughts and feelings. He was a dog: words meant nothing. He was a dog: numb grief and wild joy were the boundaries within which all feeling was stretched. His self was a dog's self, a set of known trails, ways and places to be, between these boundaries. The present was not good. He thought about it little. He ate glumly, fought when there was opportunity and snarled to comfort himself. Despite this retreat, however, another feeling crept over him, like the season tipping from summer to autumn. It seeped into him, quelling all other feelings. It was sadness and with it came, first in moments, then more often, the snowfall of despair.

Belov's business died when the dog became too quiescent to retaliate with any conviction. Officers no longer found the sight of a disconsolate naked boy with an adult's hairy body and a huge black mane all that funny. Some asked for their money back. Belov's loudly vaunted idea of bringing in another dog to stage fights never eventuated.

Romochka wished bitterly for this dog, and for true doghood. Were he really a dog, he would understand only their bodies, not their words. Were he really a dog, he wouldn't know all their names, and their kids' names. He wouldn't know and remember every word and phrase, and be paralysed by these lives that stretched before and after the station: he would know only their smell, only their aggression and torments; and what they ate.

The fight went out of him altogether. He stared dumbly, balefully without growling or snapping, unresistant even when he was pushed around. He was no longer sure that hiding his human side would get him released, but he remained a dog, unable to climb back to his boy self at will. Boy worries crept into him only gradually, flittering in pictures across his mind. Mamochka carrying a white hare, head held high. Black Dog looking guilty with Romochka's blue coat between his paws. White Sister lapping from cupped hands under a silver drainpipe. His hands. White Sister all friendly, begging from strange people. White Sister crumpling on the road.

Had he seen her stand up again?

Major Cherniak reappeared a week later. Romochka was crouching in the corner of his cell, crying softly to himself, hugging his naked knees.

'Why's this kid still here? He's crying. Have you idiots been feeding him?' There were murmurs of assent. 'Has anyone got in touch with child protection?' Every man looked at the next, and eventually there was a collective shaking of heads.

'He shouldn't be here. Get him dressed, tell them they can come and get bitten too. We've done our bit picking him up, more than our bit cleaning him up. He's their problem, not ours. And when he's gone, get this cell steam cleaned. That smell is horrible.'

Next morning Romochka was held down and forcibly dressed in some soapy clothes that smelled of Belov's tobacco and were too big for him.

Belov laughed. 'Give him to that idiot at the Anton Makarenko Centre.' He made a rude gesture. 'Rehabilitate this, dickhead!'

Cherniak laughed with the rest. 'Just call the usual number. If they want the Makarenko people involved, that's their business.'

Romochka considered he had been amazingly well fed in the cell and felt physically strong. He understood from their talk that he was to be moved, and his spirit rose like the sap in spring. He took pains to be particularly docile all morning, retrieving his boy self as consciously as he could. He stood on his feet, eyes cast down, never growling or baring his teeth.

It worked. He was marched quietly out to a white van without manhandling, flanked by three militzi and two paramedics who spoke gently to him. At the moment when the paramedics went to take over and load him in, he ducked, slipped his hands from their grasp and bolted, sprinting as hard as he could while holding his overlong trousers up. There was uproar behind him as they gave chase, but he was faster.

After a little while their shouts and exclamations, their heavy steps, receded behind him. He heard a siren and shot off the road into a winding lane, then darted into an alley. He found himself, still running top speed, on another road with a wide footpath and many people. He left that too, as soon as a likely alley joined it, then zig-zagged through a sequence of laneways and passages until he was sure he had lost them.

He quietened down to a trot, his heart still hammering. He scented his way to the river. He was on the home side, upriver from the bridge, and, to his great joy, he could see it. He made his way steadily back and began to trot along the cold trail he and White Sister had taken more than a week before.

He sweated with the horrors of that place. He looked around. There was no mark to show what had happened, and his ridiculous boy-nose would never be able to find White Sister. Despair flooded back. He was alone, his family lost, his sister hurt: all his doing. And he didn't know how to get home. His ears buzzed and his sight blackened, shutting the world out.

Then, as suddenly as he had been caught, he was knocked down by the squealing, wriggling, yabbering force of White Sister. Chewing and slobbering his face and arms, shoving her head into his belly, throwing herself bodily at his chest for the embrace. He sobbed in happiness into her neck and held her so tight she snapped this way and that, struggling to be free. Then she capered around him in wild joy, her eyes shining. At last she sprang up with buoyant purpose, looking back at him repeatedly: *Let's get out of this horrible city, now!*

At dusk it began to rain, and, to his delight, a trickle ran onto the footpath from the wide silver drainpipes that ran down the outside of the older buildings. He scampered over, bent down and put his open mouth under one of them, then cupped his hands for White Sister. They trotted on through the evening and the first part of the night, winding in and out of lanes and roads, backtracking from each cul-de-sac, waiting fearful in the rain for traffic to clear on roads they had to cross, but angling always back to White Sister's point of certainty, then heading off again at a run. White Sister was thinner even than before but, to Romochka's relief, her interest in people had been snuffed out. She turned to him, insistently, repeatedly, and to him alone. They stopped only to check dumpsters for food.

They slept in a large railway station that sheltered more bomzhi than Romochka had ever seen. Then, just before dawn, Romochka gave White Sister a chunk of bread from his pocket and they were off again, running into a wind-driven rain, but warming up. He ate as he ran.

At midmorning, they found themselves around the corner from the Roma. Romochka yipped and White Sister jumped for joy. They ran round the back. They had never been there in daylight; the lane was deserted and the restaurant shut. White Sister coursed about, whimpering with happiness as she smelled a cold trail of the family. Romochka scratched and whined quietly at the locked door but there was no sound inside. Laurentia wasn't there.

Hungry as they were, they felt they were as good as home, and they set off on the familiar path as though it in itself were food and could give them the energy to keep going.

By late afternoon, they were in the allotment, trotting wearily with glazed but expectant eyes. No one was home in the lair, so they threw their aching bodies down on the bed and slow-licked each other's faces while they waited. Bliss and weakness filled Romochka. White Sister was so much bonier than when they were here last. He ran his fingers over her. It seemed a long time ago. It seemed just this morning.

They heard the joyous crescendo of the clan as their trail was found, swelling to a scrambling, yelping climax in the courtyard, and then dog after dog piled upon him and White Sister, whining and wriggling and squealing. Even Black Sister, her reserved body swaying in delight, approached both of them with teeth low and, when Romochka threw his arms about her and licked her face, she shuddered. Held in his arms, she licked his ear, and then reached out to lick White Sister's face too, once. Black Dog and Grey Brother capered madly around the cellar, ears back and haunches low, then chased each other just to have something to do with their happiness. Pregnant Mamochka wriggled her surprising big belly into Romochka's arms and kept biting his face through her yabbering, as if she had to do more than lick to believe she had him back.

They had food. They had dropped it outside out in the allotment as their excitement took them over. They raced out once everyone settled and returned with a soft summer hare and three stiff ravens.

Ж

Romochka could not stay away from the metro for long. He was wary since it had kidnapped him but unbearably curious. He hunted with the dogs around the mountain for a few days, but his ears were tuned to people more than ever before. He scavenged for clues about the wider world and was astonished: that world had been here all the time, inaudible to him. People here knew Belov. 'Major Belov,' he heard the one-legged man say, 'pimps, beggarmasters, baby trade, you know...the Roof. He's the one you got to talk to.'

He changed most of his coins for a precious collection of tickets. At rest in the lair, he played with them, shuffling them into patterns and getting the family to smell them.

Soon he was drawn back to the station, tickets in pocket. He opened his ears, realising quickly that stations had names and learning the name of his. He found metro stations throughout his territory and bit by bit worked out how to catch the trains for one stop, then trot back home. Then two stops, and three. White Sister remained his sole companion, seasoned as she was in the underground trails and their dangers. The others accompanied him to the metro entrance but no further, and not even Black Sister showed any resentment. He quickly ran out of money, and life became more dangerous when the beggarmasters realised he had started collecting cash as well as scraps.

His exploration of the underground territory opened his ears and eyes to people, and with this came an awareness of the uses of money. He couldn't enter shops, he knew that without trying. But street and metro kiosks were for everybody. So easy! He was amazed that he hadn't considered it. You simply held out some coins and pointed. If they waited, or gestured, or said something, you pulled out one more coin.

He began buying hot food—stardogs, pirozhki, cheese-filled bread, boubliki and shaurma from the kiosks, which he and the dogs gulped down in ecstasy. Sometimes, if he pointed to the dogs, he would get some scraps too, especially if he bought food at the same time. He ran out of money as quickly as he got it.

Mamochka loved the new grease on his hands but hated him going down the escalator to the metro. She tried to steer him to hunt on the mountain or in the forest, but he went rarely these days. The metro pulled him into its arcades of glory, its bazaar of hot, greasy, pastry-covered foods and its enticing human world.

Mamochka watched him as he went, watched every move he made, troubled but passive. Sometimes she even sat on her haunches, immobile, and he mistook her silhouette for the old image of Golden Bitch at sentry. Her watching annoyed him. He would push her, pull her, cajole her to the nest. She licked him thoughtfully for a while, then stopped, preoccupied. Even after her two puppies were born, Mamochka worried. This autumn he made no move to suckle. He showed no interest in the puppies. He was out, always, at the metro. Long hours, returning late, sometimes even with no fruit of a hunt.

In the dark before a late autumn dawn, Mamochka entered the lair carrying a strange smell. Everyone looked up, noses and ears questioning the dark air. Her steps were awkward, slow, and it was clear from the broken rhythm that her legs were braced and splayed in the effort to carry something heavy and alive.

She stumbled and then dragged her burden over to the nest. Romochka sat up. She was carrying more than a strange smell. She was carrying—dragging—a whimpering human baby by the clothes at its scruff.

III

It was almost too heavy in her jaws for her to manage. Romochka growled before anyone else did, although his night vision was the worst and the others must have smelled it long before he did. Mamochka ignored him, plopped the child down and began to lick its face and hands. The two small sisters, Little Gold and Little Patch, tumbled and shoved around it. It began suddenly to sob and wail, thinly at first, then louder and through more jagged breaths. Everyone's hackles rose. Even Romochka could smell the fear puffing into the dark lair from under their tails and necks.

Romochka couldn't settle. His skin prickled and itched. Fleas annoyed him more than usual. He snapped at Black Sister and drove even White Sister from him. Then he suffered until dawn, proud and furious, too cold to snooze. His Mamochka didn't even look his way in the dark. *Where have you been, Mamochka,* he sent out in the dark. *What have you done, bringing that here?* He would have felt better if he had sensed her looking his way, answering, but no answer came to explain her betrayal.

He could hear the new child suckling and mewling. At dawn he heard a sound, familiar yet alien to the lair: a baby chortling. He got up, stiff and cold, grabbed his club and stalked towards the daylight. Black Sister, White Sister and Grey Brother immediately followed him and he felt better. They went looking for trouble. Today, he thought angrily, they would steal shopping off someone. They hadn't done this since the harsh winter before.

Romochka stayed away from Mamochka and her baby. She in turn ignored him. He hunted long hours and brought home shopping bags full of the fruits of daring theft. He remained proud and aloof, noting with wounded pleasure that Mamochka herself didn't have to hunt: that she fed herself, the two puppies and this new boy with food he provided.

After two nights had passed, he missed Mamochka too much to keep it up. As late dawn seeped into the lair, he crept over to the side of the nest. Mamochka looked up from the two puppies and the boy and growled. He lay down. He tucked his threatening hands into his groin, kept his eyes low and waited. Sooner or later, he knew, she would stop and lick him.

By midmorning, after Mamochka had cleaned his face and ears, he was able to sidle in and have a close look. It was very small. Much smaller, he was sure, than he had ever been himself. In the gloom of the lair he could see that it had pale eyes in a moony face, light coloured hair and the tiniest most useless nose he had seen up close. It was hairless and chubby, dressed in padded fluffy stuff under the ripped jump-suit by which Mamochka had carried it. It smelled too dirty for the nest, but interesting dirty. It clearly made a very special poo, sealed in by its clothes. It would have to learn not to poo while in the nest, nevertheless: everyone knew not to poo in the nest.

He pulled the jumpsuit off it to have a closer look at what was underneath. He undressed it completely, garment after garment, while it squealed and giggled and pulled at his hair with hands surprisingly strong for their size. Mamochka was very interested in getting at the skin underneath too, and every bit Romochka uncovered she licked clean. Once the sodden clothes were off, it was even clearer that the little boy was not wise about poo. Mamochka cleaned it all off painstakingly, with Romochka helping her by pulling limbs and skin this way and that to expose dirty and sore bits. The little boy screamed and his skin turned a fascinating purple in the gloom. They ignored him. The puppies tumbled about, chewing hands and feet, and the little boy screamed harder, kicking furiously. Romochka pinned him down and shoved the puppies off.

When they were finished, the little boy was shivering and whimpering, but clean and nice spit-smelling. Romochka felt a rush of pride. The little one looked much better. Now to dress it. The pooey clothes and nappy were no good. He pushed them into one of the many plastic bags lying around and hurled them into a far corner of the lair. Better there than outside for some stranger to sniff. He got one of his old jumpers from his bower and dressed the little boy in it. This new puppy would need clothes if he was going to be so hairless. Then Mamochka curled around Little Patch and Little Gold and the boy. They drank, tugging and making loud sucky noises. The boy looked funny in Romochka's clothes. A bit like him but much smaller, much weaker. He can't even fit into that old thing! Romochka thought to himself as he lay down beside them and licked over his own hands and forearms happily. It would need a name, this human puppy.

Puppy settled in quickly. He learned to poo outside the nest for Mamochka to clean up the same way she did with the other puppies. He rolled about in rags Romochka had long outgrown. When the dogs were out, he made tunnels under the blankets in the nest and curled up in them with Little Gold and Little Patch. He could stand up and walk the way Romochka did, but without grace or speed. He fell over a lot.

Romochka watched him closely, pleased with every sign that showed Puppy to be weaker and younger than himself. He wasn't very gentle with Puppy; he enjoyed making him yelp in pain or scream with fury. He hated the way Puppy fled to Mamochka for protection and he smarted from the nips Mamochka had begun to give him. He had not been nipped so much for a long time. Not since he was new and didn't know anything. He hated the way Puppy always forgot and forgave him, and crept into his arms when they were all asleep on the nest. But he never threw Puppy off. There was something tantalising in Puppy's smell and his hairlessness. Romochka liked to slip his own arms under Puppy's clothes and sleep with his bare skin against Puppy's, and he liked to breathe in the smell from the top of Puppy's head, even though it made him uneasy. Puppy sometimes murmured simple words in his sleep, *Dyedou, Baba*, and Puppy had nightmares no dog would ever have. Romochka would lie awake, holding onto the sleeping boy with a bad feeling in his stomach.

Everything about Puppy filled him with unease. He slowly began to accept that Puppy was a member of the family, to be hunted for and looked after, but the sight of him still made Romochka itchy with annoyance. He started to treat Little Patch and Little Gold too with a degree of distance as he saw how attached they were to their litter-mate. He hoped they would grow up soon and join the real dogs.

One day he entered and Puppy was nowhere to be seen. He looked around, vaguely disappointed. Then Puppy and the two little sisters pounced on him from behind the woodpile, barking and yelling. He growled at Puppy and tried to grab him, but Puppy was off, laughing infectiously and something in Romochka gave way. He would play, he decided, now and then. When he felt like it.

The snow came in surreptitiously, without wild storms. One day the air chilled, and the snow, seeming to fall upwards more than down, dusted everything and didn't melt again. Then the next day there it was, gentle, swirling, filling up all holes and blemishes and making everything smooth and mysterious. Squirrels became more visible overnight. None of them had ever caught a squirrel, so they didn't try. That little flash of red and grey movement turned their heads, but Romochka knew only baby dogs would give chase.

'Schenok!' All the dogs looked up in surprise at the sound of Romochka calling his brother the way a human calls a dog. Romochka was pleased: they'd see that Puppy was not one of them. Puppy slunk to his hands, body wriggling, eyes hopeful. He licked Romochka's fingers, arms, cheek. Romochka pushed him down and over, growling nastily, and Puppy lay completely still, eyes almost closed, body braced passively, ready to receive whatever punishment Romochka wished to inflict. Romochka sighed in exasperation and lay down next to him. Puppy slowly relaxed and began to whimper softly. Romochka felt like crying or screaming. He reached out his hand and stroked Puppy, feeling the happiness course through his little brother, and then feeling that small body settle into sleep.

Romochka refused to smell Puppy. He refused to lick Puppy. But it wasn't working. Even Romochka could see that the little boy was becoming a dog, and the more he tried to prove to Puppy that it was not so, the more he, Romochka, seemed to become human.

He was keenly aware of just how perfect Puppy was. Puppy spoke only the language of dogs. Puppy seemed able to smell out everything there was to know. Puppy would smell and smell at something, standing long in contemplation. Puppy would wake up and smell every corner, quickly, appraisingly, for all that had happened in his absence. Puppy ran, fleet and fluid, on four legs.

The more Romochka noticed Puppy's transformation, the more irritable and snappy he became with everyone. He became aware that he, Romochka, used sounds no dog ever used, that he used sticks and nailboards and clubs in fights more than his teeth, that he used his hands to eat: most of all that he was a boy, a human boy, and he walked upright exactly as one of *them*. These things—his words, his grasping hands and his carriage, all things that had made him so formidable in the family, and so useful in being the one unnoticed by *them*, now stood out to him as unbearable defects.

One day he tried to run with four legs, but it was a terrible mistake. He hadn't run like this for more than a year, and

Puppy was, for all his bumbling, floppy gait, more doglike, more at ease in a dog's form. Romochka felt unnatural, hampered, with his hands to the floor, as if he had grown out of precisely what Puppy was so rapidly growing into. He slunk to his mother's bed and growled when she came to lie down. She licked him in his bad temper, and then went and lay down near the entrance.

He lay on the bed alone for a whole day and a night and refused to go hunting. He snarled and swung his club at anyone who came near. If Puppy had approached, he might have really hurt him. But Puppy stayed gambolling by the entrance with their mother and the other puppies while Romochka watched him balefully, chin on hands. He is a boy, not a dog.

A boy, not a dog, he thought miserably. Even thinking it, he knew that this was true of them both. He watched Puppy in a slowly spreading despair. Puppy had Little Patch by the ear and was shaking, tugging, rolling over. Romochka remembered that some time ago Puppy would also have been giggling. Now he just gurgled and growled.

Perhaps Puppy was not a boy anymore.

Romochka turned to the wall, curled up and tried to sleep, with Puppy's voice in his ears and Puppy's distinctive smell in his nostrils.

It was a remarkably easy winter and Romochka's memories of the two winters before became dreamy and remote. If it hadn't been for the desiccated carcasses he and Puppy played with in the lair, he would have forgotten the Strangers altogether. It wasn't just that the winter was milder: Romochka was bigger and knew a lot more. He was well dressed this winter. He had

153

to seek out and steal clothes for Puppy whenever he could, and took the opportunity to clothe himself too. He had a hard time begging, as other beggars now reported him on sight either to their masters or to the militzia who protected their territory, and his begging for scraps suffered too because of this.

Food was nonetheless plentiful, if monotonous. A craze for shooting ravens swept Moscow, rapidly escalating into an unregulated winter sport. Young house men cruised around in their cars, looking for the grey and black birds. Around the mountain and in the forest, people and dogs fled and hid at the sound of gunshots, but the steady supply of dead and injured ravens drew them all into the city. Romochka so wanted warm bird that he would go to where he could hear the gunshots, hoping to find something wounded or just killed. When he found a warm one, he would stuff it under his shirt and race home to eat in peace in the lair, sharing it with Puppy before it froze. The dogs brought home so many ravens that Romochka was able to make a raven bower for Puppy at the other end of the lair.

Out at the mountain, women sat around the fires roasting the plucked birds on sticks, stirring big pots of soup made from the stripped carcasses. No dogs were eaten this winter.

Ж

Everyone loved Puppy. They let him do what he liked, even sometimes pinch food from them. Romochka too, was disarmed by him. Puppy was smart, cheeky and good-spirited. He would play at the slightest sign of playfulness, and he was fun.

Romochka refused to allow Puppy out of the lair, even in late winter when his brother's litter sisters were well grown and had begun play-foraging out into closed paths with a minder. Whenever Puppy tried, Romochka beat him viciously; if ever one of the litter sisters tried to take Puppy with her, Romochka snarled at the two of them until they slunk back inside.

Romochka didn't really think about why, but he knew that with no hair and no tail, Puppy would stand out. His sense of the danger Puppy would represent to all of them if he were noticed was acute, and Mamochka backed him up. Puppy was only allowed out into the roofless building—never to the street, except to pee. Either Romochka or Mamochka had to stay near the lair to keep Puppy inside during the daytime.

In his confinement, Puppy had an insatiable need for novelty. Romochka began a new kind of hunting. The lair filled with colourful balls, animals, blocks, bells, a drum, a plastic sword and shield, even a toy pedal car. Romochka spent hours tinkering and playing with the toys he collected for Puppy, while Puppy scampered around him in delight. But when Puppy too settled and squatted to play, deeply engrossed, Romochka stroked him lovingly, with real pride. They built things together. They drove the car, Romochka pushing Puppy (with Puppy's eyes sliding this way and that like a scared but obedient dog). The little boy raced around in joyous relief when it was over.

Romochka began to prey on little kids. He and Black Sister held up prams and strollers to get the toys. Black Sister, finally chosen for a special hunt, refused to allow any other dog to accompany them and trotted beside him with proud intensity.

155

She was efficient and effective; she only had to get in close and lift her lip over her long white teeth, gurgling and chortling through her muscly jaws, and any mother would snatch her child from the pram and scream gratifyingly. Romochka would be into the pram, rummaging and snatching at any fallen toys, then they would be off, quick as rats. Black Sister barely showed how much she enjoyed it, but he knew she did.

This was a daylight hunt, and risky. As the thaw began, Puppy needed new clothes too. He took many of them off and lost them, especially now, in early spring, but he needed clothes to protect his skin from the nips of the dogs. Romochka was worried, too, by the feel of Puppy's body. He could tell, sleeping with that little ribcage in his arms, that Puppy was thinner than he had been before. He wanted good clothes for Puppy, not miscellaneous damp rags collected on the mountain.

Romochka began stalking little boys to find out what they did, where they went, where they lived, what they wore. Stealing clothes was hard. You either got a spare boy with them (and Romochka really didn't want Mamochka getting fond of another boy) or the clothes were safely hung up in shops or houses. Romochka and the dogs were at a disadvantage in shops—Romochka was suspected from the moment anyone saw him, and the dogs were liable to be kicked or shot at. He decided to try houses.

He thought he should be able to get into apartment buildings. He had seen bomzhi stand at the street doors in winter pressing buttons on the keypad until they got lucky and someone buzzed them in. He chose an older building at random and set White Sister to watch.

He pressed lots of buttons but nothing happened. Then a

drunk appeared at the corner, almost a bomzh but cleaner, and Romochka pulled back warily. He didn't run; he wasn't particularly afraid of drunks. The man swayed at the door, cursing and pressing buttons, eventually smiling broadly when he managed to get his apartment code. The door buzzed and Romochka slipped in behind him, leaving White Sister outside. The door clanged shut. He held back in the gloom by the doorway as the drunken man stumbled to the lift and jabbed the buttons.

Once the man was gone, Romochka padded across the cracked concrete to the blue-tiled stairwell. He loped silently up to the second floor. This building reminded him of another from long ago, although it seemed smaller. The door from the stairwell to the communal corridor was ajar. The dimly lit hallway smelled of old cooked food, alcohol, sweat, soapy skin and stale smoke. His heart beat fast. Grown-ups might like dogs but in his experience they hated kids.

He slunk up the dark corridor, checking each of the padded apartment doors. His heart was thumping now. A deep-voiced dog barked a warning somewhere ahead and he jumped, so edgy he nearly bolted back down the stairs. All the apartment doors were locked. He came to the door behind which the dog was now going berserk. He stuck his nose to the crack between door and jamb, and snuffed loudly then growled. The big dog's panic scared him—it had no idea what he was. He was deep in closed paths here, with no easy escape. He stood up and soft-footed back towards the stairs and up to the next floor, leaving the terrified animal behind. There was no sign that people were home, so far. Only the dog, crying now in fear and loneliness below.

He lost his nerve when he heard the lift clanking and winding. He scuttled noisily down the stairs to the street door, remembering at the last minute that to get out he had to press the big button. He could reach it easily, and then he was outside under the grey sky. He yipped, and White Sister came bounding from behind a rank of dumpsters.

Stairwells and communal corridors were not going to get him what he was after. He would have to look carefully, if he wanted to get into apartments, and find a way in from the outside.

Some older five-storey buildings had external drainpipes that ran near windows. Once he had found a few he looked for the apartments that still had the old-style double-glassed windows: inner and outer casements set either side of a wide sill. They were always closed but they sometimes had small rectangular ventilation windows set into the bigger frames, and these were often open. Eventually he narrowed his choices down to three third-floor apartments that each had a drainpipe he was sure he could climb.

For a week, he watched them from the street. One he ruled out because he couldn't be sure there was no one home in the daytime. The second was too exposed on the outside; someone was sure to see him climb the pipe. The last one had kids that he glimpsed at the window in the evenings, and seemed empty during the day. He spent another week building up his courage.

White Sister whined at the base of the drainpipe as he worked his skinny frame through the little window. Once he was wedged on the wide sill between the two large panes, he looked down at her, flicking his muzzle, and feeling his ears dip reassuringly at her. She continued to pace and whine, to his annoyance. She thought she could make him come down.

He crouched low. He was visible from the street, and if anyone was in the apartment they only had to part the lace curtain to find him sandwiched in their window. He had probably already made quite a bit of noise getting through the outer window. The inner ventilation window was closed and latched. He had begun to work at the cracked frame of the inner casement when it suddenly gave, opening inwards. He waited a little, then jumped quietly down through the curtains and into the room.

He was in a tidy bedroom with yellow walls and a high white ceiling. A little bed with rails was near the window, and a very large bed took up most of the room. Behind him the heating pipes were draped in pretty clothes too small even for Puppy. A picture on the wall showed a forest not unlike his home, with autumn birches in the foreground and a river much cleaner and bluer than any he'd ever seen running between green banks. He felt a wave of nostalgia for the time when such a place would have been all he needed for a good hunt. A time before the need for toys and puppy clothes.

The big bed was covered by a beautiful pink, green and mauve patterned quilt and matching pillows. He snuffed the air. The room smelled of washing powder, perfume, burnt cloth and, faintly, of wee. He was worried: the apartment must be bigger than he thought, for this room was only a bedroom, nothing more.

He moved soundlessly on all fours to the door, listening. There was no ticking or subtle shifting of body weight, no muffled rustle of someone waiting. The apartment was empty. He reached up and softly turned the handle, then dropped down low and eased the door open. The apartment was huge: there were three open doors off the corridor, inside doors, not the heavy padded ones of discrete apartments. The corridor was filled with furniture and ornaments. He was a little spooked but pleased to see children's clothes hung on heating pipes under the window at the far end of the long room and toys scattered here and there. He could smell a dog too. He wondered what the dog would think when she came home. He was in closed paths here, but would a tame dog know what to think?

He was crouching, still looking around and considering the crisscross of smells when a small white dog sprinted, snarling and gulping, out of the next room along. He screamed as the dog leapt. At the last minute he averted his face and the dog was on his head, sinking her teeth into his mane of matted hair and shaking him hard. He wriggled and threshed with arms and legs to fight her off. She latched onto one of his arms and he yelped and yabbered. He rolled into the children's room, yowling in fear, trying to wrestle the bristling little animal off him. His arm was bleeding. Then she launched again at his crotch, but this time he was ready for her and caught her by the throat. She was quite hard to hold as she snarled and snapped and writhed. He held on tight, pinning her with his knees as well.

Between his hands and legs he could feel her shaking terror. She didn't know what he was either. He tried to tell her that in crossing her closed paths he was strong enough to do as he wished; and that she should be offering him stiff deference. He held her down with his body weight and sniffed her over. She smelled all wrong: like soap, perfume, people. He tried to let her smell him, but she wasn't listening, or didn't know, and began to fight harder.

No wonder Mamochka avoided these crazy dogs. This little bitch didn't have the sense to know that he was dangerous and that she was small and risked everything if she fought him. He was suddenly furious with her and shook her hard. He buried his fingers deeper in her throat and sank his teeth into her rattling neck. Why didn't she see that he was a much bigger dog than she? But she threshed and slavered and wriggled and was altogether too much a ball of muscle for him to throttle her easily. He stopped biting her and spat out her soapy hair. Then he felt her starting to waver. Her fighting fear was giving way to despair. He could feel it. His rage drained out of him too. He felt sad, now that they weren't biting each other. He stood up on hind legs, yanking her with two hands off the ground. She went limp.

Just then he caught a glimpse of himself in a mirror on the wall and forgot about the dog altogether. He put her down slowly, staring open-mouthed. She slunk away and lay down a little way away from him, growling miserably, with her eyes low and her ears flattened.

He saw a very big dirty boy dressed in rags with a huge head of wild black ropes and tendrils, hair unlike any creature he had ever seen. He looked into his own eyes. Black, frowning. He wasn't what he thought he was. His teeth were flat and tiny like Puppy's. His new tooth, which he had hoped would become long and pointed, was indeed sharp, serrated, but very much a human tooth. The hairlessness of his body was a shock. He raised an arm. His callused paw and scarred forearm were stringy, bald, filthy, long. Wrong.

He certainly wasn't a dog, but he didn't look like a boy either. He suddenly felt annoyed with the little dog. She didn't know what he was and didn't like him either way, but she preferred him to be a boy, that was certain.

It was unbearably hot in the apartment. Watching himself all the while, he stripped down to his underneath layers of clothes.

'Good doggie, good dog,' he said in a soothing human boy's voice, watching his own mouth move in the mirror. His voice came out like dry leaves on bark, first; then cracked and unmusical. The little dog growled unhappily. 'Good doggie, good dog,' he repeated in a low voice, watching her in the mirror. She licked her nose and averted her eyes. He turned, squatted down and called her over, clicking his fingers and using a human voice, insistent until she couldn't disobey. She slunk towards him, her eyes low and her tail curled tightly under her. He patted her gently and she licked his hands. Her tail didn't lift but wagged rapidly between her legs.

'Brave little doggie,' he murmured. 'You fought the monster, even though he was as big as a Stranger and you were small. Brave little doggie.' He felt his words changing everything, not just between him and the dog, but between him and the place. He sensed his limbs: long and smooth, a boy's legs and arms. His ears, he knew, were flat to the sides of his head, not pointed and hairy. No dog would see his ears dip or prick—they were fine shells hidden under his hair.

The little dog squinted and rolled over, baring her throat, tail twirling. Then she followed him with eyes big and body miserable as he went through the apartment. The living room and the bedrooms were separated, and it was full of pretty things. He straightened his shoulders. He was a boy, not a dog, going through an apartment full of boyish things. He could enjoy this.

It was full of kids' stuff in every room. The room in which he had fought the dog had two beds and toys, not just scattered all over the floor, but in boxes, on shelves, even on the beds. A boys' room. Two boys lived here. There were two beds, two large fluffy toy bears, two distinct smells in the clothes, two of everything. Romochka climbed into the first bed and snuggled into the cream linen, tucking it around himself in movements that were somehow easy. The quilt had a picture of a stripy orange cat stitched onto it, with big teeth and yellow eyes.

'A *tiger*,' he said out loud, delighted with his own memories. He closed his eyes. 'Good night,' he said, experimentally, and the little dog whined. 'If you don't shut up and go to sleep, I'll fuckin skin ya!' he said to her, giggling.

He noticed that his hands had made blackish finger marks rather like a picture of claws on the cream sheets and pillow. He leapt up and hopped into the second bed. This one had a many-coloured blanket covering the quilt. But Romochka found he couldn't stay still, and he soon wriggled out from under the bedding and began pulling all the toys out of the boxes and the clothes out of the wardrobe.

Two boys, brothers, one bigger, one smaller. Romochka and Puppy. He stopped. Puppy's name wasn't a word. 'Schenok,' he said out loud, standing in the middle of the room. His joyous feelings cooled. He didn't like the sound of his own voice, all of a sudden. He had better get some stuff for Puppy. He sniffed through the clothes and toys, wondering what Puppy would like most. There was no way he would be able to carry all this stuff, so he would have to choose.

He rummaged through all the drawers and cupboards, filled his bag, emptied it again, and filled it again with other things. He became bewildered and overwrought with the huge array and the choices he had to make and now he was sick of the smell of their clothes. Without thinking, he peed on the door and the side of the beds, and then did a poo in the corner by the wardrobe. The poo and wee smelled all wrong in here too, so he threw some of the clothes over them. Then he remembered with a jolt that people would not like it, and he tried to wipe the wee up and clean the corner, but ended up smearing the poo up the wall and spreading drips of wee on everything.

He got hungry and went looking for food. The kitchen was tiny and very pretty. He loved it. He had never seen anything like it and ran his fingers over everything. It was covered in pictures of flowers, many of them in colours he had never seen on flowers. It had a white gas stove and oven, and, above the stove bench, white tiles decorated with small blue flowers that reminded him of the blooms that had just opened in the sodden snow of the vacant allotment. There were white lace curtains on the windows, and a plastic tablecloth printed with large mauve flowers and light brown leaves. The soft lino floor was a yellow field with pink flowers and lilac leaves. Everything was very clean.

The kitchen was so well stocked with food that he almost abandoned the idea of collecting clothes and toys for Puppy and hunted instead. He pulled everything out of the refrigerator and took a bite out of whatever was edible. He emptied the pantry cupboard onto the floor and crammed biscuits into his mouth. He felt for his pockets, realised he had taken them off, and crammed even more into his mouth. He wondered whether he should perhaps burn the mess he had made, but he could find no matches or firelighter, so, full bellied, he went back to the room that now smelled slightly better and sat down on the pile of clothes and toys and bedding.

The little white dog crept in close to him and stared at him. She looked away whenever he looked at her. Finally, worried about getting drowsy, he stuffed some trousers, jumpers, coats and hats into the bag. A pair of boots. He looked in bewilderment at the toys and couldn't choose.

Just then the little dog shot out of the room. He followed her, nervous. She was at the door, ears pricked, tail up, body stiff—listening to something way down below. Then she started barking, desperately. She knew help was at hand.

Romochka raced back to the bedroom, grabbed the half-full bag, toyless still, and raced back to the front door. In the entrance he saw one last toy, a red and yellow plastic bone that squeaked as he grabbed it. He shoved it in and ran for the door, slipping on the cold blood from his fight with the little dog. She was in a frenzy now, all focused on the door. He pushed her aside and wrestled with the handle. It was locked. He could hear steps on the stairs. The little dog sang out the whole story with such urgency that even people would be able to hear it.

He shrieked in panic, scrabbled his fingers briefly at the door, and then raced for the parents' bedroom and the window. He jumped up through the open casement onto the sill, but he couldn't squeeze his bag of stuff through the little window. He thought of abandoning it and pulled himself up. He tried to get his feet, shanks, knees out, but what he had managed to do when calm he now found impossible.

The little dog was yabbering, practically howling. He heard the door to the apartment being unlocked, opened. He was too late. He jumped back to the sill, picked up his bag and crouched in the room. There was no hiding place. He was whimpering now with each breath. He turned towards the door, and, with his bag over his shoulder, he ran.

There were three people, holding their noses and exclaiming in horror. Romochka roared and ran straight at them, dodging sharply through their startled lunges, through their exclamations—'Phuuuuu!! Oujas! What *is* it!?' 'Catch him!' 'Bomzh thief!' 'What a smell!' 'What *was* that?'—and then he sprinted, with them behind, down the strange corridor to where he thought the stairs had to be. He was faster, even hunched over with the bag on his back. He rattled down the last flight of stairs with tumult behind him and ran as fast as he could for the street door. Someone opened the metal door from the outside just at that moment, and he was through.

White Sister appeared out of nowhere and snarled into the faces of the startled men and women who were filling the doorway behind him with angry uproar.

He ran all the way home to try to keep from freezing in his thin shirt and long underwear.

He played at home with Puppy for a few days, feeling diminished. Gradually his ears sharpened to points, his teeth lengthened, his chest lost its flat human plane and he headed out again to hunt the forest and mountain. And, inevitably, the city.

Once his sense of himself was sufficiently doglike again, he gave way to his desire to hunt toys, telling himself it was Puppy who needed them. But he gave up houses. The mirror had made him miserable, and he couldn't forget the little white dog.

Ж

Romochka and White Sister were making their way warily through the slush in a strange alley. One side was filled with rubble and had the occasional familiar nest of cardboard, broken crates and old blankets. The other had a thin puddled pathway through a slurry of plastic bottles, paper, nappies, broken glass and onion skins. The hairs prickled on the back of Romochka's neck just as White Sister stiffened. They were being stalked from the laneways leading into this alley. They were being stalked but not stealthily. And at that moment the alley behind them filled with people, whooping and yelling.

'Dogboy! Dogboy! Don't let him get away!'

Romochka and White Sister turned and sprinted along the clearer side of the alley, their footfall loud and spattering, covering each other with black oily mud as they ran. They were in an unfamiliar part of the city where Romochka had been seeking a degree of anonymity for his hunt, and he didn't know the way out. They were running in ankle-deep sludge now, half-clambering through large piles of rubbish by two over-turned dumpsters—a bad sign. The cries behind them had the high excitement of a hunt reaching a climax, and Romochka wasn't surprised when the alley turned and ended suddenly in a brick wall, still piled with black snow.

He and White Sister spun to fight. But as the gang rounded

the corner, quieter now, he knew it was hopeless. They were a very large pack, all nearly grown. Big short-hair boys. He crouched and swung his club low, legs apart, waiting. White Sister bared her teeth and snarled in rumbling swells, snapping and slavering to show all she had. But he knew that they were just two dogs, and it would not be enough.

He woke up to the sound of White Sister snarling and yelping in pain. He kept his eyes closed, listening. She sounded angry and submissive at the same time. He could hear that she was afraid. He could hear laughter, swelling and bubbling in response to her cries. He could feel someone hovering near him, leaning in. His head hurt. His hands and feet were free but no part of his body was touching the floor, he realised. He was hanging, naked, by a bunch of hair drawn from his brow and crown. He couldn't touch the ground, but the person in front of him must be standing on it. Cold water was running down his face, and he could feel from the breeze that his face was completely uncovered.

He waited, made a guess from the sound of smiling breath, and kicked the person in front of him in the face as hard as he could, opening his eyes and snarling at the same time. His body swung as he snapped his foot out and the kick was far weaker than he had hoped; hard enough only to startle and enrage. The youth jumped back, clutching his face and yelling. The others turned and laughed.

He was in a large darkened warehouse space, filled with pipes and pillars. The gang were lying around at rest, or gathered around White Sister. Her head was pressed to the floor, pinned with a large nail driven through her folded ear.

He just had time to glimpse her scrabbling in desperation as they goaded her, before the one he had kicked smacked his head with something and darkness fell.

He was thirsty and hungry. His scalp ached. There were fewer in the room now but still quite a pack. They had become bored with White Sister. She was trembling in the middle of the floor, trying feebly to stop her exhausted limbs sliding out from under her. He could smell food, hot food. They were eating out of paper bags. Stardogs and Subway. He made a noise and they turned. A dark spiky-haired youth in a leather jacket came up to him, grabbed his foot and swung his body. He swayed dizzily from side to side, scrabbling to stop himself with hands and feet. The others laughed, choking on their food. They looked at him with bright eyes and he knew this was not good. The boys were not bomzhi. They were all short-hair boys. They had house clothes, jeans and warm jackets; he could smell that someone washed their clothes and bodies.

He felt terribly afraid now. House boys hated bomzh boys so this was going to be a clan thing, not just a lack of appreciation. He glanced around surreptitiously as the boy swung him against the wall again. This was their lair, but they lived elsewhere, in houses, apartments, flats, with their mothers and uncles. They seemed unreal to him, somehow. He tried to picture them as sons of the women he had robbed. In the apartment with the little dog. He found he couldn't imagine it.

The lair was furnished with some broken-down sofas, a ramshackle improvised fireplace with a warm fire blazing in it and a table. The boys played with noisy flashing toys Romochka didn't recognise. Most of them had knives. Their eyes slid sideways, always, to see what other boys thought of them. Following their glances, Romochka realised there were also two girls or very young women in the lair. One was asleep on one of the sofas, her long bare arms glowing orange in the firelight. The other was staring at him with a bored expression from the back of the room, where she was leaning against the shoulder of a very tall boy.

'Dare ya to fuck it!' one boy said suddenly, pushing the skinny boy next to him.

'Fuck it yasself!' the skinny one said, shoving back.

'Fuck IT, fuck IT, fuck IT, fuck IT!' the other boys started chanting, giggling. They scrambled to their feet and formed a semicircle, clapping their hands in tune with their chant and miming hip thrusts. The skinny boy grinned and lashed out at them with his fists.

'I'd rather fuck the dog,' he said and they all fell about laughing, and began pulling him towards White Sister.

'Fuck yourself,' Romochka croaked, and they all turned and stared at him in sudden silence.

The boys surrounded him, poking him with sticks.

'Say it again, again, again!' they chanted.

These boys wanted him to speak, so he spoke. They wanted him to cry, so he cried, fat tears running down his cheeks and chest. They wanted his fear, so he gave it to them.

He wet himself for them. He held his penis for them. He sang for them. He begged, pleaded, drummed his heels on the wallboards. He fought them each in turn, dangling and swinging like a marionette in a puny helpless dance of fists and feet. He kept them entertained and away from White Sister, all the while thinking *Mamochka, Mamochka, mother,*

mother, come for me, come for me now. Come quickly and bring all the teeth we have. He eyed a long naked knife one of the boys had left lying under the far table. How impossibly far away that wonderful lone tooth was.

Night fell. The boys slowly lost interest in him as a toy, a doll with a range of human emotions. They had become fascinated with his endurance and were now experimenting to find out just how much he could take. They pierced his ears. They burned his arms with cigarettes. When they cut the lines into his chest with the point of a knife he howled until his voice was gone. He knew they would kill him in the end, probably almost by accident. He had killed the orange cat almost by accident. He felt himself receding from his outer body, gathering all of himself deep inside, coiled, ready and waiting. *Mamochka, Mamochka.*

You haven't had your birthday?

He shook his ears, giggling. Fancy Mamochka taking birthdays seriously!

We'll have one then. Here is your crown.

He let her put the peacock crown on his head. He sat beside her in the metal-toothed bucket of the red tractor. White Sister came through the wheatfield first, carrying a warm pigeon. She placed it at his feet. Golden Bitch appeared with a feathered chicken. Then Black Sister with a bloody vole. Each walked with ceremonious step and sat beside him, having placed their presents at his feet. Black Dog came through the golden seed heads carrying a heron, Grey Brother brought three speckled eggs. Then Brown Brother...Brown Brother! Bumbling and joyous with a fresh hare. Brown Brother had never caught a hare. Little Patch and Little

Gold followed, carrying a loaf of bread between them. The pile of goodies grew and everyone stared, drooling. Puppy appeared last, bounding up unceremoniously to hand over a plastic bag filled with hot pirozhki. The smell of the hot potato pastry and meat filled the air, drowning out the rich scents of blood, and wet hair and feathers. The dogs quivered, held back only by the importance of the occasion. All the while Mamochka sat by his shoulder, warm and approving. She was unflustered by the maddening delicacies at his feet. She looked grand and wise, sitting there in the big red bucket beside him.

Happy Birthday Beloved. Shall we? She indicated with her muzzle. He turned to her, urgent, expectant.

What have you got for me, Mamochka, Mamochka?

All the teeth I have. Coming quickly, darling. As quickly as I can.

He felt fast and sure on the inside but his outer body had slowed. He took a while to notice that White Sister was taut, her free ear swivelling. It broke in on him slowly: Mamochka and the others must be outside.

He dragged himself back to the surface, to the laughing, the hard grip and the pain. A boy was burning his long ropey locks, one by one, holding his nose and exclaiming over the rich crackle as they frizzled. The others were bored, he could tell, and the boy was looking for a more exciting reaction. He tried to moan, to draw attention away from the door, and although his voice found only a whispering thread of soundless breath, they were looking at him when the room filled with dogs.

The knotted end of Romochka's greasy hair ignited. His elflocks parted and he fell to the ground. He seemed to sleep for long seconds, although he could see the marvellous swirling violence sweeping the room, could feel the glorious strength of dogs as if it were coursing through him. His body did not obey him. The bored girl was stamping out the flames in his hair, swearing through her cigarette, shaking her head at him as she did it, then she was gone into the melée.

He had waited so long, made himself so ready on the inside but his body would not come to life. Then he realised he was already crawling across the floor, legs and arms heavy, unbelievably slow. He was flooded with a fierce joy: he felt the loving wall of hair, tooth and muscle close around him, heard their snarls and the house boys' screams. He scrambled across the floor to White Sister. He licked her bloodied face once and scrabbled on his belly over to the knife. He didn't think. He took the knife in both hands, sat hard on her head and, sliced off her swollen ear. The knife was brilliantly sharp.

The next thing he knew he was out on the street, dizzy, naked, his arms around the trembling bloodied body of White Sister, pulling her away, as the ruckus continued behind them. He had no idea where they were but White Sister did. She shook herself weakly, and with halting, feeble steps, nosed out the thread of the others' trail. They stumbled through unfamiliar streets in darkness. Now, in the midst of his relief, ballooning terror shook his jaw, clattering his teeth. He wished he had not dropped the knife. White Sister was picking up his scattered parts with her bloodied muzzle.

Then they were in the awful alley, lit now by homely bomzh fires. White Sister turned away. She didn't want to enter it—she knew this part too. But he begged her, and they crept to the blank wall, to their forgetfulness. He scrabbled around in the rubbish until his fingers found his club.

They headed into known trails and were soon joined by the others, all battle scarred but jaunty. They hemmed around his shaking naked body, each in turn slipping in to lick his hands and face, to lick the cuts on his chest, the sides of his mouth and White Sister's blood-soaked head. The breeze on his naked skin froze him and his wounds stung. He shook all over, clammy and sick. He wanted to close his eyes and sleep on the road, but the thought of recapture drove him on. He looked around, big-eyed, fuzzy-headed. Maybe he was dying, after all. He could barely hold onto his club.

They entered the lane leading to the last meeting post as a tight, jostling mass. Then Romochka saw Pievitza. He knew her straightaway. She still had a floating, sinuous walk, completely unlike anybody else's, although now she was walking carefully. She came slowly up the lane towards them, staring at the ground, her face in shadow. Her skinny daughter wasn't with her and Romochka thought she wasn't waiting back home either. Pievitza gave off the unmistakeable scent of grief.

He melted with the dogs into the shadows and watched her pass. She was thinner across the shoulders. Once she was close he could hear the occasional hiss of her breathing through her strange mouth, and he could smell her. He breathed in deep on that: ash and chemical, sweat and semen. The smell of harm and hurt. The dogs lifted their muzzles. Pievitza, he suddenly knew, was pregnant. Her long hair was uncovered, pale under the orange velvet sky. He saw the flicker of that long-ago fire in her shining hair. He couldn't see her face or her mouth but he burned now as if he were filled with fire. His teeth stopped tap tapping. His shaking stilled. He stepped out silently into the path behind her and stood up tall, naked under the stars with the dogs quiet around him.

He touched his fingers to the congealing blood on his chest and raised his bloodied hand to her receding form, just as Laurentia did to him. Then the wall of hair and muscle and teeth hugged him close and he drew the cleanness of the night air deep into his stinging chest.

The following morning he woke up shivering, sweating, hot and cold all over. He couldn't bear the dogs to touch him but needed them to stay nearby, warming him as best they could. He couldn't get up without falling over. Puppy was alternately overly compassionate and overly boisterous, but it was Puppy who held him while he shivered, and Puppy who curled in his arms, carefully distant from his wounds, when each storm had passed. Romochka lay in the nest, dizzy and miserable. His wounds were too inflamed to be licked. He couldn't eat the freshly killed offerings everyone brought for him. He kept thinking over and over that his mother and uncle were going to miss his birthday.

For three days Mamochka licked the sick sweat from his face and ears and slowly worked her way down to the oozing scabs on his chest. He shut his eyes tight and put up with the pain for as long as he could. He remembered the sores that healed in springtime after she cleaned them. On the fourth day, he ate some baby mice White Sister brought for him and played with Puppy.

He recovered his strength in a week. He imagined again and again heading out to find the singer but he didn't leave the lair. His hair was still long but didn't quite cover his face and he felt exposed. White Sister had recovered quickly and hunted specifically, lovingly, for him. Each time she returned, her lopsided silhouette at the entrance hole jolted him, and he fingered his own slowly healing scars. White Sister brought him rats, mice, birds, a fox cub and miscellaneous edible refuse: he could tell that she was hunting the mountain and the forest, not the city.

Romochka spent his time playing with Puppy, making the most of all the toys obtained on past hunts, building elaborate cityscapes. Romochka made streets and housing estates out of all the blocks and broken toys or rocks they could collect, while Puppy barked in anticipation. This city had to have the vacant lot, the meeting place, the open paths, and then the exact streets Romochka knew. Puppy's eyes shone at the magic of it all.

Once Romochka was happy with the city, he made people out of small sticks and pebbles. People milling about in groups too large to stalk, people shopping, people in buildings; and always one lone pebble far from the others. He walked his fingers through the alleys, imitating with his eyes and manner the moves of a hunt, getting Puppy to crouch down, hold his noise. Then his fingers would leap out, Puppy leaping too in imitation, and the two boys barked and snarled as Romochka's fingers backed the hapless pebble up against the wall of a teetering building.

Sometimes he would abandon the lone pebble and stalk the crowds, leaping his fingers at them, scattering the shocked pebbles, making them run this way and that. Puppy dashed and lunged at them by his side, eyes flaming, white teeth bared, shaking all over with excitement. Then, after scattering all the pebbles, Romochka would trash the very city with the power of his hunt and Puppy would go wild with delight, standing up and running around on his hind legs like Romochka and uttering strange war cries.

Ж

Romochka stuck his nose out of the lair, struck by the thought of just going out the way he used to. He was bored playing with Puppy, bored with the lair, bad tempered with the dogs and dissatisfied with the tidbits they brought home for him. He pulled himself out and shuffled into the ruin and then the courtyard. Late spring sang and shimmered. The dandelions were high and bees buzzed over the high grass. He could see that he had missed a lot of things hiding from the house boys. He squatted in the green, eating the bitter-delicious leaves, snatching at them and gobbling like a dog with a tummy ache.

He looked around. The birch would be dancing with many greens in these light breezes; babies would be out in the leaves with their mothers watching over them. There would be nests and mottled eggs in the forest. He loved eggs. He wished he had some now. The dogs were useless, wasteful egg eaters. Smash and lick, that's all they could do, swallowing sticks, shell, plastic and road grease as they did it. Stupid dogs. *He* would bore a little hole at either end with a sharp stick, and then suck, feeling the white and then the yolk swell through that little hole and fill his mouth. He sighed. How could he tell them to go and get him some eggs? If they weren't dogs, they'd know the word *egg*. Stupid dogs.

He sniffed the air. Only cooking fires burned out beyond

the mountain. The reek was mingled with pollens, the air laden with the best things in life. Birds whistled and warbled, marking their territories with sound. So many crisscrossed invisible boundaries, trails, nests and lairs. So many fights to be had for dog, cat, man and bird. So many eggs for the brave.

He grabbed large handfuls of dandelion and climbed back down into the lair.

Puppy was sleeping with Little Gold and Little Patch, and Romochka tiptoed around them. Little Gold opened an eye and yawned but didn't move. Romochka settled himself in his bower with his treasures. He stroked the soft tatty fur of the cat's tail. That was a brave cat and as orange as autumn, as orange as fire. He smiled. He stuck the tail between his bare buttocks but it wouldn't stay, so he curled up and sucked thoughtfully on the bony tip of it. *I don't eat dog, I don't eat human, I don't eat cat.*

He was, all of a sudden, very pleased with himself.

The next day, with the warm spring wind stronger and humming across the entrance hole, sucking from the lair a booming music, Romochka couldn't stay a second longer. He wanted to hunt, to explore, to rediscover the shining world. He hugged himself in glee at the thought of visiting the Roma, a thought filled with expectation of delicious food and, perhaps even more delicious, Laurentia's tears.

When Romochka started hunting again, he was lean and fast on the streets and in the rain-spangled forest. He snarled savagely at children when he saw them, terrorising them and their mothers; making his own family insecure and close-hackled around him. But he wouldn't chase cats. When he saw

178

them, he stood and nodded thoughtfully to them, exactly as his singer had once nodded to him. Cats stopped arching and spitting at the sight of him and just slunk away, turning at a safe distance to blink their shining eyes.

He liked to see a cat at the start of a hunt, and, whenever he did, was convinced the hunt went well. He screamed, bashed and bit the dogs into leaving them alone. When Golden Bitch and Black Dog carried a cat into the lair, he infuriated everyone by snatching its mauled stringy carcass and climbing the ruined cupola to hide it where they couldn't reach it.

Ж

Romochka knew, as soon as he entered, that Puppy had done something wrong. Puppy didn't race to greet him but stared at him from the family nest, big eyed. Romochka stiffened and stared at his little brother with menace. He let the others jump all over him. He threw his bags of scraps to the side for them to smell over, all the while keeping his eyes fixed on Puppy's face. He waited. Puppy crept on his belly to Romochka's hands, licked them, then crept back to the nest. Romochka swung away from him and headed to his bower. He could feel Puppy's eyes following him.

Puppy had been in his bower. Romochka could smell him and could sense each tiny displacement of his space. Puppy had been many times in his bower: they all had, but only by invitation. His eye caught the loose brick in the wall, subtly dislodged. Puppy had been into his secret place. Filled with a cold rage,

Romochka slid the brick out and felt over his things, all fouled by Puppy's touch. His fingers missed it first. He felt over everything again with care, then scraped the collection of beaks and claws into his other palm. There was no doubt: the crown was gone. He turned with a savage snarl and towered over Puppy, who was lying on the ground right behind him, face averted. Romochka roared and reached for his club. Puppy fled to the nest just as Mamochka entered the lair, leapt forward and snarled at Romochka full in the face. He nearly clubbed her. She saw it in his eyes and blazed at him in full attack readiness. He crept away ashamed and shocked. He refused to eat and refused to sleep with any of them afterwards. He froze until midnight, then headed out miserably to roam the mountain with Black Dog.

The crown was not to be found. Puppy had eaten it for its beauty.

A day later Puppy was scampering about, barking happily. Romochka was surly; however, as he had clearly lost his aloofness, Puppy was ridiculously elated. Romochka started trying to catch Puppy in order to thrash and maul him, but his attempts to catch his little brother only increased Puppy's playfulness, and soon Romochka was running around the cellar too, with Grey Brother and White Sister joining in, until he tired of the game and flopped down in the nest. Puppy sat in front of them, eyes wide, grinning, poised to duck and race off as soon as any of them made a move in his direction.

Romochka really wanted Puppy to fall asleep so he and the others could go out. Eventually Puppy flopped down on his belly, sighed and rested his chin on his hands. Romochka got up slowly. Puppy blinked at him and closed his eyes. The dogs watched from the floor above as Romochka built a barrier out of slats that should have kept a dog inside the cellar. With a spring in his step, he jumped up the rubble pile to the entrance, ready to get a little bit of fresh air, soak up some sun and to smell and see the mountain before dark. They all stood at the street door and tested the air.

Romochka glanced back and roared in fury. Puppy had scrabbled over and was landing on all fours; then he too jumped up the rubble pile and sat, wagging his tail-less rump, begging, bright eyed. Romochka knew that if he raced over and savaged his little brother, Puppy would just roll over and squint at him.

Romochka's envy bubbled up within his rage. Well, why not? If Puppy wanted to come. Puppy was going to be too big to be stopped *forever* from coming out of the lair. There had to be a first time. So what if people saw him? Puppy was quite fast; and as a pack they were invincible when they were together. Another little voice deep inside said: he is a human boy, after all, and can't live with us forever. He'll grow up, for a start. Humans will want him back.

He flicked his nose sweetly, deviously, towards the outside world and Puppy raced, quivering in delight, to his side.

He was still cross when they reached the allotment but then Puppy's crazy joy infected him too, and they both scampered in wide circles, yipping and barking. Puppy had startling blue eyes and long, pale yellow hair. Romochka almost stopped playing to let his eyes take Puppy in. He was a much bigger boy than he had been. The straight golden hair flicked and sparkled in the sun, the pale face was flushed, red lips parted over those funny flat white teeth. Puppy was the prettiest child Romochka had ever seen. His easy gait and speed over the ground were amazing. Romochka was filled with pride that

181

Puppy was theirs. He spent some time catching grasshoppers for this new Puppy, and feeling a strange solicitude as he watched the beautiful little boy crunch them up.

A dry golden haze hung over the warming world. They chased each other around the allotment, racing each other to eat the white and yellow flowers that spangled the undergrowth in the field.

After that no one could stop Puppy from going out. He was uncontrollable. He ran up to people; he followed them and dashed into houses. He barked at prams and then tried to jump into them. He accepted sweets, in fact anything people gave him. He leapt on the world as if greeting a returning mother. He wouldn't shut up. He listened to no warning barks and dodged all bites, chased butterflies rather than melt away; and he rolled over on his back when he saw a militzioner.

Within a week he disappeared.

Ж

For three weeks Romochka hunted for Puppy, but all trails faded. In the lair, he played with their toys, miserable and lonely and snapping at everyone. At the end of the three weeks, he woke up from a nap and needed more than anything a taut belly full of pasta.

Laurentia beamed when she saw them.

'My darlings!' she chirruped, bustling in to get them something to eat. Then she stood and watched, singing. Romochka bent his face over the lovely food, shovelling it in with both hands. It was safe at the Roma, safe enough to drop his guard and concentrate on eating.

'They caught another one like you, caro,' Laurentia said suddenly, breaking mid-song. Romochka looked up. His jaw stopped moving and the gnocchi fell back into his bowl.

'But this one a real real dogaboy.' She wriggled her fingers in the air, making her big hand lope like a dog. 'It was in all the papers. Funny, eh? I wonder how many bambini...'

'Where did they take him?' Romochka asked intently.

'Oh, some special internat, some name, in N. district,' Laurentia said.

'What *name*?' Romochka almost screamed.

'I'll remember in a minute. Hold on! Eat. I'll remember... Makarenko, Romochka. Calm down! Eat!'

Romochka was shaking, eager to be gone. He bolted his food, yipped at the dogs and ran off into the darkness. He stopped at the end of the alley and turned to wave his thanks to Laurentia. She was standing under the streetlight, waiting. As always, she raised her huge paw in return.

Romochka found the centre easily enough. He and the three cornered a gang of young bomzh kids in the carved stone metro station and scared the information out of them, including which metro to catch and from where. They told him that kids got taken there never to be seen again, and that experiments were done on them. Romochka didn't understand what this might mean, so he snarled at them to shut up.

The stations had changed over the last two seasons. He had to keep moving or militzia would materialise, and then he would have to run. He was so afraid now of militzia that he felt a disabling weakness at the sight of them. These days it was as if, in the stations at least, the militzia had developed as good a sense of smell as dogs. They were uncanny trackers. And the trains themselves still made him jumpy. He preferred to trot from station to familiar station as the giant worm was screaming through its hole far beneath his feet.

But he could catch one if he had to. He had found out long ago that if he made himself small in a corner of a train and then snarled, slavered and rolled his eyes when anyone approached, people left him alone, including the uniformed ones who weren't militzia. And this time he had no choice. He would have to take the metro, at least the first time, in order to follow the instructions the children had given him. It would be the furthest he had travelled since he got lost on the wrong side of the river.

He took White Sister. Since she lost her ear her old charm was diminished and her manner more aloof. Her bond with Romochka was unbreakable now and her city hunting so seasoned that he still relied more on her than on the others. She gave him her total attention and could not be drawn from him even by the proximity of a spitting cat.

His trip to the centre was uneventful but his fear rose as each station passed. He could feel the train rushing towards the river, that outermost boundary, and his scalp crawled. Then the station the kids named was called out. He breathed again. This couldn't be the other side of the river, not yet. It was too few stations, too fast.

The station was unfamiliar, beautiful and completely without bomzhi. He didn't wait and look around. Bomzhi-free was not good. At best there had just been a purge, at worst they were driven out or arrested the moment they showed up.

He found himself at the head of the metro stairs in a leafy, unwholesomely clean city. He guessed he was not all that far from the area in which he and White Sister had been lost, although he knew he was upriver and on the right side this time. He also told his hammering heart that he knew his station, knew his home in human words and could scare information out of kids any time he needed it. He couldn't get lost again.

The cars shone. The pavements, although crumbling, were swept. They had nothing for a dog to eat. Cats sunned themselves on walls without even looking at him. He broke into a panicked trot and was relieved to see the white building of the centre exactly as the kids had described it. It was an old building, newly painted. It reminded him of a bomzh man emerging from the welfare centre—shaven, washed, disinfected and dressed in fresh clothes. He and White Sister jumped the flaking street wall so as to be out of sight from the city and then they settled in to watch.

The building had many windows winking in the sun but getting in would be hard. Although it was old enough to have external drainpipes, each window had metal bars in front, made to look like fingers spread in front of a face. Pretty, but very hard to wriggle over or through. He could see that these windows had an inner grid too, and that would make it impossible.

The building was a low four-storey, much longer than it was high. The gardens had many recently established shrubs near the wall and a few large alder and chestnut trees that must have been the same age as the building. He could see a new-looking playground to the side, and in it four children dressed in bright T-shirts: red, blue, green and purple. Red and blue were playing and shrieking without caution, and Romochka's lip curled. House children.

Once he felt he had scowled for long enough at Puppy's new home, he headed back to the metro to brave the journey home and make sure he could repeat it without getting lost.

He visited the centre three days in a row to stare, frowning deeply, from behind the street wall. He explored the lane behind, prowled through the car park and scaled the locked gate into the gardens after dark. The car park was open and temporary— there were no bifold tin boxes for the cars. This meant no one lived here, except for the kids. The staff all had homes somewhere else, although they came and went at different times and there were always some cars here, even at night.

The guard dog was a loud but timorous fellow who by the second night adored Romochka and eagerly showed him around. During the day Romochka watched the people coming and going. If Puppy was in there, he wasn't coming out with any of those people.

On the fourth day he dressed in an assortment of his least ragged clothes. The cleanliness and beauty of Puppy's new territory troubled him; perhaps he should hunt for a good jacket and trousers that he would keep just for going there. He looked down at himself, standing in the rain outside the ruin. Well, he looked good in these old things for now. He brushed off a little caked-on mud. Very human. This time he would be the boy, not the dog, and if they called the militzia; well, they would get a surprise at what he was hiding. He squared his shoulders.

Outside the centre, he got White Sister to wait in the gardens, acting like any old stray, while he walked right into that forbidding white building, his heart leaping up his throat and trying to strangle him.

He froze, ready to flee. Three closed doors, the door behind, and the stairwell ahead. The tall windows would be useless, he knew that already. He listened to the door behind him close, making sure no lock clicked, and clutched his club, legs apart, knees bent. The woman behind the desk stared with bulging eyes as her hand crept up to hold a small piece of cloth in front of her face. She tapped, leaned forward, and wailed into the empty air above her desk,

'Dr Pastushenko, you are needed in reception!'

She was scared of him, and he felt a little better.

The entrance echoed and stank. Soap and something acrid. The woman smelled of sweat and some unfamiliar tang. Not flowers nor fruit nor meat. Not animal. The high walls were freshly painted but the iron balustrade leading up to the next floor was chipped and flaky. He could smell children's home, old bad feelings, a hovering sadness. He could hear the children still shrieking outside and the drumming of young footsteps on the floors above. He couldn't smell Puppy.

'Dr Pastushenko!' The woman squeaked, leaning to put her mouth down near her desk from behind her cloth. Her eyes slid again and again to a door beside the balustrade, so Romochka watched it too and waited.

He was startled when a young woman burst in from another door entirely, wafting eddies of a chemical and flower smell into the space. She had a swathe of shining brown hair as long as his own, but curly, not tangled.

She bounded in, past, then froze like a young elk to stare at him with dark eyes. Her hand too rose to her face, then she deliberated and lowered it. There was a silence as she drew him in.

'Dr Ivanovna! Dr Ivanovna! Do something. Please! I have been paging and paging Dr Pastushenko!'

'It's OK, Anna,' the elk woman said softly. That voice. Mellow, rich, all colours. Not shining like Pievitza, but glowing. Coals. Romochka reeled: if Pievitza had a Black Sister, this elk woman was she. She smelled like a woman who is with a man and carries herself and him together on her body to warn off others. But she had nothing of the harm and hurt of Pievitza. He was scared now, bewildered—and worried that he would forget how to find Puppy.

'Brother Schenok!' he croaked.

'Aaaaaaah,' said the voice, low and clear. 'We really do need Dr Pastushenko.'

Romochka's heart beat hard. Puppy was here, somewhere, or she wouldn't be so knowing.

An adult step clattered on the stairs and, as a man's legs appeared, a dry, rasping voice shouted,

'Anna, I am here! Ouj...what is that *smell*!' And with that last word he appeared and stopped short. Elk woman turned to him as Anna fluttered behind the desk.

Elk woman smiled, breathing through tiny intakes.

'He wants his brother *Puppy*!'

The man started at the word. '*Puppy*,' she said again, as if goading him.

There was a long silence.

The light from the stairwell windows was behind the man, and Romochka couldn't see him clearly. He was tall and lean, and it was his smell that elk woman had in her keeping.

'Your brother is here,' he said, his voice sere and rustling like autumn leaves. 'He is well cared for.'

When the man stepped forward, Romochka saw his eyes first. They were grey, clouded with a mixed sadness and yearning, but kind. He came quite close, and although he didn't seem to notice Romochka clench the club, he knelt and took on an unthreatening pose. He was close enough for Romochka to smell his true smell in his scalp and see flecks of white in the thin straw-coloured hair. This man had no qualms about holding his nose between thumb and forefinger and speaking in a nasal rasp.

'What is your name?' he asked. It was the first time any of them had addressed him directly, and Romochka wished he had a dog snarling next to him, keeping them at bay. He dithered for a moment, wondered whether to bolt, growl or swing the club. All three. Then he blushed.

'Romochka.'

The man stood up.

'Natalya, let us take Romochka to see his brother.'

She laughed, eyed the man from under her lashes, and the three of them set off together up the stairs, with sweat springing from every pore on Romochka's body. He walked to one side of the man, the safest place. The woman looked faster and seemed more determined. Underneath a muted reek of adult male, the man smelled of leather, soap-scrubbed hands, and...wood. Autumn. Romochka had never smelled anyone like him.

IV

Pravda Moskvii, 10 June 2003

MOSCOW DOGBOY CAPTURED

Moscow child protection authorities have confirmed rumours that a latter-day Mowgli was caught in recent weeks around Zagarodiye on the northern outskirts of the capital city. The two-year-old boy was first sighted barking and running on all fours in the company of a pack of wild dogs.

Experts say that he has lived with the dogs since babyhood. He is very small and malnourished, with noticeable hair all over his body. He is able to run at great speed on his hands and feet. He uses dog sounds exclusively.

The age of Moscow's dogboy makes him a rarity. Recent cases of older street children living with animals are well documented. However, while feral children actually raised by animals have been a recurrent subject of fiction, all previous real-life instances on record are of disputed authenticity.

Nothing is known about the long-term physical and mental effects of an early life with dogs. Our Russian dogboy will be kept at the Anton Makarenko Children's Centre, where he will be studied by leading scientists while receiving the very best of care. The dogboy's progress will be of considerable interest to the scientific community worldwide.

Dr Dmitry Pastushenko put the newspaper down and sighed. If only it were that simple. Three weeks ago this story would have been sufficient; now they would have to make a statement. A dogboy with a brother just didn't seem to be the real thing. Yes, he was exposed, now. Open to ridicule, and not just on the subject of dogboys. His smug confidence! His hopes.

His views. He had said more than once over dinner that the human was an animal at heart. *Healing young humans involves getting the animal part right first—making sure that shelter, food and loving touch are a given in any child's life.* What did that really mean? The memory of his own voice mocked him. *Indeed, we never completely dissociate from our animal selves; think of how we use animals in art, or as metaphor. Animal myths and legends—avatars, significant interaction between man and beast. You have to agree these stories articulate something fundamental.* He had actually said that, his voice urbane and convincing.

He looked up from the paper. His office was full of animals. He collected ancient animal artefacts: small bronze or stone figurines. He even collected the mass-produced bears carved out of wood that could be found throughout the Ismailovo market; and he liked cuckoo clocks.

Yet just now he felt an upwelling of revulsion at everything animal.

'Of course we are animals,' he said out loud just as his Mayak cuckoo clock whirred, pumped its bellows and sang out the half hour. He knew what he meant by this. Animal was the basis, the hidden foundations; but human—that was the building, the amazing sculptured artefact of personality.

Ж

Three weeks before, Dmitry had been smarting from an early-morning argument over a dog. Natalya wanted them to get one; he hated the thought. One of their neighbours owned a Moscow watchdog, ovcharka crossed with Saint Bernard, 'which gives them,' Yuri Andrejevich had insisted, 'strength, intelligence, wiliness and *surprising* agility.'

The dog was called Malchik. Dmitry, bored almost to tears by his neighbour's adoration for it, had once theorised to Natalya that attachment to animals revealed some deficiency or need dating from early childhood. Attachments between species were nothing more than projections, and in that sense it was revealing that Yuri had named the dog 'Boy'. A human who became fond of a dog was expressing a disorder or deprivation in the same way as a lone rabbit that bonded to a faun. Or a cat that suckled a hedgehog. Unfortunately, for some reason this had strength-ened Natalya's resolve that they should have a dog.

Dmitry also felt contaminated by contact with animals. He held his breath in the SPF animal house at the university labora-tory. He shuddered at the feel of hair over alien musculature, even on a laboratory rat. He washed his hands immediately after touching any creature. This morning he had finally admitted as much to Natalya and instead of comprehension and sympathy, he caught a glow of triumph. When he added over breakfast that he also feared he might be allergic, he had to turn away, knowing he would lose his conviction if he looked at her.

Natalya laughed, her lovely voice ringing. 'Oh you *wish* you were allergic.'

Dmitry, genuinely stung, stated then and there that he loved animals but something about them made him uncomfortable.

He went to work churning; it seemed they would be getting a dog. Natalya always got her way. He knew his discomfort demonstrated a proper awareness of the philosophical and scientific divide between man and animal, but he had been unable to express this. As always in Natalya's company, he lost clarity and eloquence. No one argued with Natalya; most people did the bidding of that marvellous voice and soaked up the sunshine of her approval, her certainties, without even questioning whether they ought to be listening.

Yet he considered Natalya, for all that she was a brilliant paediatrician, a bit nutty. She was the only scientist he had ever met who'd asked him his star sign. It was the first thing she said to him and he still remembered with discomfort the smile, the keen glance she gave him, as if his answer had given her some new knowledge about him.

Such a naïve village soul, Natalya. Such childlike certainties, despite her intelligence. He would have asked her to marry him but he couldn't think why she would say yes; he was stunned she had even agreed to move in with him. But it was he who furnished their apartment. *I left my stuff at home*, she'd said, and he had never had the courage to ask why.

His childhood had been hard compared with Natalya's. Perhaps that was it: people who have had a hard childhood are more likely to realise that pets are a foolish indulgence.

The *hypocrisy* of dog-lovers! Russian kids were dying every day on the streets—Natalya knew this as well as he did—yet there was a public outcry over exterminating dogs. What other city in the world would fund the castration of strays? Propose rewarding pensioners for feeding them? Despite all this, according to Natalya, happy Russian women had dogs.

Natalya had been the perfect daughter (a talented gymnast, intelligent, warm hearted); she was now a compelling lover (independent, passionate, fascinating) and would become a brilliant wife (albeit less domesticated than some). She was going to be a wholesome mother, beloved aunty and most Russian babushka of babushkas: and all this quintessence of contemporary Russian womanhood was incomplete without a dog.

Dmitry smiled and sighed. He'd do his best to delay it for a while. And that very day the dogboy arrived, and Natalya dropped the subject.

When he first saw the tiny, hairy child crouched half naked, shivering in the corner of the militzia van, Dmitry felt an upwelling of revulsion and pity. Then, as he pulled back a syringe of tranquiliser, a strange thrill of delight tempered by shame. This was a frontier. Voilà! The human animal: a living manifestation of a failed attempt to cross over that great divide.

The child bared his white baby teeth and snarled, a useless defensive display. Dmitry shuddered. *You dog-lovers, with your sentimental anthropomorphic fantasies—you should see this.*

Of all the mangled and stunted children Dmitry had worked with, this one struck him as the greatest tragedy and the most amazing survival. He found himself horrified, yet hopeful that the 'raised by dogs' part would prove verifiable.

'Let's call him Marko.' Dmitry walked into Natalya's office after lunch and stopped short. Her body was taut, her back turned to him as she typed: she had rearranged her desk set so that she could look out of the window, not at the door. Who else would do that? Who isn't a little defensive in their office? She tapped faster at the keyboard and waved a hand apologetically. Her hair was a rippling copper swathe covering her shoulders. He could smell her shampoo. Dmitry hovered behind her chair, eager for her to approve the boy's name. He also wanted to ask her whether she had had any new thoughts on dog ownership but it occurred to him, on the basis of previous inexplicable reasoning, that she might think today's events had advanced her argument somehow. And he wanted to kiss her. To disperse the discord of the morning. 'A fighter's name—commemorate his Romulus-like early years!'

Natalya looked up, her eyes dark, and he felt a little rush of pleasure. He knew from the shadows that flickered across her open face that the dogboy had made a huge impression. Then the sombre eyes were sparkling.

'Be careful—he'll end up overthrowing the government!'

'We must just hope, Natalya, that he will in time stand up or speak.' He blushed. He so often managed to sound pompous, his words huddling together, when he talked to Natalya. Whereas she shone, it seemed to him; she rang clear as a bell and in her company he became inept with dumb joy.

'Well, perhaps a strong name like that could help his chances of survival,' she said brightly, impatient as always with any hint of gloom.

In Natalya's assessment, however, the boy was frail. There was something doddery in his movements, she said, that could relate to some trace-element deficiency. Tests would be in on Friday.

Dmitry was hopeful. His research on the rapidity of

language and cognitive recovery among stimulation-deprived children was now known all over Europe, and just this year had been translated into German, French and English. His university lectures were very well attended. *Children found with minimal language but otherwise normal capacities consistently show hyperdevelopment; in several cases they have rejoined age-appropriate levels within a few years.* He could hear his own voice saying that, and being believed.

Ж

Dmitry was at a peak in his career when the dogboy appeared, almost like a reward: a spectacular icing on a very satisfactory cake. His position as Director of the Anton Makarenko Children's Centre was the fruit of many successes and a studious avoidance of overt ambition. He was conscious of the accolade and cautious of provoking those who had conferred it. The Centre was a showpiece, funded in response to a damning international report into the endemic abuse of children in internats and orphanages. It was a show-and-tell for foreign journalists, but he loved being here, where he had the facilities to make his research really count.

And the staff: he had an excellent team. Natalya was indispensable, welding everyone else together. Around her enthusiasm they all felt elevated. His behavioural and developmental psychologists were the best in Moscow. The neurologist was a high-profile public figure and an excellent practitioner, who divided his time between the centre and the university.

Anna Aleksandrovna, the administrator, kept the whole organisation running as if effortlessly, and had been Dmitry's secretary in a range of posts before he was appointed to the centre. And his closest friend, Konstantin Petrovich, the security manager and driver, also happened to be a pedagogic psychologist (with Cuban qualifications). He was a gem. The specialist teachers, nurses and general staff were handpicked and headhunted, pilfered from all the ministries and university departments Dmitry and Anna Aleksandrovna had ever worked for. The whole team, from the janitors and cooks to the medical unit, were proud of what they did here.

Only the building left something to be desired. Dmitry was abraded every morning that the transformation of this old children's home had been such a rushed job. They had the best equipment and had had some rooms modified, but the paint job was patchy and the children's rooms still had the old metal beds from before. Just fewer to a room and with nicer linen.

The centre at this moment housed and educated thirty-five children, all rescued from the internat system. It wasn't as though the children they left behind were ineducable, necessarily. There were intelligent, if deprived, children in overwhelming numbers. They visited one regional internat where 80 per cent of its 112 children passed the special test for aptitude Natalya and Dmitry had devised, showing normal cognitive function once the results were mediated for stimulus-poor environment. Some were screened out because they had been too long in the internat system—by age four they were thought to be irredeemable—some were screened out for extreme behavioural problems; some for physical rather than mental defects (in these cases recommendations were made).

The government wanted only success stories or forefront-of-science cases to come out of the centre.

Dmitry tried to approach the unpleasant task with clinical detachment, but Natalya was from the start ruthless and manipulative—in a way he admired when he was with her and cringed at when he thought it over afterwards. She would see a kid who was, from Dmitry's point of view, unresponsive and beyond their scope, and she would set her jaw: 'We are getting that one out of here.'

She usually spotted her child within seconds of entering the room, apparently choosing sometimes out of pity. Ugly, stunted or crushed children attracted her, although she treated Dmitry with frosty silence the one time he said this out loud. She manipulated him, she falsified reports, she fiddled with the stats and the results, she bribed without hesitation (using not just her own money but also the centre's) to get damning mental health reports to disappear; and, with his discomfited collusion, she got every subject she selected out of the internat and into the centre. Worse still, she had never yet been wrong: apart from a couple who had died, her subjects thrived.

This was what kept Dmitry awake: perhaps none of the children they saw and assessed as normal should have been left behind. After Natalya started to erode his detachment, he found he didn't want to do field visits anymore. Even his favourite children's home, run by a compassionate and efficient ex-military woman, dismayed him, despite the conscientious care the children received. He found himself wishing that the major too would bend rules and falsify her reports; even cultivate favourites. At his most despairing, he thought that discarded children were too big a problem for him alone: in unimaginable numbers they either died or were abused on the streets; or were deformed through physical, emotional and mental deprivation in the homes.

He was often furious with Natalya. Right now he knew she was in the basement teaching the kids gymnastics, moulding young lives to resemble her own. She was optimistic about the children they rescued and refused to think about the ones they left behind. Amazingly, she could switch off. There were no Madonna mothers between the metro and the university now: Natalya had reported every one of them. She called the militzia on principle whenever she saw one, making herself late to conferences and restaurants. She looked at their outstretched hands and filthy rags, even the weak blue babies they held, as though they were remote from her; an affront to everybody. And she acted. But Dmitry was sure she never thought about them at all. He commented once that the babies at times died of hunger or gangrene from unchanged nappies, and speculated about the link between various kinds of depravity and the degradation of maternal feelings.

Natalya had said brusquely: 'Don't get philosophical, Dmitry. It doesn't suit you. You didn't father the baby or corrupt the mother.' His heart had filled, then, with a flood of things to say to her. *What if my mother was such a one?* Natalya, walking just ahead of him on Pyetnitskaya, turned at that moment with a face so fresh and unscathed that his thoughts scattered and he reached for her hand. Once close to that fire, he just wanted the warmth of it.

Natalya was startled when people didn't agree with her but she changed nothing, no matter how cogent their criticisms.

Dmitry told her once, working himself up for a couple of days to say it, that she was incapable of admitting a mistake. She laughed, said, 'Rubbish!' and went on unaffected. Really, Dmitry told himself, daffiness and arrogance were a terrible combination in a character.

Natalya stretched her neck and shoulders as the children chimed their rote thank-yous and filed out. She had insisted on the ritual from the start and their naïve, raw voices pleased her. She felt her age in the stiffening of her body after gymnastics but considered herself young, nonetheless. Gymnasts might be old at thirty-two, but paediatricians were babies. Her technique was still impressive so why shouldn't the children get the benefit of it? Dmitry—well, if these children were fed, nurtured and educated to the most basic shared standards of parented children, that was more than enough for Dmitry.

Natalya raised her arms, bent at the waist and put her palms to the floor to shift her irritation. She tucked her head to her shins, and became a strange, four-footed entity, narrow, with a tail of hair reaching from the back of her head to the floor. She lifted one leg to the vertical, then the other, into a controlled handstand. For a moment she was an inverted statue, then she dropped, rolling along the half moon of her spine to stand in one fluid movement.

He was so passive about all this! She had had to scrounge for the equipment in this ugly basement while Dmitry the orphan quietly derided and disapproved of the vantage point, the insights her own childhood had given her. She had had the privileges of the talented and the loved, he once said, as though she was somehow tainted by this. Well, Dmitry's prejudices would not preclude *her* children from gymnastics. *She* hadn't become a self-absorbed gymnast, but had *chosen* to become a paediatrician. He, on the other hand, had had the benefits of the once-functional state system and had focused on success with the blindness of a mole.

It was odd: only Dmitry ever argued with her. She couldn't remember anyone, not even her parents, arguing so much with her. And he was brilliant, in his twisted, complicated way: a walnut tree, clenched tight around every burl and knot. Her annoyance faded and she smiled. He still wrote his notes long-hand! He would be funny with a dog. He would end up loving it much more than she would: *he* was the one who needed a dog. And he would be such a wonderful father! She inspired the children, yes, as a great teacher should; but it was Dmitry's hand they reached for. He needed her to know such things.

She untied her hair, gathered her clothes and headed for the staff showers, feeling the sweat cooling under her leotard. Ha! He might see gymnastics as ornamental, but he certainly enjoyed her flexibility. Her thoughts shifted to his bewildered-looking grey eyes, his charm, his sexual need and directness and the planes and fine lines of his body. He was very hand-some, her Dmitry. For a forty-five-year-old.

Since age fifteen, Natalya had known she wanted a man who satisfied two criteria: he had to be physically attractive to her, and he had to need her help. She had dreamed then of an agoraphobic pianist; a gifted (and beautiful) cripple of some kind. Most of her lovers had seemed to fit this at first: one had been a drunken petrochemical engineer; another a psychotic writer. They resisted help, and she lost interest in them. But Dmitry—she was sure she could do him a lot of good.

She would cook tonight, and she would be sweet smelling; and he would flex, glisten and moan. Her belly tightened.

Ж

Dmitry sat watching Marko from the observation bay, the various test results clipped to his folder. What a surprising child. Internalised to a degree—licking his hands over and over, absent and sad looking a lot of the time. A degree of stereotypy—as now, rocking side to side or front to back, or pacing anxiously and without purpose around the room on hands and feet. Didn't know how to chew food, but he did know when he was full, which was, from Dmitry's experience with other neglected children, unusual. No single terms or combinatorial speech, but much babbling, drawn-out vowels. And signing—*doglike* signing, for want of a better word. The rapid wriggling movement of his bottom had seemed odd until Dmitry recalled seeing a large dog wag its tail, its whole body swaying. Language development, at least in the coming together of verbal and thought intelligence, had not happened; something altogether strange had taken place instead.

He was in some ways like a stimulation-deprived child from an internat, but in other ways very different. For one thing, he knew how to play—a most extraordinary thing.

Dogs are playful, Dmitry thought, leaning forward to watch through the one-way window as the boy scampered with a large yellow ball. But dogs don't build with blocks, and this child did. Dogs don't make a yellow block bark at a red block.

This child was much more responsive than any long-term internat child. He showed fear, hope, delight, anger and hunger openly. His sleeping patterns were also unusual—he was nocturnal and slept immediately after eating. His physical condition was worrying—Natalya had diagnosed cystic fibrosis—but treatable. His scores on physical tests were as odd as everything else. Good in some ways, despite severe developmental retardation, malnutrition, hypertrichosis and the deformed movement his body had adopted.

It was clear that he had lived in darkness a lot of the time. His sensory and primitive abilities were skewed beyond the range of any tests on children. His hearing and sense of smell were exceptional. Very exciting. But...

Dmitry stopped chewing his pen. What if? What if they were on the brink of some breakthrough, a chink in the theories and one that, via anomaly, showed, after all, that Vygotsky was right! The Psychology of Play, but beyond what Vygotsky and Leont'ev postulated. What a startling find—the subject at play, so unlike any deprived child. *He was compulsively constructing a non-canine zone of proximal development!* This would imply...God!—being human was elemental!

Dmitry could not contain himself. He leapt up and strode back to his office to start writing the test results up and to enter in a separate file some of his thoughts. The words ran through his head, thoughts tumbling, jostling for space. He scrawled some bold lines onto foolscap.

Age impossible to determine—teeth affected by malnutrition and individual variation—not even a wrist x-ray analysis would get a precise result on a child this young. Comparative stats unhelpful in any case. But results astonishing nonetheless: subject appeared to score highly on psychoneurological tests. The neuro-logical tests—normal function, in some brain areas hypernormal. Brain function utterly unlike that of a stimulation-deprived child...

He wrote his observations on play, and then wrote the implication. His handwriting sprawled larger than life across the page, marking this possible breakthrough, this unexpected chink in the confusion of neuropsychology. He'd have to be careful to control his tone. He chewed his pen again and reread his last paragraph. He crossed out two *astonishing*s and one *astounded*. Let them gasp: all the more effective if he stayed calm.

The psych tests were a problem—hard to administer and arguably useless. Compromised by the subject's deficiencies: fine motor skills, attachment to people, language. On the other hand, the adaptability the boy showed in play was at the *very least* unusual, possibly unprecedented. The circumstances that had moulded this subject were also perhaps unprecedented, at least in this era. He knew other scientists might dispute this and he was uncomfortable with how anomalous it would all look in the test scores. Some might even suggest that all they were seeing in this individual subject were the extremes of autism.

But the *play*—sensorimotor, representation and symbolic—it all ruled out autism. Absolutely ruled it out. Dmitry scribbled a note at the top of the first page of his foolscap pad: *This subject presents as a child who, at the outset of his short life, had nothing wrong with him and most likely had above average intelligence.*

The subject scored lowest in socialisation. He identified other children in the centre as threatening on sight, even when seen from behind glass or at a distance. He didn't differentiate between younger and older children; they all elicited bared teeth, a low growl and snarls. Yet, despite this hostility, the subject had become trusting and affectionate. This was also inexplicable.

In some ways the prognosis seemed good, and the opportunity for research was one in a million. A trillion.

Dmitry stared out of the window of his office, not noticing the children playing in the sunlight in the gardens. He was trying to imagine the boy's life. Darkness. A den. Many dogs. He fingered the smooth porcelain of his favourite coffee mug. Scratches and wounds from play-fighting with puppies and other dogs. Damp and freezing cold, except up close to dog bodies. Some alpha bitch guarding him and providing for him. A lot of rough affectionate touch. A blind world, rich in sound, touch, smell. That was the key: no sensory deprivation, so crippling and so familiar in the internat child, so visible in the little loners hunched out there to one side of the world, rocking back and forth.

How had this boy learned to play with toys? Was this simply the personality growth and flexibility conferred by a sensually rich environment? Gait, sounds, hearing, smell, and habits all suggested a subject enculturated in the life of dogs. Sighted multiple times with dogs and caught in the company of two dogs, which had initially tried to defend him from the militzia. Better collect the data of public sightings from the militzia before it was lost. Would go to proof. Why had he appeared this spring? Of course—he would have been denbound for winter. Before that, perhaps too young. He *had* to be a genuine feral child—and, Dmitry couldn't help thinking, a godsend for the centre. The Kremlin couldn't withdraw funding with the sort of attention this would attract.

Dmitry stared at the scene on his mug, the spring flowers, the silent singing birds, the wolf cub and the faun. So, how had the boy ended up partly clothed? Could he have stolen or found clothes and dressed himself? They were miserable rags, shoddy even when new. Could survival intelligence have been sufficient to put observation of humans and physical need together in such action?

The Mayak clock behind him chimed, whirred and cuckooed, and he started. 12.30. But he didn't move. No speech. Presenting with no apparent human nurture, but unusually able. And clothed. It didn't make any sense. It could ruin everything.

Clothed. He had to have had a parent or caregiver.

Damn.

Ж

Romochka couldn't stop stroking Puppy's new hair. It had been an unpleasant surprise to find Puppy shorn, but now he found that his scalp felt lovely. A little like White Sister in summertime but even better. Springy, smooth. Golden, shiny and soap-stinky.

He had entered Puppy's room warily. It was too bright and smelled sharp and nasty. Puppy's smell had changed too. He could just pick up a tiny trail of it among all the new smells on Puppy's body. Puppy had howled and yelped in an excess of delight at the sight and smell of him. Puppy bowled him over when Romochka squatted down, wriggled onto his lap and off again, and then raced around and around him in tight circles, winding his skinny arms around Romochka's neck, then unwinding them to use them as legs again, unstoppable until Romochka caught the little body in his arms and held him tight. For all the strange smells, it was a relief to hold Puppy again. He had bent his face to Puppy's neck while the little boy, breathless with happiness, squirmed uncontrollably. He would have begun slow-licking Puppy but he could not shake off the feeling that they were being watched. They explored the room together, looked at themselves in the mirrors, played with the toys. Romochka hunted for the little crack with eyes behind it but could find no telltale draught, no shift in the uniform smells of the room. He couldn't work out how they were doing it, but he was sure.

Romochka relaxed a little when he saw that Puppy liked the dry man and the elk woman here. He was so free and joyous with them, they couldn't have done anything to harm him, but still Romochka's neck hairs prickled. He listened for the tramp of heavy boots and the ripple outside the door that might hint at militzia. He was careful to keep his boy-mask on; he held himself back from sniffing Puppy too much or licking him at all. He used his hands as a boy would and stood up self-consciously, boy-fashion.

Puppy recognised this as a game and played too, pretending to be a dog with a boy, rather than a dog with a dog. He stood up occasionally, being a boy with a boy. He licked Romochka's hands, eyes shining, then held Romochka's hand self-consciously in his own, like a little brother with a big brother. He raced around Romochka's legs. He didn't even begin games that involved gripping Romochka by the throat or barging into his side to try to push him over and get his belly exposed. Romochka was proud of him, and Puppy felt it.

Puppy was curled in his lap asleep, body lax and loose. Now, resting, Romochka wanted to be gone. The charade had been an effort; he felt tired and frazzled, even cross. He felt Puppy's body with careful hands while Puppy sighed, smiled and stretched in his sleep. He felt like pinching Puppy to make him jump, but the constant feeling that *they* were watching stopped him. He looked around now and then to see whether he could catch them at it, but the room gave nothing away. Puppy was thinner, and seemed small in these new clothes. Had he fitted into Romochka's lap before, limbs spilling out all over, but centred like this? He couldn't be sure, but Puppy might be shrinking. He worried about taking this stripped-down hairless Puppy out into the cold.

His throat tightened and he longed for the warmth of the lair, to curl up with Puppy and slip his hands round Puppy's belly, licking and murmur-growling in his ear. He pushed Puppy off his lap, stood up carefully, opened the door and walked out without looking back. The hair along his neck rose but nothing happened. They didn't stop him. Not the tall man, nor the elk woman who was his mate. She came up to him, walked him part-way along the corridor, then smiled and said, 'See you again, Romochka.' He glowered at her and ran the length of the corridor, down the stairs and out into the pouring rain with her voice ringing on in his ears.

'You didn't want him to be human,' Natalya said, pointing her shashlick at him over the dinner table. Dmitry was speechless. She was wrong, so wrong! He had just wanted Marko to be purely what he was, rather than partially this, slightly that. Everything in his whole life had been partly this, slightly that—and all the rest murky. Natalya herself was the only exception. She licked her fingers, watching him. He felt the blood rush to his face.

'Well, maybe this explains the clothes.' Natalya's voice was light. She was trying to give him the positive side, as she always did. But he felt no better. This bigger boy called the younger one Puppy. Dmitry had cared for a child once whose mother had forced her to sleep outside with the two family dogs. Was this, too, going to turn into some everyday case of parental cruelty? Marko's spectacular story was tarnished, no matter what. This kid—obviously bomzh—doubtless had a family, along with all the critical threshold survival skills by which street kids were deemed to be past rehabilitation age. He was part of the normal social wreckage: one of a possible five million street kids in Russia outside the sphere of the centre's business.

He found himself lying in Natalya's arms on his leather sofa. She put a whisky in his hand. She started talking and he relaxed a little. 'Let's feed him at the centre, Dmitry. He'll appreciate it, and he'll give us a lot on Marko in return.'

Yes, observing the two together might explain some things and be fruitful for research. But still there was ink in his milk and his half-formed wish was that Romochka would disappear. He sighed. He knew himself. This wish was a fantasy, not a desire. Romochka made him see things he would rather not have seen. Having seen, there was no turning back. Marko belonged with, and therefore to, someone else; and Dmitry had wanted him to himself.

Natalya patted him out of his reverie and slipped out from under him, solicitously replacing herself with two cushions. She scampered off, most likely to the shower and bed.

Dmitry put his feet up on the sofa and sipped at the whisky, thinking back over his day. Out of the blue, an established human relationship. Inescapable. He stroked the taut yellow of the sofa. There was something about good leather: silken, yet earthy. The sofa was his one expensive piece, a modern 8 Marta, cheaper because of a factory defect. Its egg-yolk expanse filled him with an obscure, shy pleasure; as if it, too, marked a milestone in his successful life. He sighed again. Romochka and Marko were both abnormal, and this would have to be taken into account in any research. They were going to present in the end as simple aberrants, no frontier at all. Nothing to be learned about mankind in general: merely the usual morass of individual suffering.

Ж

Romochka ran all the way, rather than catching the metro. White Sister loped along beside him. He needed the singing of his blood and muscles, the air washing through him, and the exhaustion at the end. He ran on and on along a route he now knew so well that its little detours and shortcuts took no thought. The rain pelted down and his feet splattered as he ran. Puppy's things swirled through his mind: the squishy patterned mat that smelled like a car window frame; the hard coloured animals; the red, yellow, blue shapes, all clean and unchewed; the smooth, pale yellow walls, and the watery glass of the windows. The smell of Dmitry. Natalya's voice. He wanted to be home.

But the next day he wanted to go again.

Ж

Dmitry, Natalya and Anna Aleksandrovna got used to Romochka's sudden appearances in reception and built his visits into Puppy's rehabilitation program. Anna Aleksandrovna had instructions to call Natalya at the clinic if Romochka appeared, whereupon she would finish with the child at hand and cancel bookings for the next couple of hours. Natalya began an observation diary for her own interest while Dmitry was writing up his revised preliminary findings for the *Journal of Advances in Neuropsychology*.

She found the older boy fascinating and appalling; and, like any bomzh, an indictment of society, a walking human tragedy. Natalya had some firm principles. She had once ended up as the only other person in a carriage with a great reeking lump of a man sleeping on the seat opposite. She'd sat, shallow-breathing, fighting down waves of nausea, almost in tears. *This man is Russian*, she told herself. *This man is my brother.*

At first, she attached herself to Romochka with a similar feeling—but somehow the shock value of his appearance and smell wore off, and her repulsion faded. Romochka was compelling as a human subject, quite a character. The appearance, she decided one day, was not a reliable marker of everything there was to this boy; it was even a bit theatrical. A disguise, an inadvertent dress-up.

Today is the 17th of July, week two of watching Romochka and Marko. What to make of the two boys together? Romochka, dark, fiery as a furnace. The child warrior. Radiating black hair and black moods. Marko, so fair, pale, frail: a snowflake who fades, retreats into passive, and yes, melting, *adoration next to his dark brother. Romochka looks indestructible. He has the most horrible fingernails—talons would be a better word. He looks like a nuclear holocaust survivor in an American movie (costume to match). Marko looks as though he might vanish as mysteriously as he came, as if he is transparent, somehow—not quite here. His health is now acceptable, but there is something beyond physical health that holds us in life or lets us go, as doctors all know (should know). What a sight these two are. If they were in a painting, they'd look like archetypes. Funny!*

18th July. A hot sultry day, with Romochka's mood to match. Romochka has something in common with professional beggar children. He is impervious and self-contained, but I think I understand him quite well now. We have little to offer him: we can feed him, but he is too wily and experienced to form an attachment. I don't pity him or want to rescue him, anyway. Although I am convinced he is smart—despite the fact that he stands out clearly as a defective. His body language, his manner, everything is that teensy fraction out of sync, the fraction all normal humans recognise immediately. Perhaps it is his self-esteem that repels pity. He likes himself. Sees no reason why we shouldn't like him too. No, that's not the right word— admire, *more like. It is also disconcerting—self-confident defectives are not usually appealing, except to their mothers, and then only if the mothers themselves are not hopelessly degraded. Marko is the victim child, the one we all must rescue. Romochka is something much more romantic and awful. And he's proud of those hellish talons. He uses them for everything, including to scare other children—and I caught him carefully filing them on the bricks of the garden wall. I should give him a nail file so he can do his manicure in style! He is vain!*

28th July. Romochka is speaking a lot now, both with us and with Marko. He talks to Dmitry, but with far more reserve than with me, I believe. He is quite eloquent in a bizarre way. He said to me this morning in his odd little voice, 'I can get you a bird. Today is sunny, it's not fuckin easy, but I can get you a bird.' This is the longest sentence I have heard him utter. A pity I don't know all that much about language acquisition. Dmitry does, though. He thinks it is a mental or speech impediment in Romochka's case, but I'm not convinced. Dmitry doesn't do intuition—data and data only. I'll have to show him this sequence. This boy's not an imbecile, I'd bet my professional reputation on it. He is something else. Intonation is spare and flat, but his speech is nonetheless vivid and elliptical. Sometimes his language is colourful and very local. I dropped a plate when heating something for him in the microwave, and he said sagely, very comically: 'But for some piss, the world's full of shit.' He sounded rather like a little old drunken moujik. He grinned ridiculously for a fleeting second when I laughed. He was showing off. At other times he sounds like a migrant using Russian as a second language. He reuses what he hears and cobbles together phrases, manufacturing meanings on the spot. Today he said a couple of things that sounded just like Dmitry: 'What does that really mean?' and 'the human animal'. I'll show those to Dmitry too—I'd like to see him try to call that echolalia! And, somehow, he has picked up bits of Italian. He uses Italian endearments with Marko, or a funny mixture. He got up to leave, today, and said 'Scram, caro' as he pushed Marko off his lap.

Ж

Romochka and Puppy worked together to convince Dmitry and Natalya that Romochka was a boy. Romochka picked up that Puppy was special to them because of the dogs, and he felt big with secrets. He could make himself special to them any time he wanted, but he didn't want to be locked away from his family, and that was clearly what they would do. Being a dog had kept him in that cell as Belov's begging tool. Being a child now seemed to keep him free. So for the second time in his relationship with Puppy he played the human role but not, this time, to intimidate; and this time it filled them both with glee.

From that first day, he didn't lick Puppy. Nor did he yelp or whimper or ask for Puppy's belly. He was careful to avoid sniffing things. He watched other small boys in the metro stations and on the streets, and copied some of their mannerisms.

He passed these, too, on to Puppy, who mimicked him in everything. One day his special performance piece would be slapping his thigh and laughing loudly; another day it might be spitting in his hands and combing his fingers through his hair. He loved this pretence.

He terrorised the other children in the centre in subtle ways, growling and snarling at them when no one would see, but he lost interest quickly. He gave his attention to Dmitry and Natalya, and to Puppy. For his part, Puppy knew what Romochka was doing and backed him up with his characteristic joyous inventiveness.

Ж

Dmitry was careful of asking too much. He could only imagine what their home might have been like. Romochka was silent on the subject. He was silent too, on how his younger brother might have been lost and have come to live in the care of dogs, or how Romochka had found him. Maybe, as was the case with that Ukrainian girl Oksana, everyone knew about the child with the dogs. Dmitry tried once to ask about Marko's parents, and Romochka said the oddest thing.

'I am the only dish on the table.' He said it with quiet confidence, even pride. Dmitry was startled. The phrase stuck with him. He assumed it meant they were orphans, a revelation that pleased and troubled him. On the one hand, no more family members were likely to pop up, and that meant no more nasty surprises for his research to accommodate. He couldn't hide from himself how delighted that made him. This had been a nagging fear—at its worst the threat of an emotional claim made by an adult who might legally be able to take Marko away, at least until he proved her unfit, and who would taint all his painstakingly reconstructed data. But if Romochka was alone in the world, shouldn't they take him in too? Wasn't there some moral aspect independent of policy, independent of the five million homeless?

Natalya, surprisingly, reassured him.

'Romochka's lucky we let him in and feed him, and we only do that because he's harmless, interesting and unusual. We can only do so much, Dmitry. You think the rest of the children we have here don't all have siblings in horrible situations? Nadezhda has five. All drug addicted, and one who sexually abuses her. Half these children's relatives are psychopaths who belong in corrective institutions for the sake of society as a whole. Do you want them here too? The gangs, the rapes, drugs and violence—and don't even get me started on the parents.'

Natalya, Dmitry guessed, didn't want Romochka on their hands either.

The food they gave Romochka at the centre was cooked, hot, and they gave him nearly as much as he asked for. But he was hunting less and what he took home was never enough. He worried about the dogs when he spent too much time with Puppy, and he worried about Puppy when he hunted with the dogs. He began to notice weekdays and weekends because the centre was shut two days a week.

He began to look forward to walking with Dmitry, talking

219

about this and that, mostly about Puppy. He liked to try to match his stride to Dmitry's long legs, and he liked the way Dmitry's large adam's apple moved up and down his neck. He liked those kind grey eyes, and that Dmitry didn't mind being stared at. Dmitry thought nothing of holding his nose to bring his face in close and make eye contact. Dmitry never laughed, but was funny. He was comfortable with Dmitry; Natalya was a different matter. He felt a little sorry for Dmitry: he could see that he too feared Natalya.

Dmitry didn't know everything but was trying to find out so he could help Puppy. Romochka found that dry voice, telling him these dry truths, comforting, but most of all, he liked Dmitry's smell.

He watched Dmitry and Natalya, noting the kisses and endearments; and the fights. Dmitry, Romochka knew, was most interested in Puppy. But to his huge gratification, he began to notice that Natalya was more interested in him. He frowned whenever she came near him. He imagined pulling her long brown hair. She smelled of slightly rotten flowers, of Dmitry, hair, soap and girl sweat. He could smell her vulva, too—spring mud and cut grass; so different from the musk and pungent anus smell of full-grown men. Very different from the cosy, sweet smell of Mamochka. He kicked chairs over and tried to bend or break things when she came near in order to show her how strong he was. He began to perform the boy most of all for Natalya. Her body-smell seeped into his dreams.

Yet he felt safer with Dmitry.

Ж

220

31st August. Today Romochka arrived at 10.30 with a small and very putrid coat, too small for him but clearly too big for Marko. An awful object, grease-covered and stained inside and out. Dark brown and grey stains. Blood? Hard to tell what colour it once was. Shreds of matted rabbit fur around the hood. Romochka's very proprietorial with it. Carried it in diffidently, but with a certain dramatic air. The stench! It filled the whole building. Once inside Marko's room, a curious ritual took place. Romochka laid it on the ground in front of Marko. The little boy was beside himself with delight at the sight of the coat, but seemed hesitant to touch it. He seemed to regard it with something like reverence. The sacred coat. Romochka looked down at his hands, then began staring out of the window. Marko crept, belly to the ground, over to the coat and gingerly laid a hand on it, staring at Romochka all the while. Marko stayed still, extended hand on the coat. He turned his face slowly, shut his eyes and stayed like that, face averted. I counted ten seconds in which both boys stayed absolutely still. Eventually Romochka turned and walked out of the room. He left. I could hear him clumping rather obviously down the stairs. Marko fell upon the coat in a whimpering frenzy. I called Anna Aleksandrovna and Dmitry in to watch. Marko smelled the coat in deep breaths, then slowly slipped it on, then rolled about on the floor in it, then took it off, and lay down on it and went to sleep with part of the hood in his mouth. I went in after ten minutes. The smell in the room was unbearable.

Not sure what Dmitry'll make of this either. Probably some guff about an autistic child's older sibling learning the behaviour necessary to communicate, with the younger effectively as teacher. But when? How does Romochka know that Marko needs to receive a gift the way a dog would? Because that's what I saw here. Why

does Marko put it on, as well as doing all the doggy things with it?
Trouble is, DPP knows nothing about dogs.

These are strange times. What if Marko was simply born a dog?
What if he never lived with dogs, but attracts them, and this is
simply a new condition, a mutation? Not impossible. Not a theory
to share with DPP, Natalya!

But they are an odd pair.

Ж

Romochka was delighted with Puppy's progress. Being a boy
himself so much of the time made him value boyness far more
than he ever had. The challenge to improve drew him on, and
Puppy followed. He was standing and walking most of the
time now, and even making voiced noises a lot. None of them
real words, but all rather like words. Dmitry praised Romochka for all this, suggesting that it was Romochka who was
responsible. Romochka added Dmitry and Natalya to his clan
of human people he liked. Laurentia, the Singer, Dmitry,
Natalya—in that order. He murmured their names in human
voice and loved the music of it. He sang them, along a melody
line that rose and fell like a dog's howl. Until then it had been
just Laurentia and the Singer.

He didn't count Puppy as a human. Schenok in voice was,
after all, a game. Puppy's real name lived in silence in his smell,
in the woven breath of the lair. And inside Romochka.

He thought now and then about breaking Puppy out of the
centre and taking him back home. How happy all the dogs
would be! He pictured Puppy scampering about to revisit every

smell and every game. They could go back to being a proper family again. But he worried, too. Puppy was so clean and soft now. The hardened muscles and the calluses on his hands and feet were gone. He ate a lot of different things here, hot things, soups and pies and meat stews in huge amounts. Much more than Romochka ate. Would he be able to find enough food for Puppy? He coughed these days, too, all the time. Maybe he wasn't strong enough to go back to that life. He asked Dmitry eventually, with what he thought were well-masked intentions, what would happen if Puppy escaped.

Dmitry looked at him thoughtfully.

'You know, Romochka, it is lucky we rescued Marko when we did. He was a very sick little boy. He needs to live here, or he might not survive.'

Romochka must have looked doubting. Dmitry walked over to a drawer and took out a small disc. He held it up between thumb and forefinger.

'But don't worry. See this? We put one of these inside Marko's body. It sends a signal, like a little beeping that you can't hear. If he got lost the militzia could find him wherever he goes just by following the signal.'

Romochka held out his hand for the disc. It was smooth and shining. He turned his back on Dmitry and surreptitiously bit it. He handed it back to Dmitry with a metal and plastic taste in his mouth. He didn't understand what Dmitry meant but it was clear that Puppy as good as had Dmitry's rope around his neck.

30th September. Romochka arrived late today, at 11.35, with a present. He hid his face behind his outrageous hair, scowled fiercely, and held out a dripping, bloodied, grimy chicken. I am clearly a favoured person to be so honoured. I think cats give their owners mice in much the same manner. It has feet, but no head. It is very unprofessionally plucked, or rather its feathers have been torn out, but it is not cleaned. I hate to think where he stole it from. He certainly didn't buy it, although I guess he might have traded it. I took it and thanked him, and he stalked off in silence. But he has been jaunty all day, really pleased with himself, and he has hung around, chatting to everyone. He helped me move furniture with a very superior look on his face, showing off his genuinely impressive strength. He is playing now out in the garden with Marko and that one-eared dog that hangs around. They must be slipping food to it. Marko adores it of course, but we'll have to get rid of it. Pity.

4.30. I caught him again scaring other children with his mad-boy act, and he looked crushed and took off.

The awful chicken is in the fridge. I washed it, and it is fresh at least. It has bruises, so I think he acquired it when it was alive. Ha! Hadn't thought of that. Ruthless little fellow. I am determined to take it home and cook it tonight for dinner—and bring Romochka a sandwich with some of it tomorrow. I'll have to have a look on the internet how you pluck and clean a chicken. I think you have to dip them in boiling water, then pull the guts out the back end. Oujas! Babushka would know, but she'll scoff at me for asking. I'll have to make it look presentable before Dmitry sees it, or he'll get all fastidious. But a present must be respected, even if it makes me the receiver of stolen (and rather revolting) goods!

Ж

Dmitry stood at the window of his fourth-floor office and watched the boy leave. He hoped the attachment Romochka had formed with Natalya wasn't going to cause problems. Kids got attached to her all the time, of course, and she was professional about it. But this time she seemed to see Romochka as a kid she could befriend, perhaps just because he wasn't an inmate. She went out of her way to flatter the boy and was clearly, to Dmitry's thinking, herself flattered by Romochka's attachment. Now that *was* unprofessional. He was particularly annoyed today because he had seen a loyal glower beamed his way from under Romochka's hair when he snapped at Natalya about taking Romochka upstairs. But really, how could she? Even if it hadn't been against the rules, it would have been ill-advised. It did children no good at all to know that they were watched twenty-four hours a day. Not to mention that it would vitiate any future data if Romochka took it upon himself to tell the others.

That one was a mystery, unlike any child he had come across. Definitely some kind of intellectual disability. Nonetheless, the way he interacted with Marko was fluent, wordless, authoritative. Solicitous. Romochka was always pleased by Marko's progress, pleased to hear that he was sometimes walking rather than four-footing it. Romochka could make Marko do anything, and initially Dmitry had been delighted.

These days, however, he noted there was still a canine element in Marko's eagerness and aptitude, and wondered in more jaundiced moments whether Romochka was teaching him tricks for their benefit. At other times Romochka simply sang to his little brother, and Dmitry put aside his doubts. He sang snatches of songs that were all, oddly enough, Italian.

He had a raw yet musical voice. It was Romochka who managed to get Marko to make a word, repeating his own name over and over to his younger brother.

'Romochka, Romochka, Romochka, Romochka.'

Then Marko's startling sound, his only human syllable:

'Rom…Rom…'

Dmitry watched Romochka saunter along the drive below, swinging that club. That was one tough kid. Romochka was bomzh and an orphan, and well past the age to form attachments, yet he was developing a relationship with them. Maybe the idea of foster care was not hopeless after all. Their hands-off approach to Romochka's life still troubled him, especially as he observed the boy's growing attachment to Natalya. He was fairly sure Natalya was no longer so certain in her views either. In fact there was a good chance, he thought with a wry smile, she would deny ever having held them.

There was no doubt the two brothers loved each other, but Dmitry was beginning to suspect that Romochka's visits had something to do with the younger child's slight regression and physical deterioration; perhaps also with Marko's complete failure to learn to speak. He couldn't explain it. Marko's play indicated the cognitive parallel for language. He had arrived with all the preconditions for language acquisition to be rapid, but there was little sign of it. Romochka spoke, yet Marko barely noticed it. However, if Romochka grumbled or murmured, Marko reacted immediately. At one point Dmitry had annotated this, relating first the story of Viktor, the wild boy of Aveyron, who didn't notice a pistol shot but showed animated interest at the sound of a nut cracking. At the very least Marko was missing his older brother more and more during Romochka's absences. Dmitry was unsure what to do about it, other than take the older boy into care too.

Below, Romochka was joined at the end of the driveway by that big white dog. Natalya had said she would get rid of it more than a week ago. The dog licked the boy's hand, which he didn't seem to notice, and fell back to trot along at his heels. Romochka stopped by the gate, bent and sniffed it. Then, without looking around, he casually urinated, out in the open, on the gatepost. Odd.

Oh God.

It had been staring him in the face from the beginning. Two of them. He felt dizzy.

Ж

Dmitry had been walking for more than an hour, energetic, apparently purposeful, but without any destination. How did two brothers become dogboys, wolf-children? Who were they, these two, one so dark and one so fair? The memory of his own excitement over the discovery of Marko brought with it a sharp flicker of shame. It wasn't just that Romochka's existence devalued and tainted all the data. His groundbreaking studies on Marko seemed now some unwitting part of a sick experiment, larger than the 'linguistic thresholds', 'non-canine zones of proximal development' and 'compulsive human-ness' of his published papers, way beyond debunking the twenty-first-century vestiges of a belief in *Homo ferus*.

He felt as though he, Dmitry, had been part of some huge

game, even duped in some way. Certainly not by Marko. Nor Romochka. He stopped, remembering in flashes that strange boy's behaviour. Romochka, an urban feral child, had dissembled with conscious and consummate art. That child was intelligent. Gifted. But Dmitry didn't feel duped by Romochka. He felt something bigger, some greater blindness that made him the sport or the laughing stock of someone. He started walking again. Who, then? Himself? God? His peers? His discipline, science? Mysterious children? He grimaced as he watched his boots pump in and out of view. Wolf-children, once so rare they were seen as mythic, were now in plague proportions in Moscow. So many millions of homeless children to choose from, for dogs looking to adopt.

He stopped for a moment. *What if it was really nothing new?* How many of the besprizorniki of the terrible 1920s—those devouring, rampant hordes of homeless children—had sought out dogs? Teaming up for mutual benefit—wasn't it likely, rather than unlikely?

He laughed bitterly. Natalya's schoolgirl diary on Romochka would be a more valuable resource than any of his painstaking research. They could submit work that described the co-researcher as 'Bloody Dmitry' or 'Dear Old DPP'. It was all going to turn political and might spell the end of the centre. But it would have to be faced. Natalya's judgments were idiosyncratic but her observations detailed. They would have to go through her volumes with care now, salvaging everything that could be rewritten. At least, for all her fascination with the older boy, Natalya hadn't guessed either.

And Marko was constantly ill, now, even asthmatic. Marko was trying to deal himself out the game. So then, Romochka.

228

What would he do if Marko died?

Dmitry walked harder. He chided himself for his bitter-ness: *Get it into perspective. Professional pique, DPP?* He would be ridiculed, sure. All that earnest blindness. Marko and toys. He flushed. Everything was changed, explained in shameful detail. But, think about it, this was all bigger, much bigger.

What if two little boys lived for years with dogs? Not family pets like that little baby Andrei Tolstyk, not like Ivan Mishukov and his street dogs back in 1998. No—with a clan of feral dogs, functioning socially and physically as dogs themselves. Romochka was a hunting animal; Marko a puppy for whom he provided. Yet, because they had each other, they had become liminal beings—socially, developmentally. Marko couldn't speak because of course in pack life Romochka would never use speech, and Marko more than anything wanted to retain his place in that world.

But Romochka was a master of *passing*. Among humans, he could pass as an ordinary boy, near enough. With Asperger's perhaps, or mild autism, or a behavioural disorder plus brain damage brought on by abuse. He'd done so for three months now in the centre—among *experts*, no less. Among dogs...well, Dmitry could only begin to guess, but in a way Marko's early behaviour had to be a reflection of Romochka among dogs. Romochka could cross...over. Romochka walked upright and had language. He had to have begun life with the dogs well after he became verbal and once all sensorimotor, representa-tional and symbolic play skills were developed.

Was this really possible? That meant...what? Three years now with dogs? Three winters. It was astounding, unprece-dented. You could almost say one was more dog than boy; the other more boy than dog. Not to mention the feat of survival. Two!

This was exciting, now that he thought about it. He could rewrite the studies and submit an honest reassessment in the light of new information. He would note all he could remember (and those diaries would be crucial: Natalya and he could do it all together). He would study the two boys with the greatest attention. He would lure Romochka into the easy living in the centre, wean him from the dogs over a period of time. Come to think of it, he had never seen Romochka eat—all the food they ever gave him was taken, surreptitiously sniffed, and stored on his person. Dmitry's blood sang around his body as he strode. He would rehabilitate both, and perhaps be able to show the resilience and recovery of children who have had just one significant human contact in early years, no matter how defective. Marko's health might improve too, if Romochka lived with him. Marko *would* acquire language, if Romochka lost his secret clan dominance, Dmitry was almost certain. And Romochka would reintegrate spectacularly. After all, Ivan Mishukov's rehabilitation from his life with street dogs had been successful.

He found himself thinking about the time Romochka slapped him. He had been walking up the hospital corridor with Romochka keeping step by his side. They were on their way to see Marko. Romochka said something to him, once, twice, and Dmitry was thinking about this broken speech—its odd rhythms and its insistent claim on the listener through unfamiliarity. Romochka had stopped walking, suddenly, and at the same time Dmitry felt a sharp blow to his hand. He turned. Romochka was standing a couple of paces behind him, his small face grimacing in strange, helpless rage, his eyes fierce with it. Dmitry's hand burned afresh now with its own memory. He wished he had heard what the boy said. The incident stood out to him now as important. An irretrievable moment that might have illuminated everything.

If Romochka was around four when he began life with dogs, then Marko was...born later.

No. It wasn't possible. His disappointment settled even more heavily than before. There was going to be some ordinary explanation that revealed them as merely neglected.

Dmitry looked up, his rhythm broken by the slowing flow of pedestrians. He had walked a long way from the Makarenko Centre and the university. He checked his watch. 4.30. He had left the centre just after lunch. He didn't recognise this district at all. The pavement was narrow and treacherous, broken here and there as if diseased, and the buildings were an ugly, impromptu mix of structures, some faded and crumbling, some newer, Kruschev-era. Almost all post-revolution. There was some blockage up ahead. Other pedestrians leapt among cars and around each other and eventually he found himself directly behind the obstruction. An elderly lady in a dirty cream lace scarf inched along the cracked stone lip, carrying two avoski bulging with produce. Cars scudded by in the crushed ice of the puddles, spattering them both as he waited, his thoughts scattered, for a chance to pass her.

He crossed the road instead and found himself at an inter-section, unsure which way to turn. He could see no tram stop, no avtobus, and no metro. He would have to ask directions. A sad-looking black dog crossed the street with care and headed along it with some steady purpose. Where did dogs go and

231

come back to with such certainty?

He followed the dog for no real reason other than curiosity. After just five minutes, its purpose faltered. It stopped, sniffed around and lifted its leg to mark a concrete seat. Meandering around, but not randomly. It was intent on something, sniffing here and there, then marking a tree behind the bench. Dmitry looked up and saw that he was outside a fairly recent Soviet-era metro entrance.

Inside, the warmth enveloped him, and he headed to the turnstiles, relieved. He passed a group of bomzhi, men and women, begging along the wall and descended the escalator into the deep vault and arcades of the underground. He didn't recognise the name of the station and was disoriented. Definitely outside the ring route, he thought, or he would know it. He looked for the signs, unsure at first which platform would lead back home. Yes. This was one station from the end of the line.

The station opened up in a series of plain palisades, arches and pillars. A rather grand place for all its plainness. The platform was crowded with tired-looking commuters. Factory workers. Along the back wall of the platform there were more bomzhi, some asleep in piles of rags, some standing near trolleys that were piled high with miscellaneous stuff and draped with plastic bags or blue tarpaulins. They looked ready to move and, when the militzia came down the stairs, they all got up and pretended to be waiting for the train. Dmitry noticed particularly the dogs. A dog hovered warily at the outer fringe of the workers and another, in its own private cocoon, wove in and out among the people, avoiding contact, alert but unafraid. A small black dog rode high on a blue tarp, staring bug-eyed yet blank. None of them made any noise. Although Dmitry was surprised at how many there were, he was also aware that they were familiar. There were often dogs and bomzhi in metro stations. He had simply never paid them much attention before.

He stood among the workers waiting for the train to pull in. Just ahead of him he saw a plumy dog's tail and he moved to see better. It was a large thick-haired mongrel ovcharka. It stood patiently among the people, shifting if anyone came too close.

The tracks hissed and rattled, the air, shunted up the tunnel and across the waiting people, was filled with the familiar compound cacophony, and the squat face of the train filled their view. People stirred, reanimated. The dog's tail moved, and it turned with the people to acknowledge the arriving train.

The dog waited for the doors to sigh open and the first crush of people to embark, then it too hopped onto the train. Dmitry followed. The dog stood to one side and stared into the middle distance. People ignored it. Dmitry stood not far from it, his heart beating fast. The dog sat down and stared out of the glazed doors, panting quietly. Dmitry noticed how the thick pelt shifted and parted over its shoulders as it swayed. He could see its profile—wide smiling jaws, white teeth. The dog gulped now and then to clear the saliva from its tongue, then resumed panting. The steady look in its brown eyes, the wrinkled brow, didn't change. When the train pulled into the next station, it stopped panting and looked around, ears lowered deferentially, apologetically, as it moved its large body out of the way for exiting passengers. Then it resumed its stare and its relaxed swaying stance. As the train slowed for the second station, the dog stopped panting. It waited until most people had left, then stepped off among the stragglers. Dmitry watched as it trotted across to the peregod through to the ring-route station and disappeared up the stairs.

He slumped back into his seat and let his home-bound train pull him back to the familiar parts of the city. His dizziness returned. His world had shifted somehow, had swelled to encompass some fact that had always been there but from which he had been barred. Why had dogs always seemed thing-like, symbolic, when they were in fact person-like and about as symbolic as he was? Where was that dog going? Was it someone's dog? How had it learned a path that took a train, then a transfer? Or was it travelling randomly—his scalp crawled—for pleasure? When he reached home, one station short of the university, he stepped down beside a ghost image of four legs disembarking in the throng.

Here everything was familiar. Just beyond the park was his apartment, seventh floor up, with a beautiful view of birch tree trunks and golden tops, a restored church and a ring of identical apartment blocks. In it Natalya was waiting. He had a feeling Natalya would see no cause for dismay in his news, and although he was bracing himself against her enthusiasm he craved it too. He was exhausted and his legs were shaking. He found it hard to put one blistered foot in front of the other.

At the park gate he saw a dog. It was a shaggy thing lit murky orange in the street lights. It caught his glance and dropped its head to slink into the shadows, then it loped on silent feet to slip out of sight into the small alley by the Megafon shop. Three dogs further down the street were raiding the large new rubbish vat. A pale dog was up on top, gleaming as it tore at a cardboard box. The second had its front paws on the vat and was wagging its tail and flipping its nose as though making small silent barks. The third, black, its silhouette tipped in orange light, was standing four-square a little away from them, not looking at them.

Dmitry realised suddenly that they were a team. The muscle, the brains and the lookout—which was staring, he realised, straight at him. He was part of this tableau.

He turned away and pushed the park gate open.

This large, poorly lit park was considered safe. A militzia patrol was supposed to keep drunks, beggars and drug dealers out. All the neighbourhood knew the militzia controlled the deals that took place in the park, but the effect was the same: the place was safe, and free of beggars.

Tonight, however, the park was full of dogs. Dmitry counted at least seven, looming larger than life in the shadows. Why had he never noticed? He reached his bench under the birch trees and sat down. He had sat here often on his way home. He had sat here in all seasons, winding down after long days. On clear autumn nights like this the park shimmered and glittered as pale leaves tugged at their stems and then rained down with a windy rustling to the pale carpet. The army of park workers had not yet taken over. They would be along soon to rake up all the leaves and pack them into garbage bags, leaving bare ugly earth ready for the snow, but at this moment the park shone, unkempt. Everything was luminous, the sky dark and cloudless. He had seen few such nights in his six years here. He closed his eyes. Of course he had seen dogs before. He had been harassed by dogs before. Everyone had. Still, he felt shaken.

He opened his eyes at a tiny, proximate sound. Well, of

course—a dog. It was a mastiff, a Moscow watchdog, and it knew him. Its little black eyes gleamed at him in a friendly way out of its dark panda mask. He knew it too. His neighbour's dog. Malchik sat down and waited, still eyeing him with happy affection and wagging a huge tail.

'Hello, Malchik,' Dmitry said softly, and Malchik tipped his massive head to one side in what seemed almost comical acknowledgment. Had Dmitry ever spoken to a dog before? Not that he could recall. He held out a hand, and Malchik immediately got up, padded towards him and licked it. The tongue felt warm, faintly raspy, quite gentle. Sloppy, too. Dmitry wiped his hand quickly against his trouser leg. Malchik then turned and reverse-parked his great bulk right beside Dmitry. He pressed his weight in against Dmitry's knee. He tipped his huge head up and back over his shoulder to keep eye contact. Dmitry stroked that bunched brow; ran his hand down over the heavy neck and shoulders. Malchik's thick pelt was so loose on his body that it rolled under Dmitry's hands. The tree-trunk neck and rippling muscles were deep underneath all this cuddly stuff. Dmitry smiled and kept massaging the dog. He glanced up and down the dark park lane and leaned in to sniff his fingertips and Malchik's neck. This dog smelled quite nice. A lot nicer than Romochka. Yuri Andrejevich must shampoo him. This huge bulk all sudsy in a small bathtub? How ludicrous. Rub-a-dub-dub. But you'd have to wash a dog if it lived with you.

He sat back, self-consciously stroking the dog. Naming Malchik, he thought, would not have been so easy. How could you ever know their real names? Boy, Girl, Mother, Father, Pup—that was the only honest common ground. He was

236

overcome with weakness: he was not only exhausted but also famished. He sighed. Natalya was not particularly interested in food. She cooked rarely, with unpredictable results and an air of proving a point. *I do cook for you, see?* He had never mentioned her cooking or not cooking, and, bewildered, had made no comment when she raised it. Natalya always got home before him, but these days he found it stressful to walk in and find her wreathed in cooking smells, smiling triumphantly, preemptively winning an argument.

She might have shopped, though. Perhaps it was the influence of the dogs, but he really felt like otbivnaya. A dog's dream dinner: a slab of meat, bloody, seared. With onions. He would cook, and they'd eat together.

Dmitry got up. 'Come on, Malchik,' he said, and they headed home. Dmitry had never walked alongside a dog. Malchik padded beside him with a lion-like gait, his brow twitching incessantly. One eyebrow lifted in triangular wrinkles now and then as he cast an eye up at Dmitry's face. Dmitry was intensely aware of the dog's friendliness. This huge beast, this sagacious brute who could not speak his language, was radiant, somehow, with a foolish goodwill.

Dmitry pressed the buzzer on his neighbour's apartment. Yuri Andrejevich opened the door and Malchik romped inside, splattering spittle. Dmitry gestured towards the dog with a wordless smile. Yuri stared at him.

'He's a nice dog,' Dmitry said hurriedly, and waved goodbye.

Natalya had bare feet up on the yellow arm of the 8 Marta. Her hair was down and her wild curls gleamed in the light of the table lamp. She hadn't cooked, but the fridge was full and the kitchen clean. Her face glowed softly, blue-lit by the television. She looked up at him with her uncomplicated smile; and, as always, the unfailing health and warmth of her face drew him in. He felt the miseries of the day as small inert packages, defused, well-prepared for handover.

Ж

1st November. We had a long talk with Romochka, and finally all is clear. What a godsend it is that Romochka can actually talk and is intelligent! He gave most of our questions one-word answers, but was open enough. It is a strange yet somehow ordinary story. Everything is explained. Romochka and Marko ('Puppy' is a pet name) were in the care of their mother. Mamochka, Romochka calls her—very sweet. He must be one of those boys who regard their mothers with intense devotion and solicitude. They all loved dogs, and the family had many dogs, he says—they lived with him and Marko. No father in the picture; mother working very long hours, leaving the boys with the dogs. He's loyal: says she took 'very good care' of them, giving them milk and other wholesome foods, and keeping them 'very clean'. Mamochka got Marko 'as a present' for Romochka, he says, which is also rather sweet. There seems to have been a lot of love in this impoverished little family. Then, at some point, Mum disappeared. Asked him repeatedly what happened to his mother; his answer always the same: he has no idea, but he never saw her again. Romochka was, as he says, 'the leader'. He took care of Marko and the dogs, he says.

Time frame: only vague answers. We'll have to go on the behaviours Marko demonstrates and speculate a bit.

They are not really dogboys, just from a family that understood dogs well, and then had to fend for themselves with only the dogs for company. The older child in loco parentis, *as is common in neglect scenarios. Disappointing for the purists—and the mythologists. They can't really be categorised as feral children, but they have survived an incredible ordeal for at least a couple of years. Not much here for poor DPP to write up, though. Romochka's still looking after the dogs, it seems, and has them living with him. He said, or rather agreed, that they live in a nice place, with everything they need. He mentioned other people who help them with clothes and food, so maybe some kind neighbour lets them live in the cellar or attic. Dmitry is right, really—a lot of Romochka's behaviours can be explained by some mental defect and the emotional attachment to the dogs, the only enduring element of their family life.*

How do you define a dogboy? The fact he's a boy will always dominate, and these dogs were family pets. Providing warmth and affection but perhaps more a responsibility? Not really such a major influence upon the older child.

Good to have got to the bottom of all this, finally. It makes you think, it really does.

Ж

Natalya had Puppy moved to intensive care. The blood tests were in: it was pneumonia. With cystic fibrosis, this was critical.

The oxypulsimeter graph showed the racing heartbeat and the falling oxygen. The little boy flicked his limbs and she knew he was in pain. He didn't appear to recognise her but fixed his gaze on Dmitry. As she watched the bony chest labour under her stethoscope, she felt Dmitry staring across the barouche. There wasn't much to say, so she didn't say anything. She wrote up her notes without looking up. Nothing they had done had made the child sick, so Dmitry's accusing stare could burn itself out. Of course, he had more at stake here. He had still wanted to study the two boys together, and stubbornly held onto the idea that they were at least partly feral. She could do without his disapproval just the same.

She gave instructions to the nurse for the increased dosage of intravenous gentomycin and morphine and left the room. Dmitry would call her if anything changed. She was conscious of retreating. She had been fond of Marko, but she could not turn this around. Her affection had no place now, and she needed to retract it. She was the one who would be doing an autopsy on a child she'd known, not Dmitry.

Puppy's body made a tiny mountain in a vast snow plain on the barouche. He objected to nothing. Dmitry sat long hours with him and Puppy, soaring somewhere on morphine and fever, smiled each time he looked into Dmitry's eyes. There was nothing canine, or boy-like either, in this glance. Certainly there was nothing of the boy Dmitry had known. Dmitry sat, waiting for the glance, and wondering what Marko saw to make him smile so sweetly. He had the uncomfortable feeling that the boy was seeing someone else.

Puppy died almost effortlessly the following evening.

V

It is a long autumn twilight. The hour between dog and wolf. Light and dark are mixed, fear mingled with possibility. Between dog and wolf, everything seems to hesitate, everything is neither, until the point when night, like a drawn-out exhalation, spreads over the city.

Romochka trailed along the side of the mountain, striking cans and other rubbish with his club. A bitter cold wind was blowing from the north, tossing small flocks of plastic bags up the sides of the mountain for take-off over the city. The heat was gone from the world and the smell of autumn was in the wind. Sweet dry grass heads, tea, and the smoke of fires. Out at the forest the birch trees stood out, golden and orange; the larch were a high haze of dull gold, and the pine and spruce seemed taller in their dark coats. The rowan fruit hung heavy and red, as yet too tart to eat. Romochka's thick mane of hair blew across his face as he turned this way and that in aimless misery. Puppy was dead. He knew what that meant. Blood out, not in: a kill smell. Cold bones. Cold rot. He knew he would never see

Puppy again. Every creature he had ever seen die had been afraid, and he couldn't bear to think of Puppy like that.

He stared up at the bloodshot eye of the sky. What if someone, somewhere, were watching all this? Someone like Natalya, someone who knew nothing and lived outside everything, unable to smell, to touch, to rub; just watching, delighted, without comprehension? It was good, that day, standing beside Natalya and looking down at Puppy playing in the room. He had always known they were watching, and the satisfaction of finding out how blended with happiness that she had shared her secrets. She showed him the TV screens, and he looked at all the other children. He suddenly found them interesting, when they had been completely uninteresting before. It was a form of hunting. Everything the children did seemed changed, worth seeing and thinking about. He had been about to tell her his own secret, but then Dmitry found them and was angry.

A rat shot out of a faded bucket at his feet and he swung savagely. He missed, and a sudden rage flared behind his eyes. He battered the bucket with all the strength of his arms, but a rising fury swept over him as he did it. The bucket split, crackled and splayed out in shards. There was nothing satisfying about smashing a fucked-up bucket. Puppy was dead but not broken like this. Curled up. Warm…then cold. With Natalya and Dmitry watching.

His blows slowly stilled until his arms hung by his sides.

Romochka, Romochka. I am so sorry Romochka. It is bad news. We didn't know how to contact you. He was very ill, Romochka. We did all we could.

He hadn't said anything. He had wondered for a moment whether anyone had eaten any of Puppy, whether some hungry dogs had got to him when he was defenceless. Strangers. Then he had realised that Dmitry was trying to touch him. He had wanted then to smash Dmitry's face with his club.

He sat down on the spreadeagled bucket with his club across his knees and stared out. He was on the slope nearest the cemetery, overlooking the wooded graveyard and the much thicker treetops of the forest. The trees in the cemetery seemed more wintry than those of the forest beyond. The wind could shake them more easily.

Autumn was nearly over. The tall oak tree nearest him was already almost bare; the black branches with their tattered remnants reached a hand of many fingers against the darkening sky. He could see the fur of lichen making a frayed upper edge to the silhouette. Where the forest met the cemetery, he could make out the occasional flicker of movement: squirrels bustling, hunting in the leaf fall, urgent with purpose. He should be hunting too, if only for the sake of Mamochka, who was heavy and soon to pup. Winter was coming. Winter without Puppy: neither warm and comforted with Romochka's arms around that homely little body, nor soap-stinky in the centre under blankets.

He should have hit Dmitry. Puppy was Dmitry's responsibility, and he must have done something very very wrong. But he felt all twisted and knotted in his belly at that. He tried to throw up to clear his belly, but nothing came and the knot stayed. Suddenly he couldn't breathe; he began coughing to dislodge the heavy block of wood that seemed to have become stuck in his chest. He shut his eyes.

His neck-hair rose. Some dumb stray was stalking him, upwind. He could smell fear and hope and inexperience on this dog. He opened his lashes enough to see through the grey curtain they made. It was a big, thin dog, just a shape in the evening gloom. There was something wrong with it. It was rasping, making too much noise as it crept towards him, sending its weird sick smell straight at him.

He sighed twice, as though still in his own world, but gripped his club tight. When it finally lunged, he rose more swiftly than the rat from the bucket and swung with all his strength and speed. There was a satisfying, sinking crunch as the club caught the dog below the ear. Romochka's fighting snarl dropped to a growl, and he watched with something like clean happiness as the yelping dog staggered briefly, its smashed head held low, its one good eye leading. It stopped, stood with its head swaying. Then it collapsed and lay still.

Romochka walked over to the dog. His happiness cooled and vanished as quickly as it had risen. The dog was twitching slightly, but leaving. He could see that distant, fearless look in its eye. He felt his own blood draining away, leaving him weak, wrecked. He had never killed one of his own kind. The knot inside him tightened.

He walked away from the dead dog, down the mountain towards home. He wasn't hungry but thought he had better fill himself up tight, then sleep. White Sister and Grey Brother were waiting for him at the mountain meeting place, to his relief. He couldn't have borne being alone for one step longer. White Sister licked his face. Grey Brother kissed his neck as he sat down with them. They smelled him over, looking for Puppy. For them Puppy had been, for a long time, the smell on him when he returned from the centre. His rage and misery returned as he licked them both. They would never smell Puppy again. Romochka's throat and stomach clenched painfully.

A man staggered along the trail. He looked and smelled just like any other drunken bomzh, wearing a miscellany of ragged garments and an old soldier's woollen hat. His grey hair was long and lank and dangled in strings over his scarves. He walked gingerly up the pathway, controlling his unsteadiness. Then he tapped his forehead with his middle finger.

Uncle.

The man turned his thin face briefly towards them. He was unmistakeable. Romochka bit down on a cry and then stiffened into the stillness of a hunt. The dogs looked at him in surprise.

Uncle had changed. The almost-respectable suit and great-coat were gone. Even in this light it was clear that his body and face were gaunt. He was old. He was homeless. He gave the two dogs and boy plenty of room as he swayed, humming and cursing, up the path from the mountain towards the metro. In a dizzy moment, Romochka realised he knew the song the old man was trying to sing.

*'Am I to blame...Am I to blame...*Fuck...Fuck!'

Romochka felt faint. His mother's song from long long ago picked up his heart and tossed it about painfully. He followed and the two dogs fell in behind him, padding after the drunken man. They hadn't harassed a drunk for a long time now, not since they were young and silly, but they never questioned Romochka's choices.

Romochka kept Uncle close; he wanted to hear the song. Uncle trilled in falsetto over the first line, again and again, without getting any further. The whole song, as complete as when his mother sang it, plunged into Romochka's chest and rang through him, while up ahead Uncle swore and slurred. A kind of yearning entangled itself with Romochka's anger and misery. He placed his feet with the silence of a hunt, but it was the song he was stalking, not the thin old man. He picked up each halting word like a crumb, a pebble, dropped just for him to follow. He could recall each word: it seemed to become the only thing he truly knew.

'Am I to blame, for being in love?!…Fuck, fuck, fuck!'

His mother's voice battered at Romochka's heart until his body sang with pain and longing. He felt the huge block rise in his chest and throat again and knew now that it was made not of wood but of tears, teeming like a ball of summer maggots inside him.

Uncle, unaware at first that he was being followed, swayed through the twilit alleys. But at a wide street corner, he turned and saw Romochka, the two dogs at his heels, staring open-mouthed. Uncle stopped, frowning with concentration. He hummed the tune, slowly, mindlessly, as he stared back.

He gave Romochka a sudden gleaming look of drunken recognition and stopped singing. He pointed three times and left his hand hanging in the air at the end, a gesture as familiar as the song.

'You little shit. I *know* you.'

Romochka held his breath. He raised supplicant hands. He had a sudden vision of his mother in an apron, cooking porridge for all three of them, singing, as Uncle laughed happily.

'Yeah…I know you. You're that weird little dog-fucker. I saw you just now, back there at the mountain, staring like an imbecile. What are you following me for?'

Romochka didn't move. He was still impaled on the song. So broken open in that moment that, had his uncle really known him, had he shown one moment of softness towards him, Romochka would have wept. White Sister and Grey Brother, bewildered at all the strange crosscurrents in this hunt, had stiffened beside him, and he felt himself pulled away from Uncle's eyes into the same defensive stance. A strange tension flickered for a moment between the wild child and the broken old man, but Uncle's gaze flicked away nervously.

'Fuck off, stinky, and take your dogs with you.' He turned to lurch away.

The song, as soft and cruel as snow, faded from Romochka's heart. He and the dogs followed in silence, without knowing why. Uncle knew they were still behind him; Romochka sensed the moment when he began to be afraid of them.

The knot filled his stomach and a confused anger seeped back.

Uncle picked up speed, glancing back at the three now and then. His step seemed steadier. Romochka guessed that he was heading for lights and crowds, a lone pebble rolling frantically towards strength in numbers. They turned into an alley that Uncle didn't seem to know; he tried a few of the street doors to see whether one had failed to latch. Romochka felt his strength returning. *Look at that foolish pebble, Puppy! Mark it closely, stalk it, get ready...No, don't make a noise, not now! Ready...*

He could feel the two dogs beside him wavering. They didn't know this game. He gripped his club tight as Uncle turned into a smaller laneway. Romochka and the dogs rounded the corner wide. It was a rubbish-filled cul-de-sac between two buildings. Uncle stood in the middle, hunched a little; facing them with a knife in his hand. White Sister growled a low, uncertain warning.

Uncle spoke in a loud, firm voice: 'Look kid, enough's enough. Go home! I haven't got anything. If you come any closer I'll cut you, right?' Romochka could hear the undertone of fear in Uncle's voice. *Puppy, look! Mark! Watch closely. Almost time!*

He crouched slightly, White Sister to his left, Grey Brother to his right and his club gripped in both hands. He bared his teeth, lifted his face so that the matted black hair fell back. He snarled a drawn-out battle crescendo, White Sister and Grey Brother joining their voices to his, strengthened by his conviction. Uncle stepped back, and Romochka smelled his terror. *Now, Puppy!* He leapt forward so quickly that Uncle was still frozen on the spot when Romochka hit him hard in the thigh—a wide, swift full-body swing with the strength of his hard little body and his hatred behind it. Uncle shrieked and half dropped, breathing loudly in fear and pain. He lunged, grabbing Romochka's hair. The dogs growled and crouched but did nothing, uncertain about the strange passions of this hunt.

Romochka twisted in an instant, dropping the club and clawing at Uncle's face with his hands, while trying to bite the arm that held his hair. Uncle held on easily, even when Romochka got flesh between his teeth. Uncle was shaking him and yelping in pain, one knee on Romochka's writhing body while he scrabbled with his free hand for the knife.

White Sister finally leapt, then, and Grey Brother followed. Romochka heard Uncle's shriek close to his ear, then a hoarse gurgle as White Sister got him by the throat. Grey Brother sank his teeth into Uncle's thigh, and Romochka was free.

Romochka picked up his club, stood over Uncle's body. His legs wide-straddled the braced form of White Sister and the man's bony torso. White Sister had the kill grip. Romochka swung his club high, aimed, and smashed it down into the side of Uncle's head. One rolling, terrified eye reached insistently, with an urgent childish inquiry, for Romochka's glance. Romochka brought his club down again, then again; battering until that eye quieted and stared blankly.

He wiped his club clean in the dead grass on the pavement outside the cul-de-sac. The knot was gone from his stomach; he felt calm and still, floating in peace. Puppy was dead, but not like this. Just curled up asleep around a sick tummy, sick breath, then not breathing anymore. Then cold. Then after a while either frozen solid or smelly and inedible. Uncle shouldn't have abandoned Puppy.

No...He felt a little dizzy. Puppy was not Uncle's Puppy. He half turned to go back to the cul-de-sac; he looked down. White Sister had a red muzzle. He knelt and licked her face clean, tasting blood like his own. Or like Puppy's. Then he turned to go. White Sister hesitated, and followed. Grey Brother fell in behind.

They didn't understand this hunt at all.

Ж

Dmitry waited for a week and a half, then alerted the authorities and initiated the dogboy hunt. He did it without talking to Natalya, or indeed thinking of Natalya at all in the moment he

251

made the call. He was sitting at his desk, his third coffee cooling in his mug, when the unpleasant churning of feelings that had troubled him since Marko's death clustered suddenly, powerfully, at his anus, and rose like a hand through his belly to his throat. He swallowed. He didn't think at all, just reached for the phone and dialled the number.

He was shocked at the blaze in Natalya's eyes and the snarling curl of her lip. He suddenly remembered that Natalya had a stake in this story and should have been consulted.

'Have you *thought* about what you have just done?' She was shouting.

'Natalya! Of course I have thought and thought! What else could I do? He can't stay living as he is, alone with a pack of dogs!'

How could he explain to Natalya that this involved no thought? He was conscious that he had done a *volte face*, and was presenting as insupportable something they had both been happy to tolerate for months. He was exposed now in his belief that Romochka was special; he had violated their unspoken agreement that Romochka was an ordinary street kid.

She was so angry that she had turned white. Her clarion voice rang out, fierce, quivering. 'Dmitry! How *could* you! Of all the poncy, do-good, gutless…I know this boy, Dmitry: you *don't*. What will he think of us now? What is his future? How will I ever *help* him?'

'Help him? *H-Help*…' Dmitry choked on his outrage, 'Natalya, when have you *ever* done anything that was not about you? Everything on principle, so you can avoid the pain of really…seeing! You think you have nothing to learn from me, from Romochka—from any…Never acknowledging…a-and you are still…won't even show me your bedroom at home, you could not give up…Has it ever occurred to you that some people know, see, feel…less crudely than…Could you…Is… C-can…' He ran his hands through his thinning hair. 'Can you really think I am helped in some way rather than hampered by you…your know-it-all…You *arrogant* little girl! You…you, you…*blockhead*!'

Natalya was silent, her eyes huge and dark in a white face, her hair somehow electrified into a beautiful echo of Romochka's.

He wanted to catch the words, that last word, haul them back in; but it was too late. He could not move. The silence lengthened between them. He shut his eyes. He felt the full horror of what he had done and what it was going to cost him. And where had it come from? All the times…how *hard* had he tried to talk to her, only to jam up; and then to spill nonsense like this, things he had never even thought! *Under the influence of multiple stressors, the subject's usual self alters…*

A solitary life yawned before him, barren and confused, swinging without meaning between success and misery.

'Oh, Dmitry.' He heard Natalya sigh, her voice wavering slightly, but clear. 'When you lose it you really…do, don't you?' She laughed uncertainly. 'Did you mean it? No, I know you didn't. You just wanted to hurt because…' She breathed in, gathered herself up. 'Dmitry, I *am really* worried about every-thing we have done to Romochka—it's as if we have meddled unprofessionally, without direction or purpose or princip… Well, now we have this tragedy.'

He opened his eyes and sank into his chair. She was still pale, proud; but looking at him in a way that made him want to weep with relief.

'I know,' he said timidly. 'This will be very terrible for him, but it is for the best. I'll take responsibility for him personally.'

Natalya was suddenly animated. 'Dmitry!' Her eyes flashed. 'I know exactly what to do! You will do more than take responsibility for him. No institutions for this boy, no scientific studies. We're going to foster him! Take him into our home, and you bind yourself to him for good or ill until the day of your death.'

Strangely, Dmitry's heart didn't quail. He was in that moment complete, open, ardent. He did not even find her contrary or melodramatic; he saw how she too exposed herself and her affection for this boy. Something in him stilled and calmed and, for the first time since his vigil by Marko's deathbed, he did not feel wretched. He looked up into Natalya's radiant face.

'Of course, Natalochka,' he said quietly.

She kissed him then, drawing his lips into the taut circle of hers, drawing him in. He closed his eyes and melted into this new belonging for a long moment, and then felt the tears hot behind his eyelids.

It wasn't her world that he was entering, he thought, but, hand in hand with her, Romochka's. Romochka's impenetrable, unknowable world that he, Dmitry, was going to smash to pieces with no way of predicting or tabulating the conse-quences. And, amazingly, he was to take his pure-hearted, incorrigible Natalya with him.

Ж

The first major militzia attack came near home in territories they knew quite well. They were making their way single file past the abandoned warehouses towards the allotment, when Mamochka stopped and lifted her head, good ear swivelling. They all halted and listened. Romochka couldn't hear anything but all the dogs could. Then before he knew what was happening the dogs moved, fast and silent. Mamochka slid herself under the warehouse demolition fence; White Sister, low to the ground, backtracked to slip with Little Patch and Little Gold into a narrow trail that led between, through and under buildings, the long way round to the last meeting post and the mountain.

Romochka recognised a melt-away but dithered. By the time he decided to follow Mamochka under the fence, the dogs had all vanished, and even he could hear something. Then, half under the fence, he turned and peered back under the hessian. The unmistakeable padded dark blue trouser legs, many of them. He panicked and, breathing hard, wriggled through the fence and ran across the broken concrete of the yard.

He'd explored this warehouse before with the dogs and knew which way Mamochka would have gone. There was a narrow alley through to the car park behind the apartment blocks and an old tin car shed. But now, with the yelling men's voices, the clank of chains parting, and gates opening behind him, he still dithered. What if they caught Mamochka in the car park, trapped them all in that little tin box? What would they do to the dogs? He was dizzy with terror, unsure whether he should try to follow the dogs or lose the militzia by himself.

He ran over to the buckled tin facing of the warehouse loading gates and tried to pull up a piece and slip inside. He could see into the huge first floor. It was spread with the usual discarded plastic bags and occasional pieces of tatty, comfortable-looking furniture. This building was the one inhabited by kids and their dogs. The dogs who lived here were not fighters and not organised. They too were often puppies. The kids were very sweet with them, and with each other, but exceedingly vicious if they caught outsiders. There were enough of them to beat off any intruders or kill anyone they hated, especially drunken adults or lone members of rival gangs. But he knew he was safe from the kids this once—he was, after all, trailing five uniformed militzi. They would have melted away too by now, if they were awake.

The tin wouldn't budge, flimsy and old as it looked. He wrestled with it, cutting his hand. He couldn't squeeze in. He glanced back. The five men were huge. They were inside the yard now and had slowed down, holding back. Yes, he could see it: they thought they almost had him cornered and knew enough to conserve their reaction time by not getting too close. He scuttled from the loading bay, hugging the wall, looking for an opening. When he got inside, he'd lose them in the spangled dust and light beams that crisscrossed the darkness: it was a space so bewildering it was worse than darkness. But leading them away from Mamochka took him away from the part he knew, and his flooding panic was making him fuzzy and slow. His heart pounded in his temples. *Let there be an opening around this corner!* He forgot that the next warehouse abutted this one, and the gap, what there was of it, was too narrow for a dog. The men fanned out, their boots clumping through the weedy concrete, stilling as best they could into the silence of a clumsy hunt. He rounded the corner to find a pile of rubbish and no pathway. Just an impossible, narrow gap in the rusty tin and flaking brick. He could see a sliver of freedom: the sunset glowing orange off the apartment blocks in the distance through the long narrow crack, but there was no chance he could squeeze through and run down those grassy trails. He squeaked and turned to face them, crouching low and flailing too hard, breathing too hard. He'd have to draw them in close, then trust that he was faster and more agile. If he could make it out of this horrible yard and into the long weedy growth of the allotment, they would never catch him.

'Steady little man, steady,' said the tallest militzioner. 'We are not going to hurt you.'

'Hell, Vasya, he's just a bomzh kid.'

'Nup—he's the dogboy. Didn't you see those dogs with him when he went through the underpass? Didn't you see the weird way he ran? Just close in slow and easy, Misha, and catch him without hurting him.' Vasya looked at Misha, flicked the cuffs at his belt with his finger and dipped his eyes meaningfully. Misha shrugged and nodded.

Romochka saw movement at the far hessian fence; then, at the corner, closer, just behind the leader, he saw Mamochka's muzzle. Vasya was very alert for a house man and noticed the slide of Romochka's eyes. He turned to look too; saw nothing. Turned back.

'Drop the club, little man. Come quiet and easy. We've got you—you know we've got you. Just come quiet. I'll give you a lollipop when we get in the van. I'll buy you McDonald's. Bet you're hungry, hey?' Vasya kept up a stream of gentle chat.

Romochka kept his eyes on the men, on Vasya, the leader. The dogs were here and had the advantage of surprise. He couldn't give them away with his eyes, he mustn't. The sweat sprang out all over his body and he was shaking. He drew himself in, pretending to be ready to fight, waiting for the moment in which he had to incite Mamochka, and then run, *run, run.*

When Vasya made the sign to move, Romochka yelped in unfeigned terror, sharp and loud, and six of the eight dogs also slipped out of their hiding places and sprinted in hunting quiet across the asphalt towards the men. Romochka's teeth shook. In the last second, as claws scrabbled and scraped on broken glass and concrete, Vasya sensed it and spun. The six dogs were already upon them. Their snarls woke and swelled, and the men, screaming and roaring in fear, covered their faces, fumbling at their belts for guns and batons. Romochka was just in time to see Mamochka land on Vasya's back, lips drawn back over her snapping teeth, and Vasya falling, flailing with his hands in the air to fend her off. Now! Romochka ducked under the brawling and ran as fast as his shaking legs would go. He wriggled under the broken fence, scraping the backs of his thighs on the wire. Little Patch and Little Gold were waiting for him on the other side of the hessian. They ripped through the allotment and bolted together for the lair entrance.

Don't fight them long, don't lock on! pleaded Romochka into the darkness, hugging himself on the nest with the two frightened young dogs pacing in front of him.

The rest were not far behind. The dogs had made more noise and show than real savaging—Mamochka knew only too well that they had to melt away again as quickly as possible once Romochka was free. Romochka knew, too, what a fuss he had to make of them, and have them make of him.

Once Romochka realised the militzia were using dogs to track him, he knew he had to keep his smell off the ground. He clambered up onto ledges and slippery tin windowsills whenever he could. He bounded up onto parked cars and traversed whole streets and alleys leaping from one hood to another. He never let his trail lead beyond the last meeting place. Black Dog staggered under his weight but accepted this strange new custom. The trained tracking dogs knew what he had done, but couldn't communicate it; and they were being asked, insistently, to track him, not the dog he was riding.

Then, for a while, Romochka decided to clean the streets of his smell and stay in the lair with Mamochka. He had never spent time with her immediately before she whelped, and this time he found a mellow peace in lying with her, stroking her big belly, feeling the milk begin to fill her undercarriage.

Ж

Dmitry was shaken by the revelation that the militzia had captured Romochka—it had to be Romochka—more than a year before. But he spoke calmly, even forcefully to the major, his mind racing. It was a win–win situation, he said: track the dogs and you find the boy, hopefully capturing him with minimum trauma. At the same time some idea of the life and territory of the feral clan could be established for scientific purposes. Everyone had seen feral clans, yes—even as close to the Kremlin as Neskouchni Sad there was a well-known, rather annoying clan given to chasing cyclists. But they were a phenomenon that had never been studied, and the mere fact that this one had included two human boys made them worthy of attention. Dmitry was glad Natalya wasn't with him.

Dmitry was troubled that Romochka had disappeared. The boy hadn't been sighted for a week now. Romochka's dogs were recognisable as a pack, even without him. They had been seen twice. He stared down at the large photos Major Cherniak had put in his hands, pictures of the dogs running with Romochka, a blurred sequence taken on a rainy day. One image caught his attention. The dogs were spread out: one white, one grey, three pale yellow, two black-backed, one gold with an eye patch. All large, with husky mask and tail, all clearly related. Romochka hunched in the centre, his head turned towards the camera, his legs caught in a wide lope. One of his hands resting lightly on the dog running next to him. Dmitry felt a frisson of excitement and a knot of strange dismay looking at these images. It was like seeing the image of the last of an extinct species, something precious and, even in the moment of being photographed, doomed. It was also like seeing a photo of what he had once imagined Romochka to be.

Major Cherniak sighed. 'Look, Pastushenko. We'll give it one try. You supply the equipment and personnel. We'll catch you one of the dogs. We've got a unit that does castrations on street dogs: they are pretty experienced. If it's no good, and if he's sighted again, then plan B. I've got journos and politicians breathing down my neck on this one, you know. It's really bad'— he pointed vaguely at the roof and waggled his finger— 'that there have been two of 'em.'

Romochka, on the lookout, stared up at the sky. A bitter wind was tearing through the ruin. Tatty clouds, spread out like a clan of dogs hunting, scudded low beneath the leaden sky, each with a heavy black belly bearing a small flurrying snowstorm. The snow melted as soon as it landed, but the earth and streets looked slick, darker than the clouds. Romochka saw Black Dog creep back into the ruin with the snow melting on his shoulders. His head hung low, his ears were flattened, his usually jaunty tail was clamped between his legs and his back hunched in pain. He looked broken hearted.

Romochka scrambled down from the cupola. He entered the lair to see them all pull back from the big dog. Romochka alone dropped to his knees, threw his arms around that thick neck and buried his face in Black Dog's coat. Black Dog smelled terrible. He gave off a sickly-sweet acrid stink—people, and a harsh alcohol. He smelled also of blood, but Romochka couldn't see a wound in the dim light. He pulled the big dog over to his bower. Black Dog lay down and began licking himself to try to clean the smell off while Romochka felt him over. The others hovered around looking disoriented by all the strange smells that assailed them.

The hair had been shaved off Black Dog's foreleg in a square patch. Black Dog licked it as if it hurt after Romochka had found and stroked it. Romochka pushed him onto his back and found the dried blood between his hind legs. Black Dog's nose followed Romochka's fingers, and then he began licking the open wound where his beautiful egg-sized balls had been.

Romochka felt around the empty sac and whimpered softly with the big dog. Mamochka crept up and began licking him too, cleaning off the terrible stink with her own reassuring saliva. Romochka's hands felt for that big head to cuddle it and the others all came closer and began licking as Romochka held Black Dog's head in his lap. He caressed the thick jowls and the familiar scars. His hands moved over Black Dog's head and neck and back. Then his fingers found a thick lump under the skin at the back of Black Dog's neck. Black Dog yelped as he fingered it. It was solid, small and round. He squeezed it and Black Dog spun round and bit him. He snarled back warningly and held onto the lump. He smelled it. To one side of it there was a small wound. He leaned low over the dog and began to lick the wound gently. It was like licking an insect— small spiny threads stuck out of it every which way.

Everyone was now lying in the bower. Black Dog still smelled terrible but they were getting used to it, and they could all smell themselves on him again.

Still, none of them could settle. Something had invaded their lair with Black Dog's strange smells and nothing felt safe. It was near midnight. Romochka suddenly jumped up. They would go to Laurentia's and have a big hot feed. He hadn't been on the streets for ages, and Mamochka was hungry. It would be good to get out. They all followed. Black Dog was too weak to carry him, so Romochka had to cross the allotment on foot.

The city seemed as safe as it had been many seasons before. They encountered no troubles, but they ate quickly at the Roma, hurried on by Romochka. He hadn't settled—if anything he felt worse. This was a bad idea. He hovered near Black Dog, unsure what to do. Everyone was heading home, belly full, but he knew clearly now that above all they couldn't go back home with Black Dog. He wasn't completely sure why, but somehow Dmitry had done something to Black Dog. First Puppy, now Black Dog. He reached over and felt the lump again. It was a little swollen from his attentions. Black Dog growled.

The militzia would find them. It was certain that the militzia would find them. He remembered, dizzy with foreboding, that Dmitry had had no doubt. Romochka's heart was pounding and Mamochka eyed him strangely, jumpy too now, as if she could hear the beat and smell what he was fearing. He would have to be quick. Black Dog would fight and would hurt him. He tried to calm himself and Mamochka and the now uneasy Black Dog but he couldn't.

He couldn't wait any longer. They were in a long dark alley. He tried to reach and touch the disc, but Black Dog knew his touch was not loving and snarled at him. He trotted hunting-quiet, stilling his heart for the moment. He pictured the disc and the little wound to the side of it. *Now.*

He leapt with all his strength and speed. He ripped at the thick hair with his hands, raising and parting it, and he sank his teeth deep into the wound, feeling his jaws clamp all the way round the disc. Black Dog spun savagely, raking Romochka's head with his teeth. Romochka had turned his thick hair that way, hoping to fill those huge jaws, but he still felt his scalp part. He held on with hand and jaws as Black Dog scrabbled and twisted for a better grip. Romochka tucked his elbows in and held on. In a second Black Dog would twist and whip round the other way and bite into his face. His mouth was full of blood. He could feel the disc coming away. He was vaguely aware that the others hadn't attacked him. Nor had they attacked Black Dog. Black Dog was up and turning hunting-kill quick. Then the disc was his, and he rolled off in a ball, guarding his face and belly with his back and hair.

Black Dog stood over him snarling, bewildered. Romochka could feel Black Sister behind him, tense, growling too. He thought for a moment that he would need Mamochka to help him fight the two of them, but Black Sister did nothing.

Romochka whipped round and stood up over Black Dog. He growled a low, reassuring warning: gentle, warm—speech for a puppy who has not understood. He spat the blood from his mouth and the disc into his hand. He held it out to Black Dog to sniff. The others all came up to sniff the alien thing sliding in Black Dog's blood. Romochka growled out the danger of it, long and low. Then he threw it far from them and turned to run home. Black Dog fell in behind him.

Romochka was at peace. Mamochka would clean his bleeding scalp. He would lick Black Dog's wound clean and hold Black Dog tight and all would be well.

Mamochka pupped in the pre-dawn. Romochka alone lay with her, stroking her, feeling the mysterious pressures and currents ripple through her body. Not even Black Dog was allowed near. Romochka received with her each slick, squirming sac, helping her part the skein to find the blind mewling baby inside. He helped her clean them in turn. Mamochka's sage eyes shone in the gloom, and Romochka helped each of the four cleaned newborns to their first milk. He sat on his haunches staring down at his exhausted mother and the new babies. He was filled with a vast calm. The raw flesh smell was sweeter and stranger than food, mingled as it was with Mamochka's unique scent and the dribbled sticky-sweet first milk. Everything depended on him, and he could be, and do, anything at all that might be needed. He stroked Mamochka's sunken flank, his cheeks wet with tears as mysterious as the glistening, struggling sacs of life she had pushed from her body.

Before when the clan had small pups, he had always considered Mamochka no fun and had tolerated and despised the little ones themselves for weeks following their birth. This time Mamochka fascinated him, and he noted every small change in the puppies. He felt truly grown up, even feeling, as he once had, that he owned these creatures, the grown and the new, his mother and his brothers and sisters and all her children; but this time it was different, because he also felt that they owned him. All of him, to the very last gristle of his strength and intelligence; and they had a right to demand of him sustenance and safety for every breath they took.

For a week and a half, Romochka stayed close to home and stole food for Mamochka from the army of dumpsters that had now crept into the neighbourhood. He watched her become easy with the pups sleeping alone, and become proud when the others sniffed and licked them. The rituals of greeting began to encompass them too. Romochka was there when the biggest opened his bleary eyes for the first time.

Ж

A full moon hangs high over the cold city. Howl of dog, siren, swell and ebb of mingled engines, car horn, squealing tyres, backfire, gunshot. Moonlight washes everything, covering and revealing. The city is dressed with wide swathes of cold light and deep velvet shadows. The air promises frost and numbs fingertips and noses. The gaps between buildings are stark bars of light. The gaps between trees invite. People roam for as long as they can stand the cold, their thoughts open to *what if...* Dogs lope; their eyes glisten. Nothing sleeps. On such a night, for human and animal, anything could happen.

Romochka is dangling his legs over the edge of the cupola above the lair. He has seen few such nights in his four years as a dog. Romochka breathes in the cold air of the magnificent city. He sighs. He misses Laurentia, Pievitza, Natalya. He misses human company. He yips for the dogs, nagging Mamochka to leave the sated, sleeping puppies. They all head for town.

Ж

Laurentia looked pale and unhappy. She handed Romochka the bowls in silence. He placed them on the ground in the alley in front of Mamochka and then signed everyone out of the shadows. Laurentia handed him his meatballs and spaghetti, and stood back in the shadowed doorway, face averted. She wasn't singing. Something was wrong. He started to eat but with a bad feeling in his chest, in his stomach. All over his skin. He glanced up. Tears were rolling down Laurentia's cheeks. His neck hair stood on end.

'I am sorry, *bello*. So sorry. The militzia…they give me big trouble.'

He stopped chewing, his mouth half filled and trailing spaghetti, and stared at Laurentia. His pulse picked up. She was sobbing, now, in heaving, messy gusts. He heard a strange, soft thud behind him and turned.

Mamochka had fallen.

His bowl dropped to the ground and smashed.

He is at Mamochka's side, on his knees. Everything is silent, except his pounding heart. Mamochka shaking and crying through clenched teeth, his arms around her neck, his mouth open, but he cannot hear himself. Her faint whimper comes from far away, up in the sky. He holds her chest to his chest and lifts his eyes unwillingly to the others.

The whole world slows—one beat, then the next, then the next, measuring everything. The beats rock him, slow, slower, Golden Bitch staggers, tries to run, falls. Black Dog almost reaches him and Mamochka, tumbles, begging, slow, slower, his bewildered eyes fix on Romochka's face. White Sister heaves, stumbles…Grey Brother, Little Gold, Little Patch each…crash…slow, slower. Black Sister, eyes intent, staggers forward, falls, against his thigh. The world is filled with whispers. Their voices all leaving him in sighs, silent yelps…Slow… slower. Their coats, black, grey, gold, white, shine in the street-lamps and moonlight. Their beauty is unbearable. Their eyes glitter. They blink at him, asking, asking.

He is losing them all.

Romochka's heart burns in his chest and throat; he is crying unawares. Slow…slower…Slow…slower…

…Still.

Mamochka is dead in his arms. A frightening smell seeps from her in a last slow rush.

Militzia, like a nightmare, like a dream, are tumbling in from the corners of his mind. He closes his eyes and begins to slow-lick Mamochka's dead face.

'Get him off! Get him off! He might get some of it in his mouth!'

He is wrenched off by many hands. He waits, feeling deep for his upwelling rage, feeling for his strength. He hangs limp for seconds, like a meek human child, like Puppy, then he explodes like a cat with all the fighting strength that he has in him.

Ж

'His name is Romochka,' Dmitry shouted, pushing through the throng of militzia, searching desperately for Major Cherniak. Natalya was just behind him, and he reached for her hand.

Dmitry had their attention and lowered his voice.

'He can talk; please stop barking at him. The famous dogboy Marko, who was in my care at the Makarenko Children's Centre, was his brother.' He no longer had much clout anywhere on the subject of Marko, so this was a gamble. Militzia also were a problem: they despised the centre, he knew, and tended largely to the view that street children were the larval stage of killers and drug lords. But he had to keep

268

Romochka out of the internats somehow. And he had to fulfil his promise to himself and Natalya.

The young officer who had been barking looked sheepish. Dmitry squeezed Natalya's hand tightly, and pitched his voice to carry over the din Romochka was now making in the back of the van. 'I am Dr Dmitry Pavlovich Pastushenko. I am to foster him. He knows me.'

The militzia were hovering, looking haggard. Destroying strays was more accepted these days, especially since the Sokolniki rabies case, but many of them were still quite squeamish about killing dogs. Then that Italian cook had shamed them, sobbing like that over the corpses. But you can't have feral dogs terrorising the district and you can't have homeless kids becoming canine. And now that they had the dogboy wreaking havoc on the interior of the cage vehicle, they were unsure what to do next.

'He's like a wild beast,' an officer holding a bleeding arm said doubtfully.

'He knows me,' Dmitry insisted, although the noise now coming from the van shook his confidence. Finally, he found Major Cherniak, who looked relieved to see him. 'You can take him to the secure section at the centre to begin with, but I expect to transfer him to my home once he calms down and has had some health checks.' He leaned in close and murmured. 'Don't panic anyone, Major, but everyone who has been bitten must go immediately to Emergency for rabies immunoglobulin and a course of vaccinations, just to be safe.'

The Major turned to look at him, shocked for a moment, then nodded. 'That would be just about all of us,' he muttered with a wry smile.

They watched the van pull away.

'Why didn't you try to talk to him?' Natalya asked.

Dmitry didn't answer immediately. Why indeed? Would Romochka have listened? He might have calmed the boy down. Why the reluctance? Had he feared what he would see? The noise was inhuman, bestial. That, yes; and what else? Then he knew: he was wary of being associated with the capture. No act in that moment could have been right for the boy he was going to foster, so he chose not to act.

'Why didn't you?' he asked coldly.

'I don't want him to hate me!'

That's why she had held back meekly and uttered no word, waiting for Bloody Dmitry to act. Dmitry felt anger wash over him and then leave as quickly as it had come.

There was a silence. They both thought it: Romochka must surely have heard Dmitry; and maybe he had smelled them both. They had made an awful mistake in leaving him as if he were an animal screaming in the van. Waiting for that van to make the journey from wilderness to hospital, from animal to human, before they would touch him or help him.

Natalya sighed. 'Oh well.'

Dmitry suddenly felt very sorry for her and for her sadness, and sorry for both of them and all the mistakes they would be making together. A strange streak of joy shot through him, completely at odds with everything: here they were, inexpert and foolish, together, as parents. Their love story, so small and ordinary, would include all the ordinary mistakes too.

He reached his arm around her shoulders, patting her awkwardly.

'You'll be the best foster mother,' he said.

Dmitry pored over his map as Natalya frowned at the skyline. The city was unfamiliar. Even the names were strange to him and the topography bewildering. He rotated the map through one-eighty degrees. Here it was. Yes, they were in the alleys of Zagarodiye now, the known territory of the pack, and very likely the precise area in which the lair was situated, according to the militzia. The restaurant was a very long way from home for these dogs. Incredible as this hunting range seemed, there was no doubt: Dmitry had the tracking routes marked in orange on the map from the brief five hours that one of the restaurant dogs had had the implant. He had planned on going everywhere but this forgotten fragment of Moscow was disturbing and his resolve faltered. He felt as though they had entered an alien land and were strangers. They were attracting attention—watched with hostility, skirted as though diseased.

To Dmitry's dismay, he noticed they were being followed by a silent gang of children and adolescents. A cold sweat broke out all over his body. He knew all the theories on gangs and the reasons why children and youth gravitated to them (the twin drawcards of power and group belonging), and the miraculous fact that if they lived, they grew out of the need for gangs at a certain point. But he had always felt gut-clenching fear at being followed by kids like these. They had secret codes, secret incomprehensible wars. These ones all had 88 or 18 on their shirts and bomber jackets. The only certainty was that they were merciless.

He glanced at Natalya. Except for a quickening of her step,

she seemed unconcerned, ridiculously unafraid. Natalya, he knew by now, had never once seriously considered that rape or violent death might come her way. Natalya had a stand-up-and-talk-your-way-out-of-it reaction to all confrontations, a dangerous, naïve confidence that her small universe of right and wrong could prevail and, with the force of her eloquence and personality, be imposed on anyone. She was often right.

But Dmitry knew she couldn't be right here, now, and he was annoyed that he had to have the double terror—for her as well as for himself. He couldn't trust her to follow his lead. She might do something crazy like talk to them. He would fight for her with all his strength. He was ready—but what if he failed? His heart pounded as he tried, unremarked, to assess their numbers. About fifteen, at least half of them past puberty. He felt his feet sliding in the sweat that filled his shoes.

After a while the children veered off, and Natalya slowed, making him slow down too. His terror settled. She must have had some inkling of danger, or she wouldn't have quickened her step. He wanted to hug her as he glanced back to make sure the 88s had really disappeared.

They listened hard now for anything that might give them a sign of dogs. A pack of eight dogs, and one of the bitches had had dugs. There should be puppies. It was autumn, though; perhaps too late.

Where would you hole up if you were a dog?

To their left, pale gold grass half covered a meadow dotted with miscellaneous rubbish. In the middle distance the grass ended at the feet of serried ranks of huge apartment blocks, once cream- and blue-tiled but now streaked with grime and riddled with snow crazing. They were typical of their

272

era. Probably a thousand people per building, Dmitry thought. He had heard about this precinct Zagarodiye, he realised. Popularly known also as Svalka, Rubbish Dump. He had had something to do with a couple of teenagers, juvenile killers, who had lived, he guessed, in these same apartments somewhere.

Tiny squares of washing fluttered gaily on myriad far balconies. Really, these buildings were just like hundreds of others clustered around Moscow's outer ring route, yet Dmitry found the whole tableau, even these flags of lace and gaily coloured cloth, awful somehow; tainted by the fact that a boy (two boys) had lived with a pack of dogs here and been unremarkable. To the side of the blocks, unfinished constructions were slowly disintegrating in a weedy waste land. They looked blackened, even burnt in places, and Dmitry guessed that gangs or bomzhi lit fires in them. High up on the bare façades burnt holes showed here and there, with fire marks around them like theatrical eyelashes.

With a foetid chemical-and-rot smell in their nostrils, they crossed an empty allotment, as big as a communal garden plot. The smell was getting stronger, until it was almost a physical barrier, pushing them back. Dmitry had the feeling that it was coating their lungs, infecting them somehow. He pulled out some tissues, clamped one over his mouth and nose, and handed one to Natalya.

Then Dmitry realised that the great flat-topped hill to their right was made of rubbish. A mountain of rubbish. He had never known that Svalka was literal, not metaphoric. The mountain loomed over the forest and the land, compelling attention with its height and breadth and stink. They walked down the lane towards it, and the city dropped away behind them, leaving Dmitry feeling as though he had entered a different world. This wasn't Losini Ostrav National Park, that was for sure. This was forgotten land. Waste land, marsh and forest, stench-blasted. You could see occasional dachas here and there, looking unkempt. Pre-mountain, no doubt.

They passed a developer's sign that depicted the rubbish mountain as ski slopes and Natalya snorted into her tissue. Dmitry looked around with a new awareness. Actually, this was all extremely valuable. Vacant real estate. In Moscow. Incredible. If he were ever to consider buying a little block of land, this would be the place. Perhaps it was already too late; perhaps all this had already been sold for impossible prices. Powerlines buzzed audibly overhead, sagging almost to treetop level in between huge steel pylons. He could see movement on the mountain now, although nothing that resembled the brightly dressed skiers of the billboard. Tiny stooped figures inched over the rubbish in the middle distance.

'There,' Natalya said, pointing again and holding her nose. 'Somewhere in those buildings—Oh! It's a cemetery.'

They made their way slowly in that direction with a quiet footfall, listening. Natalya grimaced, looking around, and then said almost in a whisper, 'Remember what Dostoevsky had to say about animals? *God gave them joy untroubled. They are without sin, and you, in all your greatness, defile the earth by your appearance on it, and leave the traces of your foulness after you…* something like that!'

Dmitry laughed. He kicked a plastic bottle towards the place marked for a future chairlift. 'But which is our dogboy to be, Natalochka? The sinless or the defiling?'

Natalya thought of Romochka, locked now in the spare room of their apartment: bereft, wild, furious, betrayed. Shaved. He would be awake by now, groggy. She was thankful for the sedative; and trusted Konstantin to prevent the boy doing himself any physical harm.

She was even more certain now that this was their one chance to regain the boy's trust: to convince him to stay and, long term, to give him a life. He had an exceptionally strong and healthy body. Worms, sure; and the worst ear mite infestation she had ever seen, but they had been able to clean, microchip and inoculate him; and treat practically everything while he was unconscious. Lab results were back, too. No HIV; and one big surprise: Romochka was completely unrelated to Marko. She'd given Dmitry the data summary. But she hadn't told Dmitry everything: certainly not what she had seen, looking at Romochka's naked, cleaned body.

On the plus side, clean, asleep and shaved, Romochka had a striking face, and, unlike many severely neglected children, the look of a child. Despite the scars, quite beautiful. Faintly Tartar. But—she couldn't get it out of her mind. *Who had carved the word* собака *into the child's chest?*

She had a strong sense that the whole story was more tainted by human cruelty than they could ever know. The story of Mamochka who loved her sons was merely something they had been told because they wanted to hear it. She said nothing of these doubts either. Something about her former certainty made her feel vaguely ashamed—an alien and unpleasant sensation. Well, she told herself, Romochka had lied brazenly and put on a very convincing performance, and she didn't want Dmitry getting cold feet because a child was not what he seemed. Not now when she could see clearly that he needed this child in his life.

The word on Romochka's chest would be there for life. Natalya was more determined, having seen it, that it wouldn't define him and that she would see to it that he was rehabilitated. That word 'dog' made her really want this boy.

Dmitry was losing hope. Yes, he agreed, on the balance of probabilities, there might be puppies, but even in the territory the militzia map had identified, finding them would be near impossible. They wandered around with their ears straining for every tiny sound under all the sounds, finding this quiet dead land, to their surprise, too busy, too rich in noises. Underneath the buzzing all manner of things twittered and clanked, revved and rattled. Ravens yowled, gulls screeched, engine noise ebbed and flowed nearby; in the distance the steady whisper-roar of the great motorway. Natalya was not confident that they hadn't missed what they were seeking amidst all this racket.

'See, Dmitry! We are becoming dogs to try to keep him!'

'Let's smell them out then,' laughed Dmitry, releasing his nose briefly. He was mulling over something Natalya had said when they first thought Romochka too was a dogboy. *This boy was better off living with dogs than with humans.* In a way she was right. No drugs, for starters. No glue or petrol. Probably no rapes. Eight-year-olds living in the street were almost invariably victims of all three. And even if they had once been Romochka's family pets, these dogs had evolved to function as a pack. They were close enough to being feral, and probably very loyal and protective. His readings on feral dogs gave him some confidence: how organised and disciplined their social

276

structure can be. What strong codes and laws they live by. The whole clan remaining one family, working together to feed each other. Most females and males remain non-breeding. An outsider is not even approached, even if it is a bitch in oestrus. So rigidly familial that, were they to survive in peace for any length of time, they would become hopelessly inbred. Genetically speaking, they needed disasters to smash the clan so that lone survivors could begin new clans with unrelated dogs.

Well, disaster had struck, no doubt about it.

But really, a very focused and disciplined life. A homeless boy could be a lot worse off, all things considered. Romochka had scars and parasites, but no major diseases. And physically he was frighteningly strong. His clan had been sleek, healthy, fast and, if the rumours were to be believed, very dangerous. Dmitry smiled, remembering a headline: MUTANT DOGS TERRORISE MOSCOVITES. According to that article they were smart enough to use limited sign language and catch the metro to whatever part of Moscow they wanted to hunt in. Humans were on the menu, it seemed: bodies found here and there, partly eaten.

Dogs did catch the metro. He had seen that for himself.

They turned a corner into a lane that seemed almost a potholed farm track. A woman was walking towards them. She was dressed in a bulky military overcoat gathered with string at the waist. Her head was covered with a lace kerchief, perhaps once white, from which dishevelled ropes of long straw-coloured hair fell over her shoulders. She stopped and looked them up and down from a little distance away. Dmitry could see a broad imbecilic smile, but the rest of her face was strangely hard to make out. She held out one hand in a gesture to welcome or perhaps delay them, wrestling with the overcoat and rummaging in her bodice with the other.

She pulled out a bundle of rags which she began to cradle in exaggerated movements, lifting her gaze from it to nod and smile widely at them both as she approached. She seemed a figure in a pantomime, playing with a prop. A thin birdlike piping came from the bundle and Natalya caught Dmitry's eye with an angry look. It really was a baby. The woman stepped nimbly to head them off as Dmitry shifted his weight. She wasn't going to let them past. She stopped rocking the baby, looked up and leaned towards them in awful intimacy, as if they shared something. Dmitry realised she wasn't old. Her face was young, thin and horrifically disfigured by the scar of a deep knife or axe wound that had cut through her brow above one eye, through her nose, and down through her lips and her chin. It had healed without stitches to give her an unnaturally sinister expression, with the cut somehow dividing her face into uneven halves. Her small deformed nose had been severed too, he realised, and was half gone. Saliva pooled behind the two flaps of her bottom lip and she sucked, hissing now and then, to control it.

She grabbed the baby by the rags at the back of its neck and thrust the whole bundle towards Natalya. The baby was only weeks old, its malnourished face almost like that of a baby chimpanzee: small, wizened, with bulging vacant blue eyes and blue lips. Its mouth was dry and crusted. It reeked of petrol.

The woman caught Dmitry's eye and held out her other hand in an unmistakeable request. She winked, pushing the dying baby into Natalya's face, fending off any move from either of them. He was about to give her something for her pitiful child, and for her terrible disfigurement, when she suddenly broke the shuffling silence between them.

'You're late, doctor,' she said, hissing softly, but with a startling voice. 'But a deal is a deal, isn't it? 5,000 roubles? That's what the Roof said. Clean, too; no drug baby, this one.' That voice. Melodious, nuanced. Deep and lovely. His scalp crawled: it scared him. She was raising her arm high to make her coat drop. She grabbed her sleeve in her teeth and held her exposed arm towards Dmitry. It was thin and smooth, without needle scars. Dmitry looked at it numbly, as if the arm could help him, then shook his head and held up both hands to the sky.

'You...ah...y-you have made a mistake,' he stuttered. She shook the bundled baby sharply to halt Natalya, who was trying to edge by.

Natalya shuddered and pushed past. Dmitry followed. As he passed, he reached for the young woman's hand to press some money into it, but Natalya swung round and stared at him so fiercely that he retracted it, feeling all the more ridiculous for having tried at all. He looked back as they stumbled down the cracked pavement and away. The young mother was smiling again. That was how her face fell out in repose, he realised. It was no smile at all. Her face couldn't say what she wanted it to. She stared after him, then shook her head at him, the appalling smile unwavering, before she turned away.

They didn't talk. Dmitry concentrated hard on the map, although he knew already which of these little orange trails they were now stepping out. He felt completely jangled, as if he were an instrument and someone had banged his strings all at once with an unloving hand. He couldn't get that voice out of his head. That monstrous face, that smile. Natalya stomped on in angry silence.

They had all but given up when their newly sharpened hearing picked up a faint yabbering. High-pitched, forlorn. Natalya smiled in relief and triumph. In front of them was a ruined church. The single cupola was burnt and had fallen in, leaving wooden framing like a gaunt half-closed hand and the odd beauty of ornamental brickwork casements silhouetted against the sky. Long grass grew along the tops of walls, even along the top of the brickwork of the cupola. It had never been a prepossessing building. Even new it would have been modest, bordering on plain. A small village church once, perhaps, long before the city crept up; then abandoned as all communal life drained from centres of worship. The countryside around greater Moscow was dotted with these ruins: Natalya had seen a few but this was the only one she could recall seeing in the city itself. Mostly such useless buildings had given way long ago to housing developments, or had been restored and made useful again.

Natalya pushed cautiously through the crumbling gate and stepped into the tiny courtyard. Dmitry followed. Five dead apple trees were festooned in coloured plastic bags, clearly the work of some human hand. These insane flags fluttered and snapped over drifts of rubbish blown off the mountain. Inside the building itself there was nothing except rubbish and rank weeds under an open sky. Its desolation made it seem emptier than bare concrete. The path to the corner was clear. They picked their way through until they reached a jagged hole in the floor. They lowered themselves gingerly through the cracked floorboards and scrambled down the rubble tunnel into the dark den.

It was a large cellar, much larger than they had expected: almost as long as the building itself. Natalya looked around in the gloom, overwhelmed now by what they had taken on. This awful hole had probably been his home, their home. Any clinging faith she had in Mamochka vanished. She now imagined Romochka and Marko's mother as a female Bluebeard, a Fagin, someone like the grotesque Madonna mother they had just encountered.

The floor underfoot was sticky. The smell was disgusting, overpowering: the air was thick with the rankest dog smell she had ever experienced, and more. Death and decay. She switched on her torch and breathed in sharply as its yellow light played over the mess around her. There was a huge pile of rags in a corner, covered in dog hair. Plastic bags everywhere. She noticed bones lying here and there at her feet, then the torch picked out the splayed and dismembered carcasses of some large animals—a glimpse of ragged skull holes and an intimate dirty grimace. These bones were brown, not white. She counted three skulls and several shredded lengths of desiccated skin and hair. A rib cage with a battered plastic sword was threaded through it.

She shuddered. They looked like big dog skulls. Did they eat each other? That idea pulled another out of the tumbling darkness in her chest. She tried not to look further into the shadows, suddenly fearful that there might be human bones here too.

She was both shaken and affronted that a human child had lived here among these ghastly things, and had most probably taken it as normal, invisible. Nothing could have said more starkly that they lived here on the very brink of death. Against the far wall she picked out the supine form of Lenin, staring upward in blank-eyed serenity, and shuddered. It all seemed to have some deranged meaning. Worst of all, wherever she looked there were children's toys. A broken pedal car was upturned against Lenin's shoulder. Large red, yellow and blue building blocks lay scattered around, all half chewed.

She looked down. She was standing on two battered peacock feathers. There were more of them, lying all about. She stared at them stupefied for a moment, then remembered when Khan had escaped from the Moscow Zoo. So this is where that prized jewel had ended up. There was something terrible about that. Frightening. Nothing lost was ever really lost. A peacock was once here, had lived and died rigidly a peacock. It died purely from being a fraction out of line, a fraction outside the boundary of where a peacock in Moscow should be. A boy was here—two boys—lost but not-lost, with nothing so firm about their weird jelly selves.

And, of course, at last, there were puppies, cowering and silent now in the mound of rags that she had seen first. She inched her way over to Dmitry, who was squatting near them. Three living; one, out to the edge of their putrid corner, dead. All grey-gold with paler masks. They were very young, eyes just open, very weak. It had been two days now since Romochka was caught.

She touched the edge of this bed, feeling that with every breath, every touch, she was being contaminated by something far worse than a dog-den church cellar. What had they been thinking, that they could rehabilitate an eight-year-old boy who had slept in this for three or four years? They were the experts, for God's sake. They knew full well that he was past the plastic stage, incapable of any kind of grafting into life. She avoided Dmitry's eye, dreading the moment he would scent her rising fear and begin to crumble.

She felt a touch at her waist, and Dmitry put his arm around her. He was no longer holding his nose. He looked at her in the gloom and breathed in deeply, as if savouring it. 'What a boy, eh Natalochka? What an amazing kid—he was king here.' He grinned. 'He'll have to learn how to be a pauper, now.'

She knew Dmitry didn't for a moment really mean this. He was nothing if not a realist. She laughed, shakily.

'He'll be pretty unhappy, I should think.' Her voice sounded thin. Of course Romochka was unsaveable. Clever, yes, but irredeemable. The same as any experienced bomzh child beyond the age of reclamation. Really, she thought then, they should kill these puppies too, put them out of their misery. Then wash their hands very thoroughly so Romochka didn't smell it on them. Romochka probably couldn't get the care he needed except in a specialist institution.

She could hear Dmitry smiling as he spoke.

'He *is* human. All this is because he is human. There is no turning back, Natalochka, either for him or for us.' He reached for the snarling mites, shoved them into his overcoat pockets and led her stumbling out of the revolting hole.

Natalya felt better as soon as they reached clean air. She shuddered, laughing, trying to shake out the wild darkness that had clouded her. 'Phuuu! We stink! What a place. Here, let me carry one; too many might bring on your asthma.'

She had left all but a vestige of her defeat behind in the ogre's lair. They walked to the nearest metro station, itching furiously and scratching themselves under their clothes and by the time they sighted the welcome red M of the entrance, Natalya had commandeered all three puppies, juggling them between hands and pockets, teasing Dmitry about his imaginary allergies, trying to erase her awful uncertainties with bright and busy talk.

Ж

On the landing of their floor, despite padded doors, they could hear Romochka screaming in alien shrieks and growling riffs. There was no time to feed or wash the puppies.

'Let him do it,' gasped Natalya, rushing up the stairs, handing two of the puppies back to Dmitry.

They let themselves in quickly and locked the padded outer door. Better not let the neighbours hear much of this shrieking. Outside the door of their spare room they paused, looked at each other, then walked in.

The room stank of fresh faeces. Konstantin Petrovich was standing by the door looking harassed. He had bites and scratches rising in raw welts on his arms, and it was clear that Romochka had thrown shit both wildly and with excellent aim. The sight of the boy was a shock to Dmitry. He barely recognised him. Romochka's hair was shaved off, leaving an unexpectedly small face, a small child with a red raised scar across his scalp. He was naked and, like Marko, quite hairy. He had been dressed in a white shirt and some sort of white pyjama pants, but these lay at different corners of the room, shit-smeared. Konstantin had cuffed the boy's hands behind his back.

Romochka looked at Dmitry, disoriented. His rage and feeling of nakedness receded and he was overwhelmed with confusion. *How could this be?* He could smell a cold hint of Mamochka. He could smell home and more. *How? How?* He could sense Dmitry's excitement and nervousness. He was bewildered, fuzzy headed. Raw sound hurt: his ears were new roaring air tunnels deep into his head. He was terribly exposed without his hair. Dmitry had betrayed him, but what now? *What had he done, where had he been?* The teeming pain of it all welled up and he screamed with fury and grief, squeezing the terrible tears from his eyes and shaking his head to clear them.

Dmitry was horrified. This unrecognisable Romochka snarled and shook himself from side to side. The pale face was twisted, his teeth prominent in an animal grimace, his body held low in an inhuman form. The scarred simian body, the tear-stained cheeks, bared teeth and wild eyes, this posture, all added to a most alienating appearance. His torso, criss-crossed with terrible scars, was awful to see. He seemed wolf-like but at the same time unnatural: truly degraded, worse than any wolf. Dmitry could see the shock and revulsion in Konstantin's face. He waited until Romochka had stopped screaming and was looking at him with dull black eyes. He signed to Konstantin to release the boy.

'Romochka, Romochka,' Dmitry talked while Konstantin reluctantly snipped the plastic cuffs at the boy's wrists. The boy growled all the while. 'You know me. I am here to help you. Remember Mar…Schenok.'

Romochka lunged but, before Dmitry could stop her, Natalya had stepped in front of him and was roaring at the boy with a spectacular and savage snarl from all her adult height, at the same time pulling a suddenly mewling puppy from her coat. Dmitry saw her as if in a painting, frozen: a goddess or witch, with a helpless beast in hand, arched over a cowering caliban.

'THEY ARE NOT ALL DEAD!' she was roaring into Romochka's shocked, young-boy face. 'We found three for you.'

Romochka dropped back to the wall, his face suddenly blank and truly eight years old. He covered his ears with his shit-smeared hands, cradling his own face. No one moved or spoke. There was a silent tableau in the room as two tears rolled down his cheeks. He reached out his hands for the puppy, waggling one hand in a strangely demanding gesture that was made all the more odd by him simultaneously dropping his eyes and averting his face. The hand wagged and flapped imperiously as if independent from the rest of his body. Dmitry pulled out the other two puppies, tears prickling his own eyes. The boy reached greedily for the yabbering babies and buried his nose in them, breathing in deep, licking their faces, tongues, open mouths, whimpering now into their dirty fur, worrying his fingers over their hungry bodies.

Romochka sat on the floor with the wriggling, yelping puppies scooped to his belly and chest, sobbing, head down.

Dmitry squatted down next to the boy and began stroking the black stubble of his head, avoiding the red welt. Romochka didn't stop him.

'They are yours, all yours, and safe if you stay here,' Dmitry said softly. He had an inspiration then. He could never have said how, but he knew, in that moment, exactly what he should say and what it meant.

'We are the only dish on the table.'

Romochka held his breath. He looked up sideways at Dmitry with a large, quiet, child's eye. His scarred wet cheek rested in his armful of puppies. His rather fine-featured face was pale and gentle. He smiled, his eyes sliding from Dmitry's face and focusing on nothing. His face was transformed, mysterious, alight behind the pallor. For a moment Dmitry was reminded of Marko.

Dmitry motioned to Konstantin, who was leaning against the wall grinning, weeping, shaking his head. They left Romochka alone with the door open, Konstantin first, hands outstretched for the bathroom, Dmitry following. Natalya glanced at Dmitry, then raced to the kitchen to prepare some bottles of milk.

Dmitry was sure Romochka would stay, even if this was the softest moment he would ever see in the boy. He was buoyant with the success of it all, charged with electric happiness at Natalya's glance. She was surprised, admiring. Impressed. It was the right thing, and it was well done—and not just because now he felt that he and Natalya were a true team: lovers and partners. Parents. A family, now, with a child and three dogs. He couldn't wait to clean him up, straighten him out and see what sort of boy he made, what sort of boy they had. If they formally adopted him, Romochka would even be able to go to school, eventually—especially if Natalya got up to her usual tricks and faked his papers. Romochka would have the best, with a behavioural scientist for a father and a paediatrician and scamming queen for adoptive mother!

He looked around his stylish lounge room. The chipped old matrioshka on the sill was a new addition—one of Natalya's few things. After their big fight she had, without a word, moved in properly and he had been surprised and humbled to find how few things she had, and that these were precious to her not for their own sake, but for the sake of the person who had given them or the use she had made of them. She brought her piano, all her slightly gypsy clothes, her matrioshka; and everything he had ever given her. This last made him suspect her of uncharacteristic tact, but then he gave up analysing it all and just felt grateful.

He'd need a new vacuum cleaner for the dog hair. Perhaps even a Kirby. Yes, there would be quite a shopping list, and it would be a long while before they could have a dinner party again. His friends and colleagues would talk about this for months, years, that was certain. Most would say he was a fool; but some might think it was noble of him. And of course: *all* would think it was Natalya's influence.

He smiled to himself, savouring the feeling of being at last a family man. They were going to be a very unusual family. Maybe Romochka and Malchik next door would get along.

Three dogs. Perhaps eventually they could wean him onto one. One was enough for the purposes of this transitional phase; and after all, what boy ever has more than one dog? Three dogs might hold him back. Make him yearn for the old life. No, it would have to be one dog, and it would have to go to obedience classes. He had a sudden vision of himself at the dog school by the Krylatskoe line, a charming, well-behaved dog at heel beside him, commuters whizzing by, looking on. He'd have to watch to see which was the most intelligent. No, the most loyal, or perhaps the most docile and least boisterous. A single dog that was gentle, smart and loyal like Malchik, but not boisterous or drooly, would be ideal. One that would tip its head back to look at you the way Malchik did.

Then he thought, ashamed, that ideal was not what he should be angling for. He should just hope they wouldn't be noisy eaters or lick their genitals in front of visitors.

Then, alone in the living room, he felt dizzy—even sick—with fear.

The shower roared and the microwave in the kitchen dinged. He sniffed his hands. They stank of fresh faeces. He held them stiffly away from his body, unable to go to the bathroom until Konstantin finished. Now he could smell shit on everything.

How does one really raise a child? This child? Wouldn't it have been better for everyone, a small inner voice suddenly chipped in, if this awful unimaginable boy had quietly succumbed to cold or disease and malnutrition out there beyond the perimeter of the known? He could have bought his Natalochka a pedigree dog. He could have let her adopt a clean, normal, drug-free newborn.

He froze. Their strengthened relationship. They could have had a child biologically and lived happy ordinary lives.

His scalp crawled with foreboding. What had he reeled in on his puppy-baited hook? What had he taken on?

Ж

If you were to look now through the window—while on the other side of the thin wall Dmitry takes his turn in the shower,

289

while Natalya in the kitchen farewells Konstantin and begins slicing onions with verve, cooking up a dinner to mark their new lives—you would see Romochka alone in that room still cradling the three puppies. The empty milk bottle stands beside him.

His face is in profile. He strokes the pups until they sleep. Then he stands and begins to weep, his shoulders tense and shaking. He turns. His face is raised towards you now, and he is sobbing in earnest, mouthing a scream. He stays like this, his body stiff, his fingers outstretched.

He stops. His breathing stills and he stands limp at the window for a while, his eyes huge and dark in a white face. Then he turns swiftly and, bending down to the puppies, bites through each of their skulls in turn.

He has chosen to stay.

ACKNOWLEDGMENTS

This book owes more than I can say to Larisa Aksenova. Without her it could not have become the book it is.

Roger Sallis put years of loving encouragement into this book; and, in the long Moscow twilight, he found the dogs.

It is published in its final form thanks to my agent Jenny Darling and editor Mandy Brett.

Many people contributed in different ways to this book. They are: Stuart Barnett, Donica Bettanin, Gillian Bovoro, Maria Danchenko, Nikolai Danchenko, Tania D'Antonio, Sonja Dechian, Amaia de la Quintana, Jenni Devereaux, Jem Fuller, Alfred Hornung, L'hibou Hornung, Richard Hornung, Alexey Kopus, Tamara Leonidovna Kozlovskaya, Aleksandr Kozlovski, Gay Lynch, Lyudmila Malinin, Michele Meijer, John Morss, Maria Nichterlein, Alexander Ovchar, Rosa Piserchia, Olesya Pomazan (www.russiangirlfriday.com), Ramsey Sallis, Tom Shapcott, Valery and Svetlana Shusharin, Celia Summerfield, Paul Voytinsky (www.unclepasha.com), Phil Waldron, Teresita

White, Claudio Zollo.

Thank you to the University of Adelaide for a fruitful residency in the first half of 2008.

Thank you to ArtsSA for funding my research trip to Moscow in 2006.

Thank you to Nexus Multicultural Arts Centre for a three-month residency in 2006.

Thank you to Rafael Sallis for the title and much more.

Special thank you to Emori Bovoro for playing with Rafael, making possible long writing hours through the summer holidays.

Finally, Halley and Rosie deserve dried kangaroo tail every day for their parts in this book.

EVA HORNUNG was born in Bendigo and now lives in Adelaide. As Eva Sallis, she is an award-winning writer of literary fiction and criticism: her first novel *Hiam* won The Australian/Vogel Literary Award in 1997 and the Nita May Dobbie Award in 1999. Her most recent novel *The Marsh Birds* won the Asher Literary Award 2005 and was shortlisted for numerous awards including the Age Book of the Year 2005, NSW Premier's Literary Award and the Commonwealth Writers' Prize.

How long would a child
remaining speaking, living
among non speaking?

DATE DUE

7/12			
GAYLORD			PRINTED IN U.S.A.